"YOUR BLOOD IS MY ECSTASY," SHE SAID.

She kissed me again. I tasted my blood on her lips.

"And now you must taste of mine," she said.

I saw her extend the tip of her tongue from her mouth and bite down. Her blood welled. I hesitated . . . then pressed my lips against hers and drew her tongue into my mouth.

I swallowed the thick coldness of her blood, felt it slide down my throat. For a moment it seemed to coil in my stomach like a living serpent, writhing to be free. Nausea twisted within me. But almost as soon as it came, it passed, and I was shocked to feel, almost frighteningly, *alive*. My senses felt predator sharp. Alert. Intensely aware.

I embraced her tightly, glorying in the feel of her strong body beneath my hands. I buried my face in her wild mane of dark, cool hair and breathed deeply of its scent. I kissed her again, my senses roaring with her taste. And I whispered, "Even Death cannot part us now . . ."

"No, Vlad," she answered, clutching me to her, "not even Death."

I AM
DRACULA

C. DEAN
ANDERSSON

ZEBRA BOOKS
KENSINGTON PUBLISHING CORP.

IN MEMORY

In memory of a vanished House of Dreams, the Manor Theater in McPherson, Kansas where one night a child and a Vampire King had their first meeting and began working on this book.

Note: This is not the first of our collaborations. The first was a novel entitled Crimson Kisses, *written under a pen name with the additional collaboration of Nina Romberg, an author whose recent novels include* The Spirit Stalker *and* Shadow Walkers. *Few devotees of the Undead, however, are aware of* Crimson Kisses. *It is rarely listed in vampirographical bibliographies, because its publisher-chosen cover art convinced most booksellers it belonged with novels devoted to romance, where Draculaphiles never found it. Long out-of-print, CK can still occasionally be found in used book stores, similarly miscategorized. And we would feel no need to mention CK here at all save for one consideration. Because the 15th century events described in this book are the same ones that inspired* Crimson Kisses, *certain similarities exist between the two. However, while history has not changed, the times in which we live have, allowing us to feed humanity's reborn hunger for Truth by revealing in this book those events in a manner far more direct. And truthful. And complete.*

—D—

DEDICATION
for
Nina and Tzigane
from
Dean and Vlad
(and for Alice, from Speedy
and all of us, with our thanks)

WELCOME

You have been told many Lies. So was I.
  I became a Vampire for lies and for love.
  I remained one for Revenge.
  Know me.
  I am Dracula.
  Learn freely and of your own will.
  I bid you welcome to my Truth.

Chapter One

1
Evil

I became aware of Evil in my fourth year of life.

I was born in the hillside fortress town of Sighisoara, Transylvania in the third decade of the fifteenth century. There, shortly after my fourth birthday, I saw my mother die a horrible death for telling me the truth.

From the front ranks of an assembled crowd I watched as two men brought her from a cell in Councilmen's Tower and carried her onto a wooden platform that had been built in Councilmen's Square. Criminals were usually executed by hanging in a different place, but this was to be no ordinary execution.

The men who carried her wore hoods to hide their faces and heavy clothes to protect themselves from the cold December wind, but my mother wore only a ragged shift, and atop the platform the men tore the shift away, leaving her naked. Then, with her hands manacled behind her, they held her facing the crowd, supporting her on each side because she could no longer stand on her mutilated feet.

A strong woman and proud, she had defied torture for three days before confessing to their lies.

A priest mounted the platform and solemnly read a

declaration that named her a Witch. Katiasa Waydja, condemned to be burned alive by her own confession.

Historians will tell you that my mother was the Moldavian Princess Cneajna. My father, Prince Dracul, an ambitious man who became military governor of Transylvania the year I was born, married Cneajna to acquire ties with the Moldavian throne. But Cneajna nearly died giving birth to father's eldest son, Mircea, and afterward could bear no more children.

My true mother, then, was Katiasa Waydja, one of Dracul's numerous other . . . *wives,* a Transylvanian woman who was officially only my wet nurse.

Father had forbidden anyone who knew to tell. In that long ago time and place, any son he fathered would have been considered his legitimate heir. But to give all his sons the same ties to Moldavian power as Mircea, he wanted Cneajna still thought fertile. And so, of course, did she.

Cneajna was cold to me. Aloof with aristocratic superiority, the Moldavian Princess made no attempt to act the loving mother to another woman's child. Any affection I knew, for father certainly never gave any, was from Katiasa.

On my fourth birthday, all but ignored by father and Cneajna, Katiasa took pity, dried my tears on her long white apron that I remember always smelled of flowers, took me by the hand into a room away from the others and, risking punishment by defying father's order, told me the truth.

I resisted that truth only a moment, then experienced a wave of powerful emotion and threw myself into my true mother's arms. I *was* loved. And I loved in return.

Of course I promised not to reveal that I knew my true birthright. But Mircea overheard. He was always spying on me. And he told father.

12

Armed men came and took Katiasa away. Father charged her with Witchcraft and told me she had lied. No one could believe a Witch, he explained, because Witches were Evil, in league with Satan, the Prince of Lies.

And now Katiasa was to die.

Bundled in heavy clothes against the winter cold, I waited with father and Mircea near the platform. To each side of us, in the front ranks of the watching crowd, were members of the Sighisoaran Court and local officials of the church and town. My younger brother, Radu, was at home in his crib, only a few months old, secretly born of yet another of Dracul's bedwomen.

Father had ordered me to shed no tears for Katiasa. But I could not help myself when I saw her on the platform, saw what they had done to her.

Gone, now, was her beautiful dark hair, shorn from her head. Gone too was her familiar smile, her face lined and twisted by pain. And her body was everywhere marred by ugly wounds.

But her eyes were the worst, eyes once bright with intelligence and mischievous wit, now dulled by pain and hopelessness. Until she saw me in the crowd. Then suddenly something of their brightness returned, and she cried out to me, "Lies, my Vlad!" Her voice was barely recognizable, made hoarse by all her screams. "I am no Witch! And I will always love you!"

I wanted to shout that I loved her, too, but because of father I dared not.

The priest ordered her silenced. The hooded men gagged her with strips of cloth torn from her discarded shift.

Pain shot through me as father gripped my shoulder, but I did not anger him by flinching. "She *is* guilty,

13

Vlad. She confessed. Priests do not lie. Wipe your tears. Do not shame me. Be strong like your brother.''

Katiasa's gaze held mine as they chained her to the blackened iron stake in the center of the newly built wood platform.

She held my gaze at they set fire to the wood stacked beneath the platform.

And she held my gaze until her pain and the stinging smoke forced her to close her eyes. Then she began making horrible, beastial sounds as she strained to scream through her gag.

But she was still alive, her flesh blistering and blackening, when flames burned the gag away, allowing her to defy them one last time.

''Lies!'' she cried, her voice a rasp of pain amid the crackling roar of the flames. ''All lies!'' Then she screamed and screamed with wordless agony. And I screamed, too.

Father stuck me. Mircea laughed.

Katiasa kept screaming.

Screaming.

Helpless, I silently prayed for my mother's death, an end to her screams. But I heard them in my mind even after she was dead. Especially at night. In nightmares. And although more than five centuries have now passed since that day in Sighisoara, I sometimes dream them still.

2
Witch

When father became Voivode Dracul, warlord-ruler of Wallachia, we left Transylvania and moved south beyond the mountains to the Wallachian palace at Targoviste. There, in my ninth year of life, on the Eve of Saint George, when the superstitious believe Evil has sway, I dreamed that a stranger appeared in my room.

In the bright moonlight streaming through my window a girl stood naked, mist swirling around her feet. She was nearing womanhood, her breasts beginning to form. Waves of raven-black hair hung to her slender waist. A tall girl, her long legs were firmly muscled. She would make a fast runner, and I began imagining running beside her through the woods, both of us naked as beasts, racing with the wolves.

The girl said, "The wolves would never catch us." She grinned. Her white teeth glinted in the moonlight. "Listen." Suddenly, from far and wide came the howling of wolves. She laughed. "What music they make! Yes?"

I fought to conceal my fear. I demanded to know whom she was.

"Your future wife."

Ridiculous. She was obviously a Gypsy and I of noble

15

blood. "How did you get past the guards, Gypsy girl? You will pay with your life when they catch you."

She shrugged, unconcerned. "I am not really here." Her large eyes sparkled mischievously. "Watch this."

She floated upward. Her feet no longer touched the floor. Again her laughter rang out. "See?"

She floated back to the floor. "This is a special kind of dream. A vision. My mother taught me a spell by which a girl can see her future husband, if at midnight on Saint George's Eve she is brave enough to go naked and alone deep in the forest to a crossroad where the blue ghost-flames glow." She raised her head proudly. "As you can see, I *was* brave enough, and my Witchcraft worked."

Mention of Witchcraft tempered my fear with anger. *"Witchcraft is a lie."* For my mother's sake, I had secretly vowed to be above such lies; I believed mother's defiant last words, not her tortured confession. "An evil superstition."

"And yet, I am here."

"Dreams care little for reality."

"But reality cares much about dreams."

"Not *my* reality."

She laughed. "Believe what you will, for now." She looked me up and down. "And *I* believe you might make a handsome man one day, if you can learn to stop frowning. Do you think I will make a beautiful woman?" She moistened her lips with her tongue. "A desirable . . ." she slowly ran her hands over her budding breasts, ". . . lover?"

I said nothing.

Laughing, she pointed at the emblem sewn to my tunic. "What is that? Some kind of snake?"

"A dragon. My father is Dracul, the Dragon, of the Christian Order of the Dragon."

16

Her smile vanished. "Dracul? The *Devil?*" Her eyes were round with shock.

"It can also mean that, especially to his enemies, the Turks, and perhaps to Gypsy girls who sneak into the palace, even if only in a dream." It was my turn to smile. "Where is your laughter now?"

Her dark eyes flashed. "You think me afraid? You know nothing! *You* are the Son of Dracul!"

"I have two brothers. We are all his sons."

"But you are the One! I sense it. And I am to be your mate! Sweet Satan! *I am to be your mate!*"

Then she vanished. And I awoke.

The moon was shining through my window, exactly as in the dream. And wolves were indeed howling in the distance.

The dying fire in the grate cast fitful shadows upon the walls and ceiling. I fought to master the disquieting fear my dream had inspired.

"Witches," I whispered. I remembered my mother. Anger again tempered my fear. "Superstitions. *Lies.*"

But this time I was wrong.

3
Hostage

Nine years passed before I saw the Gypsy Witch again. The last four of those years were spent in captivity, never knowing when I might be killed.

To gain a temporary advantage, father sent Radu and me to the Turks as hostages, part of a treaty agreement by which he pledged not to attack them. If he did, Radu and I would be killed.

We were imprisoned in a fortress on Mount Egrigoz, and in the month before my thirteenth birthday, father broke the treaty.

He still had Mircea, his eldest son, with him. Radu and I had obviously been deemed expendable, which did not surprise me. I had been expecting father's betrayal. It fit the pattern of my childhood experiences with him. But Radu was of a gentler disposition, and when the Turks came to our cell and took me away to be killed first, he was frantic with terror, screaming and begging.

Expecting father's betrayal, I had been preparing for death and had promised myself I would face it as bravely as my mother had done. So, to the Turks' disappointment, I did not scream or beg. I fought to maintain an illusion of calm.

In the place of execution I was forced to kneel and

place my head on the bloodstained block. Then, without ceremony, the executioner's ax slammed down. And missed. In my fear, I involuntarily shamed myself, soiling my clothes. The Turks laughed and laughed. Then I was taken back to my cell with the warning that next time it would be for real. But it wasn't. Nor the time after that. I did not, however, shame myself again.

When human beings are faced with hopelessness, their spirits may break, making them easy for those in power to manipulate, and causing them to hunger for oblivion. Or they may become defiant, determined to live and struggle against the odds, and laugh Death in the face.

Radu, subjected to the Turk's cruel treatment, quickly broke. As a reward, he was taken to the palace and became the Sultan's obedient toy. But, remembering my mother at the stake, I became defiant, though not, after being punished a few times, always openly. Secrecy and cunning became my best friends, and I began studying my captors, secretly vowing to have my revenge.

I became a model prisoner. I taught myself their language, learned to read their writings, came to understand how they thought, their military strategies, their religion, and their superstitions. How to frighten them. Terrify them. Defeat them.

Truth was not a thing I owed them. I taught myself to mix truth and lies skillfully, making it difficult to tell the two apart. And, eventually, I convinced the Sultan that I was sincere in wanting revenge on my father, and that I, a legitimate heir to the Wallachian throne, was ready to lead a Turkish army into Wallachia and claim that throne, the key to the conquest of all Christendom, for Turk-land and the glory of Sultan Murad II.

As the son of Prince Dracul, my training as a Christian Warrior had begun early in life. I could ride and control a horse at an early age. In Targoviste, constant training and exercise with weapons had strengthened my body and taught me mental discipline, concentration.

In my cell, I had continued to exercise and strengthen my growing body as best I could. After gaining the Turks' trust, I obtained further training from their warriors.

I was indeed, therefore, prepared to do battle with father's forces, if necessary. I had long since decided that if he cared nothing for my life, I would care nothing for his. Or Mircea's.

But, as it happened, I did not have to kill my father and brother. A Christian conspirator named Vladislav usurped father's throne and killed them for me.

Dracul was dead. So was Mircea. And I discovered I cared but little.

Later, when Vladislav led most of his Wallachian forces to fight a new war in Serbia, the Sultan decided it was time to give my plan a try. It would not take many men to capture Targoviste while Vladislav and most of his army were away. Holding the throne, should I win it, however, would be up to me.

Finally, then, two months before my eighteenth birthday, on a cold October morning, I led a small contingent of Turkish cavalry and infantry northward toward Wallachia.

After four years of imprisonment, I was finally free and going home, unaware that a Gypsy Witch waited for me there, and with her creatures neither living nor dead, restless and hungry in their graves.

4

Vampires

So few defenders were left at Targoviste that I captured the throne without a single battle. But if Vladislav, the usurper, survived the fighting in Serbia, and returned with most of his army intact, my small Turkish force would not be sufficient to hold the throne. I therefore needed the support of the Wallachian nobility, the boyars.

But leading Turks into Targoviste had understandably made the Wallachians distrustful of my motives. And most Wallachians continued to be suspicious of me, even after I had word secretly passed to them that with their help I would drive the Turks out.

And those who were inclined to take the word of Dracul's son still feared Vladislav too much to risk helping me. Vladislav had been merciless with the most prominent members of my father's court, including father's new wife. Cneajna had died years before. But my brother Mircea's wife, Varina, whom he had married while I was a hostage, was still alive. In the dungeon.

Vladislav had taken a special delight in Varina's degradation. She had been made to watch Mircea's slow torture and burial alive in, like father later on, an unmarked grave. Vladislav had then placed her in the dungeon and told the guards they could do as they wished with the beautiful noblewoman. Later, the usurper had personally tormented her with tortures designed to terrify and agonize without killing. He meant to keep her alive, naked in chains, for a very long time.

Varina's mind had shattered. When I freed her, she was able to tell me her name, but little more, until I asked of Mircea.

At mention of her husband's name, painful memories momentarily cleared her thoughts, and she told me where he and my father were buried. But she also said that they were not really dead.

The first piece of information was useful. I had been unable to find or persuade anyone to tell me the location of the unmarked graves, another example of Vladislav's evil. The second, about their not being dead, I put down to the wishful thinking of a ruined mind.

But Varina continued her story, telling me that after I was taken to Turk-land, father had made enemies of a group of Witches, who then cursed him and his eldest son to find no peace in the grave, but to become Vampires, crawling from their coffins each night to stalk the living, drinking the blood of sleeping humans.

Their coffins, she said, had been wrapped in the vines of wild roses to keep them inside. And she begged me to free her husband from the horrid thorns, so that he might return to her once more.

The coffins were buried where Varina had said they would be. And they were indeed wrapped in the vines of wild roses.

I had the mutilated bodies, dark with trapped blood and bloated by gases, but as yet surprisingly uncorrupted, cleaned and clothed in white shrouds, then placed in the palace crypt with the proper ceremonies.

That night I awoke to find the palace unnaturally quiet.

Fearing a sneak attack by Vladislav or an assassination attempt by one of his secret supporters, I armed myself with my sword and called for my guards. When none came, I cautiously went to investigate.

I found the guards outside my chambers fallen into a deep sleep, out of which I could not rouse them. Then I heard a sound behind me in my sleeping room.

Holding my sword ready, expecting an assassin's attack, I slipped quietly back into the room. But instead of an assassin I found my father's corpse standing near the fireplace in its shroud, staring at me with its dead eyes.

In the flickering glow of the candles burning in the room, I could see blood on the dead thing's lips and chin. Blood also stained its shroud.

Except for its dark lips, the corpse had turned white, and the bloating caused by death was gone, replaced by a skeletal leanness, flesh stretched tightly over bone.

Fighting shock and fear, I tried to speak, to act. But then my terror increased, for I discovered I was helpless.

Caught in the gaze of dead eyes, I was paralyzed, unable to move or speak. My sword slipped from my grip and fell heavily to the floor.

The thing moved toward me.

It pulled its purplish lips back in a rictus grin, baring sharp, white teeth.

Red fire began glowing in its eyes as if hot coals behind cold glass.

The corpse reached me. It gripped my shoulders with its cold, strong hands and leaned slowly forward.

"Your . . . blood," it moaned. Its chilled breath stank of rotting flesh.

"I . . . need," it whined.

It leaned closer. Its cold teeth touched my throat.

Then suddenly *she* was there, a woman clad in black.

23

She rushed into the room shouting words in a language I did not understand, but which made the corpse stagger back as if struck, before it had drawn my blood.

I remained unable to move or speak.

She spoke more words of command in the strange, gutteral tongue. The corpse slumped onto the floor and lay still. Then she turned to me.

Her beauty. A wildness about her. So *alive.* A woman of the forests and mountains. Her eyes large and dark. A Gypsy. Tall and slender. Hair a tangle of raven-black curls. But not clothed like any woman I had ever known.

Her tunic, britches, and boots, all of black leather, would have suited a huntsman. Her cloak was also black, the hood thrown back. A leather pouch hung from a wide leather belt encircling her waist.

Gazing into my eyes, she spoke foreign words again, this time in a gentle whisper.

My paralysis vanished. I swiftly reached down and retrieved my sword then held it ready to strike.

She laughed. ''Do you intend to slay your rescuer, Prince Dracula?''

I cleared my throat, determined that my voice would be steady. ''I might slay you still, or have you placed in the dungeon, if you fail to answer my questions.''

''Questions?'' Her eyes sparkled. ''Questions about what?''

She was enjoying herself too much at my expense. ''Who are you, Gypsy woman?''

''Do you not remember our first meeting? Nine years ago? On the Eve of Saint George?''

I did recognize her then, recognized the eyes that had haunted many exciting, adolescent dreams. A chill of fear passed through me, but I said nothing.

Again she laughed. ''For nine years have I awaited

and prepared for this night, and finally it has come!"
She bowed slightly from the waist in the manner of a
man acknowledging an equal. "I am Tzigane, Prince
Dracula. Still a Witch. And still your future wife."

Chapter Two

5

Tzigane

Standing before me was the young Witch from my dream nine years ago, now a beautiful woman.

Impossible.

As was the notion that my father's corpse had just attacked me.

The Gypsy named Tzigane said, "You have nothing to fear from me, Prince Dracula."

I had become an expert at concealing my feelings in the Turkish prison. I was angered with myself for allowing my fear to show.

I said, "Fear is an old friend."

I moved the tip of my sword toward her throat. She did not move away.

"In prison, the Turks introduced me to fear and made certain we became intimate companions."

I moved the blade still closer, almost touching her skin. To my surprise and admiration she stood her ground. Her gaze never left mine, never wavered. I forced a smile.

"The Turks also taught me about tricks. For example, the impostor who is feigning unconsciousness upon the floor."

"Impostor?"

"No doubt he is working for Vladislav, my enemy, along with you. Were you hoping to discredit my family and my authority by making people think my father had become a monster?"

"Do not call him that. He is not unconscious. Only paralyzed. He can still hear you."

"Then let him hear this. My sword will pierce your neck, should he attempt a surprise move against me."

"Your father—"

"My father is dead."

"*Un-dead.* You saw for yourself!"

"Then he would not object to my sword piercing *his* neck?"

"It would do him no lasting harm."

"I believe I will test that claim . . ." I paused, then shouted, "right now!" and punctuated the shout by loudly stamping my right boot upon the floor.

From his position, his face turned away from me, he could not see that I was bluffing, my blade still at the Gypsy's throat, but he moved not the slightest, leaving me feeling foolish.

Tzigane seemed about to laugh, but she controlled the impulse and said, "Obviously, your attitude toward the Unseen has changed little in nine years, even . . ." she glanced down at the corpse, "when you can see it."

I had not truly thought the man an impostor. But it *was* a possibility, and the alternative violated what I'd come to believe was reality. If such things as Vampires existed, what other legends and superstitions might also be true?

"Convince yourself, Prince Dracula. Thrust your sword into your father's corpse, if you wish. There will be but little blood, the wound will quickly heal, and he will still, at my command, rise and walk once more."

"At *your* command. Because of your . . . Witchcraft, I'm to believe?"

She raised her chin. "Witch I am, and proud. But it does not take a Witch to control the *newly* Undead, only someone with the proper knowledge and training." She grinned. "Which, of course, usually means a Witch these days."

Holding my gaze, she reached into the leather pouch at her belt. I still held my blade near her throat. She slowly pulled from the pouch a small knife and held it for my inspection. "Surely this tiny weapon can do little against your great sword."

The knife had a leather-wrapped handle and a pointed blade made not of metal but of black stone, the edges chipped to lethal sharpness. Symbols unknown to me were inscribed near the base of the blade.

Tzigane knelt beside the corpse. "Now, watch, please."

She used the stone blade to slice deeply into the pale skin at the back of the corpse's neck. Only a few drops of thick, dark blood oozed sluggishly forth before the wound healed, leaving not even a scar.

"Do you also think *that* a trick, my Prince?"

"I . . . don't see how . . ."

"Good." She stood and slipped the knife back into her pouch. She looked me up and down. "Your stubborn disbelief may not have changed in nine years, but your body has. You have become a rather handsome man, although you still frown too much." She waited. "You are now supposed to respond that I have become a beautiful woman."

"Am I?"

"You find me . . . unattractive?"

I hesitated. I urgently needed information from her. My experiences with the Turks made me think of using

31

force to learn what I wanted, but I suspected she was strong spirited enough to resist the persuasion of pain for longer than I wanted to spend. My stay in Turk-land had also taught me cunning, however, and a gentle approach might work more quickly with one who had spoken of becoming my wife.

"You have, indeed, become a beautiful woman."

"Tzigane. Won't you say my name?"

Again I hesitated, then, "You have become a beautiful woman, Tzigane."

"Yes! I have." Her gaze softened. *"For you."*

6

Trust

Tzigane said, "When I learned nine years ago that I was to be mated to you, the Dragon's Son, my life changed. My parents sent me away to be trained and tested for a sacred task."

"Which was?"

"I worked harder than ever I had before to learn all that was required of me. Then I used what I had learned to survive lethal tests many others had failed. Thus did I strive for nine years to prove myself worthy to return to you. *For* you. More I will explain later, but not now."

"Explain *now*."

"Not until I sense you are truly ready to hear."

The gentle approach had told me nothing useful. "In that case, you have a simple choice. Either decide that I am ready to hear immediately, or I shall chain you in the dungeon and—"

"You cannot *force* me to tell."

"Many think they can withstand great pain. Few can."

"It would be an interesting contest, my Prince, your will against mine. But I will not allow you to harm me. I have the power to stop you."

"Such as the power to make the guards outside my door sleep too soundly to be roused?"

"Your father caused that, a power the newly Undead instinctually wield, along with the power to paralyze their victims, as you experienced."

"Which *your* power can overcome."

"As you saw."

"But which you will not explain."

"But which I *will* explain, when I sense you are ready."

Although I had no desire to harm her, the needs of the throne, *my* needs, had to come first. But perhaps I would not need to hurt her. The threat of torture, merely showing a naked and chained captive the instruments of pain, often in itself loosened tongues.

She whispered three words in the foreign tongue. And I was paralyzed once more! She took my sword from my hand and slipped it into the scabbard on my belt.

I struggled to move, to speak.

She leaned closer. "I believe I forgot to mention that another of my powers is the ability to read thoughts, as I read yours just now." She moved even nearer, almost touching me. The scent of exotic spices clung to her.

She placed her hands on my chest. "I assure you, Prince Dracula, that I look forward to your seeing me naked, but as a prelude to love, not torture."

She gazed into my eyes and whispered, "I will tell you *many* secrets. Soon. I promise." Then she turned to the corpse upon the floor and uttered words of command in the foreign tongue. The pale-fleshed cadaver stirred, rose stiffly to its feet. My father. Undead.

Now under Tzigane's control, his glassy eyes stared at nothing. Unblinking. Empty. How had this happened to him? Was it as my brother's wife had said? Had father

34

and Mircea been cursed by Witches? Perhaps by Tzigane herself?

"I did not make your father Undead," she answered, again reading my thoughts, "although I know those who did. Lies you have been taught make you think it a curse. But it is a blessing, if viewed another way."

She again spoke commands I could not understand. But my father understood. He walked from the room. She returned her attention to me. "I want you to see what happens next. If I release you from the spell of paralysis, will you promise not to hinder me or what I do in any way? Answer with your thoughts."

I could make no such promise.

"Think of what the power to read thoughts could mean to one such as you, Prince Dracula. I can teach you this power, and many others."

I thought, *I have no wish to become a . . . Vampire.*

"You need not be Undead to wield powers similar to mine. I am still very much alive. My flesh is not cold." She gently touched my cheek with her right hand. At her touch, a wave of warmth pounded through me.

"Won't you trust me, my Prince, if only a little? Please, trust me and promise not to hinder me if I return control of your body to you."

I hesitated, then thought, *Trust must be earned. But I give my word not to hinder you.* She detected my true intent, however.

"You are cunning, Prince Dracula. I approve of that, of course, except where I am personally concerned. So, remember that even if you somehow managed to render me unconscious or dead, *I am not the only one of my kind,* and we are not meek Christians who think forgiveness a virtue."

She had, I decided, won this battle, unless . . .

"No help will come from *any* of your guards. All are

35

as those outside your door. So too are the people of the palace, thanks to your father and brother. The sleep of the surrounding city, however, is my doing, I am proud to say.

"But, please, do not feel you have lost a battle to me. By trusting me and allowing me to teach you, you will also win, in time."

She looked into my eyes for several heartbeats, then said, "Ah, well, if you will not promise to trust me a little, I will have to trust your ambition a lot."

She spoke the needed words in her Witch-language, and I could move again.

She smiled and took my arm as if ready for a leisurely stroll. "And now, please walk me to the courtyard. Your father and brother are already there."

I looked at her, so close to me now. A disorienting surge of desire swept through me. But were my feelings my own? Or caused by her Witchcraft?

Witchcraft! Only a short while ago, I had thought Witchcraft a superstitious lie, and now I was wondering whether a Witch were controlling my feelings, which in turn made me feel lost, no longer certain of reality.

I again wondered how many of the old legends were true. Surely not all. But I could no longer be certain. My world had suddenly become an unknown land, and if the Gypsy would guide me through that land only on her terms, I had little choice but to make the best of the situation . . . for now.

"Why the courtyard?"

"You will see. Shall we now go?"

And so I began walking to the courtyard, Tzigane close by my side, clinging to my arm and brushing lightly against me with each step.

7
Strigoi

Even at that late hour there should have been various night sounds within and outside the palace walls. But, except for our footsteps, all was silent. Along the way I saw other guards slumped helpless in sleep, reminding me of a scene from a half-remembered children's tale.

Beyond the entrance hall, we emerged from the palace into the torchlit courtyard. Father and Mircea stood staring blankly. Varina was also there. She too stared blankly. There was blood on her throat.

Tzigane said, "Varina heard her husband call to her with his thoughts, his desires. She went to the crypt and gave both him and your father strength with her blood. She will become like them, now, in their new home."

"New home?"

"You have heard legends of the Scholomance, I am certain."

"The Devil's School? Another tale to frighten children."

"And, sometimes . . . adults?" She smiled. "It is not exactly as described in the old stories. But it does exist. As do the Strigoi."

"Another name for what my father and brother have become."

"In truth, no. The Strigoi are not human. They exist beyond the realm of Earth. And I have been trained to summon and control them, as you will now see."

"Trained . . . at the Devil's School?"

"Of course."

"And the purpose of summoning a Strigoi?"

"To swiftly carry these three to their new home. Stand quietly now, please, and watch. And know that I do nothing that you cannot also learn to do, in time."

"When I become . . . a Witch?"

She laughed. "The Son of the Dragon is destined to be much more than a Witch, Prince Dracula. Someone to whom Witches bow. You would like that, would you not? To have such as me kneeling before you?"

The thought of the beautiful young woman kneeling at my feet conjured an image that led to other thoughts.

"Ah," she said, laughing, "you *would* enjoy it, I see! Though not quite as I meant it."

My face reddened. "I think you caused me to have those thoughts, Witch."

"I assure you that the interesting image that just now . . . arose, in your mind, was yours alone. But if you will trust me, you will in time experience pleasures greater than such mundane sexual ones, though neither shall we neglect those things that mortals so enjoy. Now, behold the summoning of a Strigoi!"

She turned her back to me and looked up at the dark night sky. She raised her arms, hands above her head.

For a moment I considered testing her defenses. With her concentration elsewhere, I might be able to grab her from behind and—

But then I almost laughed aloud myself, for the thought of grabbing her from behind had immediately led to *other* thoughts of pleasure, my hands on her breasts, her body pressed tightly against mine . . .

If she detected the direction of my new thoughts, or if she had caused them to form, she gave no sign. Face upraised to the star-infested sky, she began to chant in the foreign tongue, rhythmically repeating the same phrase over and over, until changing it to a new phrase, which was then also repeated numerous times.

Her voice became louder as she continued to chant the gutteral phrases. Then, after a pause lasting several heartbeats, she screamed.

In the dungeons of Egrigoz I had heard many screams, not a few of them my own, but none like the cry of agony the Gypsy woman now shouted to the sky, her hands clenched into trembling fists over her head.

To my terror, from above came an answering cry, though not from a human throat. As the spectral scream from the heavens faded away, harsh whispers drifted earthward from out of the empty sky. And then . . . *light*, in the sky, an oval glowing purple, out of which something dark and winged suddenly emerged to plummet toward the Earth far below.

I drew my sword without thinking. Then I did think, and realized I could probably do the monstrous winged thing no real harm with the blade. But the weapon's weight in my hand comforted me slightly as I forced myself to stand my ground and, perhaps foolishly, trust Tzigane's power.

The Witch screamed words of command. The Strigoi slowed its descent and hovered over the courtyard, its size blocking out the stars overhead. The cold wind from its vast wings carried a nauseating stench.

Tzigane commanded the creature again. It opened its massive talons. She rapidly gave other commands. Father and Mircea and Varina pressed themselves within the encircling talons. Then the beast gently picked them up, lifted itself back into the heavens, and flew swiftly away toward the north.

North of Targoviste stretched the mountains that, east to west, divided Wallachia from Transylvania. Legends said the Devil's School was located high in those mountains above Lake Hermannstadt. Legends. Witchcraft. I felt again my disorienting loss of reality, felt again my fear.

As the sound of the monster's wings grew fainter and fainter, in the distance to the north wolves began to howl.

Tzigane shouted new words skyward. The purple oval of light far above dimmed and vanished. She unclenched her fists, rubbed the back of her neck with her hands, and turned to me. Her eyes still held pain, but she was smiling once again.

"Thank you, my Prince."

I sheathed my sword. "I am glad my trust was not misplaced."

"You misunderstand. I was not thanking you for your trust, but for the thoughts you associated with grabbing me from behind."

I was silent a moment, and then I laughed. She joined me. A new world lay before me, and the thought suddenly seemed more exciting than disturbing. But was the excitement I felt now my own? Or Witch-sent?

She stepped closer. I did not stop her. Closer.

I fought my need to embrace her.

She moved closer still. Leaned against me so that her breasts touched my chest. "Come to my forest cottage, tomorrow." She touched her lips to mine. A spear of desire stabbed deeply. I almost gave in to my need to take her in my arms and crush her against me.

"I will be waiting. My magic will draw your horse to my door. But ride alone, or find me you never will." She kissed my lips once more.

I stubbornly did not return her kiss. A Witch! With powers such as I had never dreamed possible. Who claimed she wanted to teach me to wield Witch-powers, too. A very beautiful woman. Or was she, I suddenly wondered, as told in some old tales, an ancient crone casting a spell of illusion and desire?

"I have used no Witchcraft to influence your desires, my Prince, save that used by all women who desire a man. And I am indeed as you see me. Beneath the covering of my clothing there waits the flesh of a young woman who longs to share her life . . . and knowledge, with you."

Another kiss.

Then she ran lightly from the courtyard, her cloak billowing behind her like great black wings.

Chapter Three

8
Doubts

To follow the Witch from the palace seemed useless. I doubted she would allow it, and from what I had experienced I knew she had ample power to stop me if I tried.

As I returned to my chambers, my thoughts and emotions in turmoil over all that had just happened, the palace guards began to stir from their unnatural sleep. Sounds around the palace indicated that its residents and those in the city beyond were also awakening.

Soon came the frantic barking of dogs as they too awoke from their forced slumber and, perhaps, scented something of the Unseen lingering in the air.

Of course I said nothing of what I had seen, and I pretended to have also been affected by the deep sleep.

I learned that Turks and Christians alike remembered nightmares. A priest called it Satan's Night, and that seemed to be a satisfactory explanation for most. Prayers of thanks for deliverance were intoned. But I secretly thought about the Witch responsible, and about seeing her again.

With the coming of dawn, however, and the passing of the hours since Tzigane's departure, the miraculous things I had witnessed during the night grew less easy to accept. Doubt entered my mind, and I searched for a more reasonable explanation.

Perhaps I had been the victim of an elaborate plot meant to lure me, alone, into the forest to be secretly assassinated. But such a plot would have had to involve poisons or drugs that put *everyone* to sleep, after which I was given an antidote that caused me to awaken and see hallucinations. The elaborate requirements of such a plot were so hard to accept that a supernatural explanation seemed by comparison almost as rational.

Further, there were physical confirmations of what I had, or seemed to have, witnessed. The bodies of my father and brother were gone from the crypt. Varina was no longer in the palace. But agents working for Vladislav could have taken Varina and the two corpses as part of the plot, and I suggested that explanation to others when the disappearances were discovered.

I could not deny, however, that I found it amusing to believe I alone possessed true knowledge of the night's events, and like a child awakening from a wonderful dream, I often caught myself secretly wanting it to have all been real.

How exciting it was to think that the Witch from my dream had become a beautiful woman anxious to teach me forbidden secrets. *How exciting to think of the power she had promised could be mine!*

I tried to think but little, however, of my father and brother and what, if all that I remembered were true, they had now become.

9
Journey

Tzigane had promised her magic would draw my horse to her door, but only if I rode alone. I decided I would, therefore, ride alone. But with a group of my Turkish soldiers following out of sight.

Late that morning, under overcast skies that threatened snow I rode from Targoviste, my soldiers following a good distance behind. I was attired for battle, wearing chain mail over a quilted skirt and an iron battle helm lined with soft leather, and I was armed with sword and shield.

Beyond the city, I gave my horse his head. He began galloping to the north as if he were indeed being drawn to a destination. But after he entered the forest, he slowed, became nervous, panicked, turned, and ran back toward Targoviste.

Although I was an experienced rider, nothing I could do slowed my horse's frantic death from unseen terror, a fear that soon communicated itself to me, causing me to look back more than once, sensing some monstrous evil in close pursuit.

My ploy to have soldiers follow was not going to work. Tzigane's words had been true! It *must* have all really happened!

The feeling of pressing danger vanished when I neared the following soldiers. My stallion again responded to my control. I reined to a halt and ordered the soldiers to remain on guard at the edge of the forest until I returned. Then I rode back into the woods.

The forest held no terror this time. When I gave my steed his head, he immediately began moving along a narrow path leading through the thickly packed trees.

When we reached a crossroad, he took the path to the left without hesitation, as if it were the only choice.

The path we traveled became more overgrown the farther we went, but my horse picked his way through the masses of dead weeds and tangled roots without slowing his pace, never pausing, never stumbling.

On and on he carried me deeper amongst the shadowy trees. I often found it necessary to lean down to avoid low-hanging branches. The air grew colder, but thankfully there was neither wind nor snow.

Soon, I no longer heard nor saw any forest creatures, not even birds, and as the journey wore on, although my stallion continued to be certain of his way I began to grow confused, found it hard to concentrate, fought sleep, felt as if I were riding in a dream, no longer able to hear the sound of my horse's hooves, or any sound at all.

Now and then it seemed that my steed doubled back on the path, passing again over previously traveled ground, traveling in circles, but an increasing lethargy made it impossible for me to care enough to try stopping him as I rode on and on and on.

How long the dreamlike journey lasted I do not know, but suddenly we emerged into a forest clearing. My confusion and lethargy lifted, and I immediately became alert and wary.

In the center of the clearing, surrounded by towering

pines, sat a thatch-roofed cottage. Smoke from a fire within curled skyward. The air smelled of woodsmoke and spices.

I carefully looked for signs of an ambush, for men in hiding among the surrounding trees. But I saw only the cottage.

The door opened and Tzigane appeared. She was covered neck to ankles in a flowing black gown upon which were worked intricate silver designs.

Tzigane. Solid and real. Smiling at me. More beautiful than I remembered.

"Welcome, Prince Dracula. My thanks for coming. Please, enter my home freely and of your own will, and leave with me some of the happiness you bring."

I checked the trees for hiding assassins again, then dismounted and led my horse across the clearing.

She said, "I fear your soldiers will grow rather cold at the forest's edge before you return."

"They are Turks. I care little what happens to them."

"A secret you hide from them well."

"They are not Witches who read thoughts." I stopped several paces from her.

"Your battle attire suits you. Do you intend to point your sword at me today?"

"I think not. I do not care to be paralyzed again."

She laughed. "What wondrous things I have to share with you! Come inside and partake of my warmth. I am anxious to begin your first lesson."

"It was a long journey. My horse requires water and food."

"The journey seemed much longer to you than it did to him, a necessary spell intended not so much for you as for those who might try to secretly follow you. But do not worry for your horse. He will be well cared for while you are inside."

49

I looked again for others. "By whom?"

"Helpers. It requires training to see them." She stepped forward and took my hand. At her touch warmth pulsed through me again. "Come inside, my Prince. I assure you that you are safer here with me than in your own palace."

I stepped across the threshold and into the cottage. The air was warm and laced by drifting streamers of fragrant, spice-scented smoke. Candles burned all around. A fire blazed cozily.

I glanced carefully around to make certain no soldiers waited within.

"There is no one inside these walls, seen or unseen, save the two of us, my Prince." She closed the door behind us. "No ambushes await you here, other than those laid by your own ambitions and desires, and fate. Be comfortable. Remove your battle helm and mail."

I pulled off my helmet. "I wish my first lesson to be how to read thoughts."

She shook her head. "No. You must learn other things first. When you began training with a sword, they did not give you a sharp blade, did they? Until you learn basic things, the power to enter the minds of others might well do you more harm than good."

"What, then, is my first lesson to be?"

"It involves your . . ." she leaned close and kissed me upon my lips, ". . . emotions."

"In what way?"

Another kiss. "Magic is powered by strong emotions, death magic by hate, life magic by love, and other magics by all the emotions in between those two extremes. But you have taught yourself to control your emotions, even to deny them in order to survive what life has thus far placed in your path. Freeing your emotions, experiencing them fully, so that you will have access to them as a source of magical power is what you must learn first. And to that end . . .''

She stepped back from me, her dark eyes on mine, and slowly began raising the hem of her gown. She was naked beneath.

"Do I please you, my Prince?" she asked, almost shyly.

My pulse was pounding in my ears! "Very . . . much," I replied.

She draped the gown over the back of a rough-hewn chair with great care. She said, "This is a very special gown. It was woven and sewn and embellished by the elders who trained me, to be worn on the day that the Son of the Devil became my lover." She looked down at the floor then back up at me as if suddenly uncertain. "Is this that day, Prince Dracula? Or must I . . . wait, for another time?"

"You can read thoughts, can you not?"

I stepped toward her.

Laughing, she rushed into my arms.

10
Passion

As I lay in Tzigane's arms, upon her narrow bed, after we had made love, my thoughts drifted to my first lover, if that she could truly have been called.

Her name was Djalma, a Turkish woman placed in my cell to seduce me while my jailers' secretly watched and laughed.

I, a boy who had just recently become fourteen, soon succumbed to her seductive arts, and again on each of the two days that followed. But on the fourth day, the Turks took me to the torture chamber and showed me Djalma, hanging naked in chains.

They gave me a choice. If I swore allegiance to the Sultan, Djalma would not be harmed. If I refused, she would be tortured. To death. While I was forced to watch.

They had already tried other methods to compel my loyalty to their leader. All had failed. And so, I vowed to myself, would this one.

I turned the ordeal back on them by pretending I did not care what happened to Djalma, and by requesting permission to help with her torture. And although it sickened me in ways I dared not allow the Turks to see, I *did* help, acting as if I enjoyed hearing Djalma scream.

But long before they wished her death to come, I used the pretense of my inexperience to clumsily end her suffering.

I believe the Turks began to fear me that night. And I vowed to make them fear me a great deal more in the years to come.

I once dreamed of a forest of tall wooden stakes upon which thousands of Turks were impaled, screaming for mercy as Djalma had screamed, slowly dying as she had died.

Tzigane snuggled closer against me, her long, sleek legs warm against mine. She stroked my bare chest with a graceful, long-fingered hand. We kissed. "I am sorry for you, my Prince."

"It is time for you to call me Vlad."

"As you wish . . . Vlad."

"Sorry for me, why?"

"I am sorry that your first experience of love became one of horror."

I tensed. I had meant no one but the Turks ever to know about Djalma. Though it had made the Turks start to fear me, memories of the monstrous things I did to Djalma before she died still shamed me. And now Tzigane knew!

"Knowing about Djalma does not change my feelings for you, my Vlad. You did what was necessary, as do we all."

"It was a long time ago. Nearly four years. It's just that I . . . regret, deeply, that it happened."

"But it did happen. And it's done. And we must now think not only of the present, but . . . the future." She sat up and looked down at me. "Vlad, after what you have experienced of the Unseen, what are your feelings concerning . . . prophecy?"

I again marveled at her beauty and reached up to touch

53

her breasts. She did not stop me. As I teased her nipples with the tips of my thumbs, she moaned low in her throat, then pulled away, stood, and reached for the black gown.

"Must you dress, Tzigane? I would prefer another lesson."

"As would I. But I asked you a question. Please answer it."

"And if I do, you will give me another lesson?"

"Vlad, please."

I sat up and shrugged my shoulders. "Prophecy? I thought it akin to other superstitious lies before last night. Now? I think I had better let you tell me what to think. I can decide later whether or not I agree."

"And if your own fate has been foretold in a prophecy?"

"Has it?"

"Yes."

"Ah. And is it a good fate? With many lessons from you in it?"

"You make me feel like laughing when I am trying to be serious. Oh! You make me unsure of what I have rehearsed for so long to say!"

"I will listen without speaking, Tzigane, if that is what you wish."

"Yes, please. And afterward, if you still desire it, we can again share passion."

"I am certain I will desire it."

I reached for her, placed my hands on her hips, drew her toward me, held her tightly, my cheek pressed against her stomach. I kissed the fabric that covered her navel. I again wished she were not wearing the gown.

She laughed and wriggled out of my grasp. "I wish I were not wearing it, too. But before I remove it again, I must tell you of the prophecy. While I tell you, however, I will let brew something special for us to drink, herbs that, when properly prepared, make passion's flames burn even more fiercely.''

''They seem sufficiently hot to me.''

''I was not implying our lovemaking failed to excite and satisfy, only that it is possible to share even more.''

''I am, of course, quite willing to explore that possibility.''

I watched as she quickly placed herbs from several earthen jars in a cauldron of water steaming near the fire. I stared with something akin to religious devotion at the curves of her body as her movements caused the thin, freely flowing gown to first cling to this part, then that, and I ached to have her in my arms once more, to again feel what I had while making love, a happiness greater than I had ever known in my nearly eighteen years of life.

But a single thought suddenly changed my emotions, turned the fire to ice.

Witchcraft was real, and I was under Tzigane's spell.

I could not trust my emotions, no matter what she said. And the brew she was making might be an evil draught that would place me even more deeply under her control.

I should clothe myself and leave at once. But I did not *want* to do that. Because . . . of a spell?

She had vanquished the iron will that had allowed me to resist the Turks in Egrigoz, weakened my stubborn self-control.

Or had she? It need not be Witchcraft making me feel as I felt, but merely a young man's healthy passion for a beautiful young woman. My first *real* lover. My first taste of passions freely given and mutually desired.

Damn the Witch! I thought. *Or damn the woman and*

55

her beauty. I have lost control of my life, and she is the cause.

"No." Tzigane returned from the cauldron and sat beside me on the bed. She took my hands. "You have not lost control of your life. You are merely losing the illusion of the life you thought was yours, because it never really was."

"Do you expect that to make sense to me, Tzigane? Because it does not."

"Vlad, the life that you believed stretched before you was largely an illusion, the life of a warlord-Prince such as your father, constrained by responsibilities and suspicions, battles and intrigues, with death from war or assassination awaiting you long before you reached old age.

"But a limited existence such as that is not prophesied to be your fate. For you there is to be so much more! And you have already taken the first steps on a journey to meet that destiny, with me."

11
Prophecy

"Your name has two meanings, Vlad. So will your life."

"According to the prophecy?"

"According to the prophecy."

"I know about my name, of course. Dracul can mean both 'Dragon' and 'Devil,' as I believe was mentioned during that *dream* I had of you nine years ago."

"You remember your part in my vision-dream surprisingly well."

"It had a strong effect on me."

"And on me, on my life, as I've already told. So, you are the son of the Dragon, and history shall record the deeds of the aristocratic, warlord-ruler you were born to become.

"But although your earthly father's enemies sometimes called him 'Devil,' when I think of you as the 'Son of the Devil' I do not think of the father of your . . . flesh."

I did not like the implications in that! But I said nothing.

Reading my thoughts, the Witch quickly said, "There is nothing of which to be afraid, my Vlad."

"Of that I . . . am willing to be convinced."

She inhaled deeply and fixed me with her steady gaze. "There will also be a hidden side to your life of which historians will never know, the life of the Son of the Devil, in which you do the work not of the father of your flesh, but the father of your *soul.*"

"And that is suppose to decrease my feelings of fear?"

"Vlad, please, try to understand—"

"Tzigane, since last night you have given me cause to believe in many miraculous things, but—"

"From where do souls come, Vlad, if not from spiritual fathers living in realms beyond Earth?"

"And spiritual mothers?"

"Satan and the false God of Light are *creators,* transcending any need for the sexual distinctions we know on Earth."

I shook my head. "That makes a kind of sense, yet at this time yesterday I did not believe too seriously in souls."

"But you do now?"

"So much has happened so quickly, I am not certain what I believe, what I *should* believe. But if the Undead are real and Witches can summon winged monsters from out of the empty sky, I would be foolish to reject outright anything you tell me is true."

"I will never lie to you."

My mind, recoiling, instinctively retreated to familiar ground. "But you will lie with me."

Confusion filled her eyes for a moment, then she caught my meaning. "You promised not to speak of passion until after I told you the prophecy."

"Then tell it as quickly as you can. At the moment, sitting on this bed with you, the future I most care about is the immediate one I can comprehend, the one I prophesy will follow your telling of this other prophecy in which I am . . . Satan's son?'' I laughed. ''Forgive me, but the idea that the father of my soul is the Evil One, strikes me as—''

''No, Vlad. That is another lie you have been told. Satan is not Evil!''

I said nothing for a moment, then, ''The *Devil* is *not* Evil?''

''He is called that by his Enemy and those who serve His Enemy, but Satan is the *true* God of Light.''

''Then, the Devil is Good, and God is Evil? Tzigane, how do you live with such beliefs and remain sane? Or, should I ask, *are* you sane?''

''Vlad, the realms beyond Earth are at War, and have been for longer than humans have walked the Earth. But that War, between the forces of Satan and those of the false God of Light, has long since spread into this reality called Earth.

''The history of humans has been driven by that War from Beyond. Some women and men are called to be warriors for one side or the other. Some are created to be leaders. But you, Prince Dracula, have been prophesied to lead *all* of Satan's forces. You are the one prophesied to become Satan's Earthly King!''

12
Desires

I did not react as Tzigane had expected. I sat silently for a moment, then sniffed the air, looked in the direction of the steaming cauldron, and said, "That passion-brew you are steeping smells delicious."

"Vlad! Have you nothing to say about the prophecy?"

"What *can* I say, Tzigane? Or, rather, what would you have me say? That it fills me with joy?"

"But . . . vast glory awaits you! You must treat the prophecy seriously."

"Because you do?"

"Well, yes! I have been trained in such matters, while you have not."

"I have heard Satan called the Prince of Lies. I am not saying you are knowingly lying, Tzigane, but is it not possible that you were taught lies? It would be a cunning trick on Satan's part to convince his followers they were doing good instead of evil, would it not?"

"Do you not think we would know the difference?"

"Not if Satan had the power to influence your perceptions. If Satan is real—"

"He is!"

"—then is what I suggested not possible?"

"I . . . suppose so. But it is not the case. And besides, does it really matter to you?"

It was a thought I had not entertained. "It should." But I was now not entirely certain that it did.

"The Prophecies of Satan have named you Satan's future King on Earth. Will you accept such glory, such *power,* only if Satan is the Power of Good I believe? Will you refuse the Throne of the World if Evil is the power behind that throne?"

I thought about it, then I thought about it some more.

"Your conscious mind is confusing you, Vlad."

"My *conscious* mind?"

"Things you have been taught to believe are fighting your true desires. Your conscious mind is repressing your personal, emotional truths behind a barrier of denial. Relax your mind and let your inner desires well up within you as did your passions while we made love."

"I have experienced many things I deemed Evil, Tzigane. I saw my mother burned alive by evil men claiming to be doing good. I endured the evil things my father, whom I was supposed to love and honor, did to me and my brothers and others, and I grew to hate him. In the dungeons of Egrigoz I learned to survive the evil of my jailers from day to day, often moment to moment, while secretly vowing revenge.

"But if the Evil I have encountered was perhaps caused by some supernatural force in which I have not believed, I must hate that force as well, be it Satan or God. Or both! I therefore doubt if I could comfortably sit on a throne dedicated to Evil."

"Which only means you are not yourself evil."

"Well," I could not help but smile, "I do not *feel* evil."

"And you are not. So, if you are Satan's Chosen King, and you are not Evil, neither must Satan be Evil. Yes?"

"Ah. A good point. But—"

"Find out for certain. Allow the desires of your soul to well up within you."

"By relaxing my *conscious* thoughts."

"Yes."

"Very well. I will try. But . . . how?"

"Think of something peaceful and concentrate upon it. Perhaps the gurgling of a stream or the crackling of a campfire beneath the stars. Think of nothing save that image. Let all other thoughts and cares slip away. Then alter your attention to your inner depths and allow what is waiting there to flow forth."

I tried to think of a flowing stream.

"Close your eyes, Vlad, It might also help if you stretched out on the bed and relaxed your body."

I stretched out on the bed and closed my eyes and tried to relax my muscles, but I had little success.

"No," Tzigane said when she had probed my thoughts and discovered my lack of progress. "You are trying too hard."

"But . . . doing what you suggest is not easy. How then, can I do it if I do not try hard?"

"Vlad, please try again."

I sighed deeply, closed my eyes again, and tried another time. But try as I might, neither my body nor mind would relax. My muscles remained tensed as if for battle. My thoughts about the prophecy swirled out of control.

"Enough, Vlad."

I opened my eyes and looked at the Witch. "Even your frown is beautiful, Tzigane."

"We will try again later."

"After we have sampled your brew and had another lesson?"

"Yes. Perhaps releasing your passion will help to relax both your body and your mind."

"I am anxious to give that possibility a try."

Tzigane rose from the bed and filled two wooden cups with the steaming brew. She brought the cups back to the bed. As I watched her walk toward me, my thoughts were momentarily consumed by the anticipation of the passion we were soon to share, and the inner feelings I had been trying to coax to the surface broke through while my conscious mind was thus distracted.

I was shaken by the intensity of those feelings, and for a moment had to fight shaming tears. And when I grasped what those feelings meant, I immediately attempted to deny their message, because it seemed that what I desired most was not something a man, as I had been taught to understand that term, such as myself should want above all else.

Tzigane handed me one of the cups and sat on the bed beside me. But when she touched my thoughts, her eyes grew round with surprise, then joy.

She leaned close and kissed me. "I am so happy, my Vlad! Do not fight your inner truth. There is nothing shameful in what you feel! Give me your cup. We will drink this brew another time."

She took my cup and set it, and hers, on the floor. Then she quickly removed her black gown and stretched out naked atop me on the bed. I had not bothered to clothe myself after our first lovemaking.

Holding each other tightly, we began to kiss.

She nibbled one of my earlobes then tickled my ear with the moist tip of her tongue. I groaned and kissed her throat. She moved so that she sat astride my hips, then she guided me into her inner depths.

She moaned with pleasure, as did I. Reaching up, I cupped her breasts. She leaned down. Lifting my head,

I captured a nipple between my teeth and gently squeezed. She gasped and squirmed atop me, sending new pleasures coursing through me. Then she positioned her other breast for a similar treatment that I did not hesitate to provide.

Panting softly, she raised up, looked down at me through her tangled mane of black hair, and said, "Don't you see? Following your *true* desires will make you *stronger*, not weaker!"

I followed the curve of her sides downward with my hands then firmly grasped her hips. I grinned. "I do, indeed, feel very strong, just now."

She began to slowly move her hips. She said, "In order to survive, you came to believe yourself an aloof, independent man who neither cared for, nor needed anyone but himself, and that illusion has served you well."

I pulled her forward so that I could again touch my lips to her breasts. "Tzigane," I whispered, kissing her warm, sweet flesh.

She pulled back. "It is time now to accept your true desires, and with them your full potential, and the glory promised by the Prophecies of Satan!"

I added, "But only if you share that glory with me." Because I had learned, as had Tzigane upon reading my thoughts, that my deepest desire, the dearest wish of a warlord-Prince discovering love on the brink of his eighteenth year of life, was to have Tzigane with me always, *and to do whatever made her smile.*

A desire for great personal power was also strong within me, but for it to have meaning, it seemed, I would have to share it with the woman whom only yesterday had been nothing but a memory from a childhood dream.

Moaning softly, Tzigane panted, "I *will* be . . . with you always, my Vlad, and you with me, as has also been foretold in . . . Satan's . . . Prophecies . . ."

"But," I added, "you must also promise to stop speaking of the future when you should be focusing all of your attention upon something more . . . immediate." I suddenly thrust deeper into her.

She gave a short, wordless cry, then squeezed me tightly and said, "Then that . . . oh! . . . I promise . . . as well!"

Chapter Four

13

Gift

In the days that followed my first visit to Tzigane's cottage, little else mattered to me save seeing her again, touching her, loving her. The duties of the throne became an irritating distraction. My old primary concern, to find local support to defeat Vladislav, should he return, was replaced by my need to return as swiftly as possible to my lover's arms.

After my third visit to Tzigane in the forest, however, she made our being together easier. On that third visit, I mastered, with Tzigane's guidance, the skill of seeing in a special way. She then returned with me to the palace, but secretly, by casting a spell of invisibility around herself that could only be penetrated by the special vision I had learned!

In the palace, she often helped me as an ally. Invisible by my side, she could read the thoughts of those around me and secretly tell me of any treachery being planned or of loyalties upon which I could depend.

But she also, occasionally, took a mischievous delight in distracting me from my duties.

She grew bored during an important discussion concerning the city's defenses, and removed all of her clothing, then began performing a slow and silent dance meant to inflame me with desire.

Her dancing quickly made me grow bored with the meeting as well. I ended the meeting early. Then I began pursuing her through the peopled hallways and rooms of the palace, the sight of her naked among clothed courtiers exciting me even more.

She eventually led me out of doors and into a seldom used tower upon the palace grounds, then up a winding spiral staircase, and outdoors again atop the tower's battlements. There, where we were alone and only a creature with wings could have seen us, she *allowed* me to corner her.

Freshly fallen snow blanketed the stones atop the tower, and new snow was falling. Seeing her naked in a setting that demanded heavy clothing made her nudity even more desirable to me than it had among the clothed people in the palace. But I nevertheless insisted she come back inside at once for her health's sake. She laughed at that and explained she had been trained to withstand, temporarily, great heat or great cold. She claimed, too, that she could walk on hot coals without burning her feet.

Soon, snow or not, she had me also bare of clothing, and we made love atop the snow-covered tower, naked to the elements, wind howling about us, snow falling all around.

Afterward, with passion's fires cooling and the freezing reality of my surroundings making me shiver, she kept me naked, held me closely, chanted a spell that surrounded us with air as warm as a summer's afternoon, and promised to one day teach me how to work the spell myself.

In the days to come, she taught me other occult techniques to prepare me for learning how to read thoughts, and more. I practiced exercises she gave me to increase mental concentration and visualization. And I practiced, when no one else could hear, intoning special sounds whose vibrations, Tzigane claimed, when combined in special ways formed Words of Power such as those I'd already heard her use.

Possessing secret occult knowledge and skills gave me an invigorating sense of superiority, and earning one of Tzigane's smiles by mastering a new lesson motivated me to work harder and then harder still to learn all that she taught.

But though happy beyond anything I'd known, I was far from at peace, and not just because of Vladislav's possible return.

In spite of all I'd seen and experienced, doubt sometimes returned to plague me when I was not actually in Tzigane's presence. At such times, my old beliefs tried to reassert themselves, making me long for a return to the simple, understandable, and more controllable world I had once known, a world where all things Unseen were superstitious lies about which I need not be concerned.

And I would then wonder anew if I were experiencing my true desires or being manipulated by a cunning woman. Did I truly love her, or had I been bewitched by a spell, made weak, enslaved by passion's snare? Indeed, was my need for her merely the demanding lust of a young man hungering for the flesh of the most beautiful woman he had ever known, not to mention the only close friend he had ever had?

But all doubts always vanished when Tzigane appeared. She was *real*. The things she did were *real*. The things she had taught me to do were *real*. And so, it seemed to follow, must the prophecy she believed in be also real. Why, then, did doubts plague me when I was alone?

One evening, we were again atop the tower where we

had made love in the snow, but this time fully clothed, both wearing heavy cloaks against the December cold.

The sun was setting, casting long purple shadows across the winter landscape below. The thin crescent horns of a new moon hung in the western sky above the sunset's glow. The stars forming the constellations of the hunter and hound were brightening in the darkening east. The scent of woodsmoke from warming fires drifted on the chilled winter air.

Tzigane snuggled close to me and said, "I know of your recurring doubts, my Vlad. I also know why you still have them, and I know how to help you to conquer them."

She paused. Then she gave me a quick hug and surprised me by saying, "Today is your birthday."

"No one here knows that, nor shall they."

"But *I* know."

"I did not *tell* you. You had to read it in my thoughts. But it matters little, my birthday."

"No?" She pressed herself into the circle of my arms and kissed me. "Have you never wondered when I was born?"

In truth, I had not. Had I hurt her by not asking?

She answered my thought. "No."

"Nonetheless, I should have asked."

"Vlad, I know that the last birthday you celebrated was your fourth, at which your mother named herself to you and was later killed for doing so. And I know your not asking my birthday indicates no lack of love for me. Your thoughts, whether your lips have formed the words or not, have told me how much you love me, as I have come to love you. But just so you will know when my birthday is, in case you might want to remember it in the future—"

"Is that a hint, Tzigane?"

"—I was born on the threshold of Spring during the last night of Winter."

"Next Spring Eve, I shall remember."

"Among my tribe, it is the custom to give a small gift at someone's birthday."

"Then you shall have one at yours. Why, it would not surprise me if there were even *more* than one!"

Tzigane kissed me, reached under her cloak, and handed me a small package wrapped in black silk. "A token of my love on your birthday, my Prince, and always."

I unwrapped the silk and found within it a ring. It was a simple silver band. But in the sunset's crimson glow I saw that the inner surface was engraved with intricate mystic symbols, a few of which I recognized from my lessons.

"Give me your left hand, Vlad." She had taught me that in occult work the left hand was the Hand of Power.

When I had removed my black leather glove from my left hand, Tzigane slipped the ring onto the first finger. It seemed a bit too large at first, but a moment later fit perfectly, as if it had somehow adjusted its size.

Knowing my thoughts, she said, "Its size did indeed change when it . . . accepted you. No one but you and those trained to do so will be able to see this ring. Only because you have worked hard and learned quickly do you possess enough occult strength to wear it without being harmed."

"I . . . thank you, Tzigane." I embraced and kissed her. "Let my lips also tell you of my love."

She returned my kisses, added several of her own, then said, "The ring has also been charged with protective energy that should give you relief from your recurring doubts. I will explain further, about the ring and your doubts, but not here. I have prepared a special place for the telling. Will you come with me there now?"

"Of course. Where must we go?"

"Not far. Below the palace. Into the crypt."

14
Crypt

By flickering lantern light, I followed Tzigane among the Dead. Down narrow passageways past the crumbling remains of those who dreamed no more she led me, the sound of our footsteps muffled by a thick layer of dust long undisturbed.

In the deepest chamber, we came to a pile of stones and beyond it in the wall the shadowed opening of a narrow tunnel. Tzigane motioned to the tunnel and said, "As you can see, they blocked it when they built the crypt. My helpers unblocked it for me. When we have done what we came to do, they will replace the stones, blocking it once more."

"The helpers I still do not have the skill to see."

"Yes. Of course the tunnel and the place to which it leads were here long before the palace was built. As is often the case, a modern seat of power was built above an ancient one. Now I must ask you something, Vlad. Will you follow me farther or not?"

"Should I say yes? Or no?"

She hesitated. "Will you follow me farther or not?"

"I was teasing you, Tzigane. Did not you read my mind? Of course I will follow you."

"You must say the words of agreement aloud."

"Another part of the prophecy?"

"Yes."

"When will I get to hear *all* of the prophecy?"

"If I told it all to you, your fulfillment of it would not be deemed as valid."

"If I am already Satan's Chosen King, what does it matter whether or not I—"

"Vlad, please. You have learned much already, but there is much more to learn. Things are as they must be. Please, answer me aloud. Will you follow me farther or not?"

"All right, Tzigane. *Yes,* I will follow you farther. Lead on."

She kissed me without smiling. "Thank you."

We climbed over the pile of stones. The walls of the tunnel were smooth, unmarred by the marks of tools, suggesting to me that it was a natural formation. The ceiling was so low and the walls so close together that we had to walk hunched over and one behind the other.

The floor began angling downward. Deeper and deeper into the Earth I followed the Witch. Colder and colder grew the air, my breath frosty in the lantern's light.

The path twisted first right and then left, down farther and farther, until finally we emerged into a small chamber with a pool of water in its center.

The ceiling of the chamber, revealed in the flickering glow of our lantern, reminded me of icicles on a winter's morning.

So deep in the Earth, all was silent save for my breathing and Tzigane's. The surface of the pool was smooth as sword steel, but black as coal, reflecting the ceiling as if in a mirror.

Tzigane walked to the edge of the pool. "An old legend known to my tribe says that anyone who falls into underground pools such as this one risks having the Devil reach up from Hell and drag them down. Such deep-Earth pools are sacred to Satan. Your thoughts tell me you have never heard of the legend.''

''I am not a Gypsy. And until a few days ago I would have considered it my duty to forget such nonsense if I had heard it.''

''But now, for all you know, Satan may shoot up out of the water at any moment and grasp your hand, yes?''

A flash of fear shot through me. I laughed. ''You undoubtedly detected the fear I just felt. Don't you think it amusing that the Chosen King of Satan is afraid the Devil might appear?''

''Vlad, it . . . would frighten me, too.''

''Truly?''

''Do you think I have no fear? Do you think I know all there is to know?''

''Well, no. But—''

''But it has seemed that way over the days you have known me.''

''That it has. I am, however, I think, glad to know that you would also be afraid if Satan suddenly appeared.''

''Experiencing the presence of a deity would be terrifying to anyone. If the so-called Son of the false God of Light suddenly appeared to the Christians, I believe they would be terrified, too. But I did not bring you here to discuss human nature. I brought you to one of Satan's sacred pools to explain about your doubts and how the ring I gave you tonight can help prevent those doubts from recurring, allowing your studies with me to progress even more quickly.''

She looked at me, fixed me with her dark gaze. ''Vlad, I must now do something that is very important.

You must treat it extremely seriously and do exactly as I ask. Agreed?"

"Of course."

She nodded. "All right. Here is what I am going to do. I am going to whisper three Words of Power, composed of occult sounds you have already learned. And here is what you must do. You must listen closely and repeat the three Words aloud. But I can whisper them only once, and you must pronounce them loudly and exactly correctly the first time."

It seemed a slightly silly thing to have to do, but I tried to remain serious. "And if I do not?"

"You *must* pronounce them exactly correctly the first time," she repeated, "or all is lost. *All*. Do you understand?"

Another stab of fear shot through me. And the fear suddenly angered me. Silly or not, if Tzigane thought pronouncing three words so important, I would not fail her.

I took a deep breath, reminded myself of the concentration techniques Tzigane had taught me, narrowed the focus of my mind, and said, "Whisper the Words."

She leaned close to my ear and whispered three guttural words composed of three syllables each, syllables that corresponded to nine of the sounds I had learned. I had expected the task to be hard, but it seemed now it would be easy.

I opened my mouth to intone the three words, but suddenly doubt assailed me. I had encountered trouble remembering one of the sounds I had been taught. Wasn't it one of the nine I must now pronounce? No. It wasn't. And then again, it seemed perhaps it was.

My confidence was suddenly shattered. I was not certain I could pronounce them correctly the first time. I needed to hear her pronounce them again. But she had said she could only pronounce them once.

What would happen, I wondered, if I did not pronounce them at all? If I simply turned and left the chamber?

But I could not leave. It might well mean abandoning the future Tzigane had foretold for us. Abandoning her. Our friendship. Our love.

I felt as if I stood at the branching of a road. Down one path, the one that would result if I left the words unpronounced, I sensed an emptiness stretching into nothingness. Down the other I believed was a life with Tzigane, the future, unknown and dangerous, but far better than endless emptiness and loneliness, a future worth the chancing.

I took another deep breath, sought to steady my nerves, and again focused my concentration.

I pronounced nine syllables, forming three words.

All was silent when the last syllable had been intoned. Had I failed? Why had Tzigane not reacted? Instead, she stood with head down, her face hidden by her long hair, her body as still as stone, fists clenched at her sides.

Pain! My left hand was suddenly in agony, as if thrust into a fire. And then I saw that the silver ring Tzigane had given me was glowing as if red hot. But my flesh, though in pain, was not actually burning beneath it.

I tried to remove the ring. Touching it sent burning pain shooting into my right hand as well, but I gritted my teeth, accepted the pain, and tried to pull the ring off. It would not, however, slip free. It clung as if bonded to my flesh.

Suddenly the solid silver turned transparent, revealing the occult symbols engraved upon the inner surface as black marks against my skin, marks that began to move, to *dance,* and to become other than what they had been, serpentine shapes slithering over and under each other, restlessly moving, moving, moving.

The walls of the chamber changed too, glowed with crimson fire, became transparent, revealing in their depths impossible scenes of horror, men and women suffering vast agonies, their gaping mouths open in end-less screams I could not hear, being tortured by mon-sters, mutilated, only to heal and be tortured again, their writhing bodies spasming with endless pain.

And the pool also changed. The water vanished, leav-ing a shaft whose vertical walls were alive with writhing serpents, illuminated from far below by the red glow of the fire deep in the Earth.

Then my attention was drawn back to my left hand as the air above the glowing ring shimmered and con-densed into the ghostly image of a boiling black cloud laced with crimson lightning, and in its center was the skull of an inhuman thing, its multiple eye sockets blaz-ing as if filled with hot coals, bestial horns sprouting from its temples. Then its pointed teeth moved, its jaws slowly opening.

I tried to look away but could not. The agony engulf-ing my hand grew worse.

And then, into my mind came words that echoed into my depths and left me shaken, nine words—

In you I am indeed well pleased, my son.

As suddenly as it had begun, it was over, the pain in my hand was gone, the ring was a solid silver band on my finger once more, and the walls of the chamber and the pool in its center were again as they had been when we entered.

My heart hammered in my chest. I breathed deeply, trying to calm myself, and I saw Tzigane was now look-ing at me.

Her cheeks were wet with tears, but she was smiling. She rushed into my arms. We kissed, long and deep.

"You . . . heard?" I asked. "The words in my mind?"

"Yes!"

"And you saw the way the ring changed? And the walls? The pool? How they changed?"

"Oh, yes! Vlad, you will be troubled by doubts no more. The doubts were caused by occult attacks launched by Satan's Enemy and His Enemy's servants who hoped to thwart Satan's Prophecies. But this ring will now shield you from further mental attacks, for you have been accepted and marked this night by Satan Himself! *You,* in whom He is well pleased!" She knelt at my feet and bowed her head to me. "As am I."

I reached down and grasped her arms. "Stand up, Tzigane. I will not have my teacher kneeling before me."

She laughed as she returned to her feet. "The prophecy said I would kneel, and I did."

We embraced and kissed.

The chamber suddenly seemed horribly small, the walls too near.

"I am more than ready to leave here, Tzigane. Or is there something else that must be done first?"

"No. I too am ready to leave. I have in mind a hot bath, sweet red wine, and a soft bed warmed by passion. Does that sound appealing to you?"

"That it certainly does."

As we walked to the tunnel's opening to leave the chamber, I asked, "What would have happened to me, had I mispronounced the words, Tzigane, if I am allowed to know?"

She uttered a strange sounding laugh. "To you? Nothing, my Vlad. But it would have meant I had failed in

80

my task to prepare you for this test. And our Lord Satan does not approve of failure. In His ongoing war, He cannot afford to show weakness and mercy. I would have been severely punished for failing.''

''Punished? For *my* mistake? How?''

She quietly said, ''I would have had to join, for a span of nine nights, those whose images you saw when the walls became as glass, those who scream without end in the depths of Hell.''

I was stunned into momentary silence by the monstrous thought, then I said, ''You should not have placed yourself in such danger!''

''Vlad, *it was mine to do.*''

''Because of the prophecy?''

''Because of who I am and what I am to become!''

''My future wife. Because of me—''

''My risk was not that great. It was unthinkable that you might fail me.''

''Yet I think perhaps you could not have helped but to have thought of it. Tzigane, your devotion to your beliefs are beyond imagining, and your belief in me . . . for you to have trusted me so much . . .''

I pulled her close, squeezed her tightly. ''If harm had been done to you, I do not think the Devil would have been so pleased with me, after all. If harm had been done to you, I would have become Satan's enemy, too.''

''Vlad, please, do not say such things.''

''Because the Devil might hear?''

''Because it is a lie that Hell is the Devil's domain. Those you saw tortured were being made to scream by the false God of Light. Satan and God often fight the War Beyond Earth by wagering on the outcome of crucial tests.''

''In that case, I hope both Satan and God hear my words! I will become the enemy of *any* God or Devil or human who seeks to harm you, Tzigane." Anger flared stronger. I looked back at the pool and shouted, "Hear me Satan and God! Hear me and know my vow is true!"

But if either heard, or cared, there was no sign.

15
Vale

The next morning Tzigane awoke me before dawn.

"Vlad, I have just seen Vladislav returning to Targoviste."

"You *saw?*"

"In a dream."

Before Tzigane entered my life, I would have ignored a warning from a dream. But now I asked, "Do you also know how soon he will arrive? And with how many men?"

"Watch for me while I try to learn more."

Lying on her back, the Witch closed her eyes and crossed her hands over her stomach, entwining her fingers in a special way. Then she used a Witch-chant to help concentrate her will and slipped into a trance.

Not long before I would have thought anyone insane who claimed to be waiting for someone to return to their entranced body, yet that is what I was now doing, waiting for Tzigane's consciousness to return to her flesh.

My occult training had not progressed sufficiently to allow me to aid her directly on levels of reality beyond that of the Earth. True, I had learned enough to know in general what she was doing. But all I could physically do was to wait, watch over her body, worry, and wish I could do more.

She had told me how dangerous a trance could be if Satan's Enemy attacked while one's consciousness was away from the body. If the connection to the body was severed, one's consciousness could be trapped between worlds and the physical body become a vessel without a guiding will.

The Enemy sometimes then placed a different consciousness into the abandoned flesh. Spies in the War Beyond were often created in that way.

One need not be in a trance for a transfer of that sort to happen, however. Many humans with natural occult abilities unknowingly traveled to other realms while asleep, thinking their memories of such journeys mere dreams. And during those involuntary travels, they were even more vulnerable to attack than a trained occultist.

To my relief, Tzigane soon returned unharmed. She opened her eyes and sat up. "He travels with many men, a large army. Your Turkish forces are greatly outnumbered. He will be here in two days, perhaps less. If you agree, I say it is time for us to leave."

We had already discussed what we would do if Vladislav returned with more men than my meager forces could defeat. I would slip away from the palace and go with Tzigane to the Scholomance where my training in matters occult could continue.

And where else *could* I go but with the one I now considered my most trusted ally and best friend, as well as the woman I loved. In a year or two or more, when I had mastered many occult powers, I could find a way to gain support and recapture the throne in a more permanent manner, if I still desired the throne of a mere country after working my way nearer the Throne of the World that Tzigane's prophecies promised.

I asked, "You are certain I could not defeat him with the forces at my command?"

"I am certain, Vlad. I saw true in the trance. You and all your men would be slaughtered if you stayed and fought."

Having seen the things she could do, and having come to trust her, I answered, "Very well. Either I go back to the Sultan or with you. I think you are the better choice. Do you not agree?"

Tzigane showed her agreement with a kiss.

I did not feel I was being a traitor or coward by leaving behind the soldiers who had helped me take the throne. They were, after all, Turks, my enemies, and their scouts would report Vladislav's approach in time for them to flee, or fight and die as it pleased them, but without me in their ranks.

I felt a grim satisfaction, however, in the rage I knew the Sultan would exhibit when he learned that I had escaped his hands. The great Sultan, bested by a young man only eighteen years of age whose defiant spirit the dungeons of Turk-land had failed to break.

Thanks to Tzigane's spellcraft, leaving Targoviste unseen presented no significant problem. The Witch merely extended her spell of invisibility to include the both of us. And our horses.

By noon of that day, we were well out of the city, heading north. It was a beautiful winter's day. Snow sparkled like multicolored jewels in the sunlight.

I felt freer than ever I could remember. And happier. For the moment at least, neither the cares of a hostage nor those of a ruler were mine. My immediate future with Tzigane was my only concern.

I glanced back. Behind us came a pack of gray wolves, shaggy in their heavy coats of winter fur. "Your friends are still following us, Tzigane."

"They are your friends, too. And they shall continue to follow until I command them otherwise."

I had been concerned about the tracks our horses left in the snow. Although we could not be seen by untrained humans while within the shield of Tzigane's spell, our horses' tracks could be seen after we had passed. And hounds could follow our scent, should the Turks, or Vladislav's assassins, think of that.

Tzigane had soothed my concerns by summoning the wolves. As they traveled behind us, they trampled back and forth, as Tzigane's spell had commanded them to do, across our tracks to obliterate them and our scent.

We made camp that night well on our way to the northern mountains. Another day's journey brought us to the foothills. On the third day, we followed a well-hidden trail upward toward a mountain pass. I was certain winter snows would long since have closed the route, but Tzigane was not concerned, and to my surprise, although the surrounding area was deep with snow, her Witch-trail remained as passable in December as in August.

By sunset of that day, we had reached the crest of a strange, bowl-shaped valley. The sloping sides were bare of trees or vegetation of any kind. The bottom was hidden beneath a thick layer of fog. Tzigane called it the Vale of Fog and Flowers.

I said, "I see the fog. I suppose I will have to wait for summer to see the flowers."

"Perhaps you will. Or perhaps you will not."

"Meaning?"

"You will find out when it is time."

"Does the fog hide the Scholomance?"

"Perhaps it does. Or perhaps it does not."

"Tzigane . . ."

She laughed. "Tomorrow, Vlad. Patience."

"Then let us talk of tonight. There is no wood for a fire, and at this elevation the thin air will not hold the day's warmth for long."

"We will not be cold."

"We will have to use the spell for keeping cold at bay?"

"Perhaps we will. Or—"

"Tzigane!"

"—or perhaps I have faith in the warmth of our passion."

"And the horses? Shall they make love all the night long as well?"

"Vlad, they are both mares."

"I know that! I was just—"

"You were just frowning too much, as usual. Do not worry about the cold. I have been here before, remember? And you do not see any snow coating this crest or the valley below, do you? I have not guided you this far only to have you freeze in the night."

"No? Well, perhaps you have. Or perhaps you have not."

She laughed, and I joined her.

We made camp, fed and watered our horses from provisions we had brought along, ate a simple meal of bread and cheese and water, then sat watching the Sun dip behind the snow-covered peaks to the west, turning the sky a deep purple slashed by streaks of crimson and gold.

Suddenly, a warm breeze stirred the air, bringing with it the scent of summer flowers. The breeze was coming out of the Vale of Fog and Flowers, pouring over the crest where we camped, warming us.

I leaned close to Tzigane and whispered, "Have you noticed that a warm breeze has begun to blow?"

"Why, I believe you are correct, Vlad. Perhaps it will keep us warm tonight. Yes?"

"Perhaps it will. Forgive me for doubting you."

"No, Vlad. It is not that easy. I believe you should be punished for doubting me."

"Punished?"

"How long has it been since you were properly spanked on that interesting bottom of yours?"

"Spanked!"

"How long?"

I laughed. "You will not spank me, Tzigane."

"Perhaps I will. Or perhaps I will not."

"If there is any spanking to be done, it will be your finely shaped bottom that turns red."

"I think not."

"I think so!"

I grabbed her and pretended to try to turn her over my knee. Laughing, she tried to do the same to me. Soon, we began kissing and forgot the punishment.

Later, we lay side by side, the warm, flower-scented breeze caressing our nakedness as we gazed up at the bright and twinkling stars.

A falling star suddenly shot across the sky.

"A good omen, my Vlad!"

"A falling star? I thought the superstition was that they brought bad luck."

"You have a belief about comets in mind. Did you know that Satan came to Earth in a falling star long ago?"

"Yes, Tzigane. Of course I knew that."

She laughed and pinched my arm. "Of course you did *not*. And when He landed, it was here. His coming formed the Vale of Fog and Flowers. And that is why the Scholomance is also here, the most sacred spot on all the Earth for those of us who know Him to be the true God of Light.''

I was silent a moment. ''So, the Scholomance *is* below, beyond the fog, and my father and brother . . .''

Again she laughed, pushed herself up and straddled my hips. ''Perhaps so, perhaps no. Now, turn over. It is time for your spanking.''

''I think not!'' I cried and wrestled her onto the ground.

16
Tears

At dawn I awoke to find Tzigane standing with her back to me a few steps away. She was naked, her arms upraised, her bare skin caressed by the rays of the rising Sun. I watched her, marveling anew at her beauty, feeling as always the stirrings of desire. But when she turned to face me, her face was streaked with tears.

She wiped at her tears. "Good morning, Vlad." She smiled, but hesitantly.

"What is wrong, Tzigane?" She had seemed wonderfully happy the day before, laughing and mischievous, and happily contented when we had gone to sleep in each other's arms after making love. "Why do you weep on such a beautiful morning?"

She shrugged her bare shoulders. "Tears . . . do not have to mean anything is . . . wrong. And I am so happy, alone here with you . . ."

"And I with you."

She glanced back at the Sun. "Have you never noticed how truly beautiful it is . . . the Sun? So very beautiful. So warm . . ." Tears again sprung to her eyes and again she wiped at them.

I stood and walked to her, enfolded her in my arms. "It seems especially beautiful to me this morning, too."

"Will you make love to me one more time before we leave? Here, with the Sun shining on us. Please?"

"I would have to be either a fool or dead, or both to refuse, would I not?"

She did not laugh at my joke, but instead hugged me tightly and began kissing me with what seemed an almost frantic passion.

Embracing, we lay down upon the blanket where we had slept and made desperate love beneath the newly risen Sun.

When we were done, Tzigane did not rest in my arms as she usually did after sharing passion. Instead, she got up and began quickly dressing.

"Is there a hurry this morning, Tzigane?"

"We should have already been on our way." She spoke without looking at me. "The journey to the bottom of the Vale of Fog and Flowers will take most of the day. We would be on our way now if not for my foolishness, making love instead of continuing our journey."

I rose and began dressing, too. "Think on this, Tzigane. I might well have asked you to make love if you had not asked me. What does it matter if we start a little later this morning?"

She continued to dress but did not answer.

Again I wondered what was wrong. Had something happened during the night about which she had not told me? Had I done or said something that hurt her? Or did it have to do with whatever waited for us in the Vale of Fog and Flowers?

I touched her shoulder. "Tzigane, if I have unknowingly done anything that hurt you—"

"No. Of course not."

"Then did something happen last night which you have not told me?"

"No, Vlad. Everything is fine."

"Is there then something awaiting us in the Vale of Fog and Flowers that is upsetting you? Because if there is, we need not go there. We can turn around and leave. You can teach me occult skills somewhere else, can you not?"

She turned and faced me. "Vlad, *nothing is wrong*. Everything is as it should be, as it . . . must be."

"According to Satan's Prophecies."

"Of course. Hurry and dress, please?"

An urge to be stubborn came over me. For a few moments, I dressed *slower* than usual, then I conquered my childish reaction and began hurrying before, I hoped, Tzigane noticed. Considering her tenseness, if she wanted me to hurry I would only worsen matters by defying her wishes.

After caring for our horses, we ate a quick, cold breakfast then mounted our horses and began following a winding path downward into the Vale of Fog and Flowers.

The warm breeze from out of the valley was no more. It had stopped about dawn. There was now a cold breeze at our backs as we rode our horses farther and farther down.

We stopped briefly, near noon, to rest and eat some bread and cheese and give our horses some water, then we continued on.

Shortly after noon, our progress down the sloping path placed the Sun on the edge of the crest above, heralding a premature sunset. The rest of the journey would be through the shadows of an extended twilight. The sky above would remain bright until true sunset came, but the Sun itself would no longer be visible to us.

Just before we entered the shadow, I saw Tzigane look up at the Sun, and again I saw tears in her eyes. But, remembering her earlier insistence that nothing was wrong, I thought it best not to question her tears.

After we passed into the premature twilight, she wiped her tears, held her head high, and wept no more.

The sky was still bright above when we reached the boundary of fog. The temperature had dropped lower as we rode, until now, near the fog, it was cold enough for our breath to steam when it encountered the chilled air.

Tzigane said, "Stay close behind me, Vlad, and take care not to veer from the path through the fog, no matter what you see or hear. There is spellwork involved, and you do *not* want to get lost in *this* fog. Understood?"

"Of course."

Into the thick and swirling fog we rode. Within moments I felt confusion cloud my mind. I quickly became disoriented. I could see no farther than two arm spans in any direction. Although I rode behind the Witch on the narrow path, careful to keep the haunches of her mare in view, I suddenly heard her voice calling to me from my right.

Out of the corner of my eye I saw a dark shape looming in the fog in the direction of the voice. "Help me, Vlad! Please! Hurry!" And then the voice screamed in horrible agony. But, remembering what Tzigane had said, I kept my eyes on the haunches of her mare and did not respond to the false cry.

A little farther on, I heard the sound of galloping horses coming up swiftly from behind and men cursing in the language of my enemies, the Turks. Panic swept through me! They had somehow managed to follow and were now about to catch me! To take me back to the Turkish prison. I had to leave the path. I had to try and elude them in the fog, to—

No, I told myself. *Ignore the sounds. Remember Tzigane's warning.*

93

The sounds of pursuing horsemen reached me, swept into the air, and passed overhead, changing to chilling laughter. Then silence returned.

The air began to grow warmer. Soon, we emerged from the fog. I reined to a halt and looked in amazement at what lay ahead.

The path sloped downward through a forest of towering, broad-leafed trees unlike any I had ever seen. Green grass sprinkled with wild flowers covered the ground. But I saw no forest creatures and all was silent, while above the sky was a uniform gray, lending gloom to the scene.

"It is summer here always," Tzigane said. "Though direct sunlight never penetrates the fog, the Sun's heat reaches through, and the fog prevents the heat from escaping. Come, Vlad, we still have a way to go before dark."

And I followed the Witch onward down the path.

17
Lake

The shadows of the broad-leafed trees through which the path led emphasized the gloom of the overcast sky, making it seem we rode on the edge of a night that never came.

The dense forest remained disturbingly quiet. If any creatures inhabited it, I neither saw nor heard them, and something about the deep silence made me reluctant to use my voice to ask Tzigane if it were indeed a forest bereft of life. If she read the questions in my thoughts, she gave no sign, leading the way in silence through the gloom down the narrow, sloping path.

The path eventually emerged from the trees at the edge of a large lake, then split to go in both directions around the shoreline between the water and the towering trees.

The increased light beyond the forest's edge and the sound of water gently lapping at the shore brought a welcome relief from the shadowed silence through which we had just passed.

We reined to a halt and looked out over the lake.

Occupying the center of the bowl-shaped valley, the lake appeared roughly circular. The closely packed trees followed the shoreline all the way around, except where broken by rocky outcroppings that thrust rocky fingers of stone into the water.

The forest continued up the sloping sides of the valley all around, extending to the misty edge of the low canopy of fog.

Through a gray haze over the water, the far shore of the lake was only barely visible, a ghostly, half-glimpsed image, and the gray overhead made the water's surface seem all but black, reminding me of the pool in the chamber beneath the crypt in Targoviste, an unpleasant thought.

I wondered if the lake harbored any life.

"Tzigane," I said, my voice sounding too loud to me, although I spoke at a normal volume, "is . . . *this* where you spent all those years of training? Here? Never seeing the Sun?"

She hesitated. "Yes."

"Then I understand your tears for the beauty of the Sun earlier in the day. You knew you would not see the Sun again until we left this valley."

Again she hesitated. "I knew that the Sun could not be seen from here, yes."

She started her horse forward again, heading along the shoreline path to the right. "Come. We must go yet a way more before dark."

When the path encountered the rocky spurs thrusting into the lake, it angled back into the forest to go around them, then returned to the shoreline. Finally, after following the path into the forest to avoid a block of rock as large as a small fortress, we emerged from the trees onto a wide stretch of sandy shore leading from the water to a towering spire of rock that dwarfed even the previous outcropping.

The gray sky was darkening. I did not like to think of how dark the night here would be. Given that it was winter, the Moon's path through the sky would take it nearly overhead, and had it been full of phase and bright it could have provided some meager illumination through the layer of fog. But the Moon was currently in its dark phase, and during the summer months, when its celestial path was closer to the southern horizon, I doubted that, bright or dark, it ever breached the crest of the valley.

The path led toward the spire of rock, and at the base of that rock I saw the entrance to a cave. From within the cave came the flickering of fire.

"Is that the Scholomance, Tzigane? That cave?"

"That is the entrance."

"And that is where my father and brother—"

Suddenly a bestial cry interrupted me. My hand instinctually went to the hilt of my sword and I drew the blade even as I reined my horse around to face whatever had made the sound.

Nothing in my eighteen years had prepared me for what I saw.

I had wondered if the lake harbored life. Now, rising out of the water off the shore was what at first appeared to be a monstrous snake, black and gleaming. But soon, when the bulk of the creature broke the surface, I saw that the snake was only the long neck of a massive beast that used huge fins to propel itself through the water.

It was swimming rapidly toward the shore. Toward Tzigane and me.

I raised my sword and shouted, "Into the cave, Tzigane!" When I heard no response, I jerked my head around to see if some other menace had attacked her while my back was turned. But instead I saw Tzigane on the ground, on her knees, her head bowed toward the monster from the lake.

And she was not alone.

Other black-cloaked women were rushing from the

cave to also throw themselves onto their knees and bow to the creature.

The beast cried out again, a long and mournful sound. I returned my attention to the monster and with relief saw that it had stopped near the shore.

It screamed its cry a third time. Then it turned and headed back the way it had come, leaving the stench of dead fish lingering in its wake.

Tzigane stood, raised her arms over her head and shouted, "All hail the Dragon of Satan!" The other women also rose to their feet and repeated the cry as the creature slipped back beneath the water, and out of sight.

Tzigane looked up at me. "And all hail Prince Vlad Dracula! The Dragon's Son! And the Devil's! Satan's Chosen King on Earth!"

And again Tzigane went onto her knees, as did the other women. But this time they were bowing to me.

Chapter Five

18
Lilitu

I still held my sword, drawn to fight the lake monster. My pulse still pounded in my ears. And now Tzigane and the other women were bowing to me, a sight I found mildly angering and slightly embarrassing.

I quickly returned my sword to its scabbard, dismounted, and pulled Tzigane to her feet. "Once before I told you I would not have you kneeling to me, Tzigane."

"It was foretold it would be so, as was foretold the appearance of the Dragon of Satan when the Chosen King had come. Satan's Prophecy has again spoken true!"

"That beast, or dragon as you call it, was not taking an evening swim just because I arrived. It probably does that every day when the sky begins to darken."

"In nine years here I never saw it do so. And Lilitu has never seen it either, until now."

"Lilitu?"

"An elder here. One of my teachers." Tzigane gestured with her hand, indicating the closest of the black-cloaked women. They were all rising to their feet.

Giving a slight bow with her head, Lilitu said, "Joyous greetings to you, Prince Dracula." She walked forward. "What Tzigane says is true. I have never seen the Dragon until today, and I have lived here all but the earliest years of my life."

Lilitu's graying hair hung long and straight to her waist. A thin woman, her skin was pale, almost bone white. She was nearly as tall as Tzigane. Beneath her black cloak she wore a black robe that covered her from neck to ankles and was tied at her waist by a crimson cord. Her feet were bare. The other women who had emerged from the cave were similarly attired. Some of them were older than Lilitu, some younger. A few were even younger than Tzigane, but none were young enough to have been called children.

Lilitu continued, "I have *heard* the Dragon before, but only twice. The first time was at midnight on the night of your birth, Prince Dracula, and—"

"You knew of my birth?"

Lilitu nodded her head. "It was, of course, foretold by many signs and portents."

"Signs and portents. Not long ago I would have laughed at such a statement."

Lilitu glanced at Tzigane and raised an eyebrow.

"He believed only in what he could see and touch, when he returned from Turk-land." She smiled at me. "But he knows better, now."

Lilitu also smiled at me and gave another slight bow. "I am glad."

I said to her, "And the second time you heard the lake beast?"

"The night Tzigane proved herself worthy to be the mate of the Chosen King."

"But *I* did not hear it that night," Tzigane added. "I was rather . . . unconscious." She laughed.

"Rather!" Lilitu laughed, too. But I did not laugh.

"Why?" I asked. "Why were you unconscious, Tzigane."

"Oh . . . well, I was exhausted, you see. The final test was one of strength and endurance as well as knowledge and skill."

Lilitu grasped Tzigane's hands and gazed upon her as if a proud parent admiring a child. "She had been without food and sleep for four days and five nights. When she recovered, we held a great feast of celebration. We were so proud of her. And we are even *more* proud of her now, for having brought to us Satan's Chosen King! Well done, Tzigane." They embraced. "Well done!"

"Well done!" was echoed by many of the other women, who had now drawn near.

Tzigane stepped away from Lilitu and took my hand. "Be you all proud, too, of Vlad Dracula, Warlord Prince of Wallachia! He has learned much in a very short time, and chose to follow me here of his own free will."

I wondered at the implication of that. Would she have used spellcraft on me, had I not agreed to come? The setting in which I stood, among women who were, I assumed, Witches like Tzigane, was suddenly far from comforting.

Tzigane embraced me. She had read my thoughts and quickly whispered in my ear, "I would never have had to force *you*, my Vlad."

But the thought had changed my outlook.

The sky was growing rapidly darker. I thought of my father and brother and brother's wife, carried by the winged beast to the Scholomance, the Devil's School outside whose entrance I now stood. My father and brother must therefore be nearby. *Their corpses.* Perhaps already stirring, anxious for sunset when they could again rise and walk the night.

I remembered my father's dead eyes as he had come

nearer to me, his cold teeth touching the skin of my throat . . .

I fought fear.

Tzigane read my thoughts. "They have changed much since the night of their resurrection, Vlad. You have nothing now to fear from them. They have become accustomed to their new existence here and will be more as you remember them from your youth."

"I . . . did not care much for them when they were alive. I would rather not see them while I am here."

"Not see them?"

I nodded my head. "I would prefer it."

Tzigane and Lilitu exchanged a quick look I could not read. Then Lilitu glanced at the sky and said, "It is time to go inside, Prince Dracula, if it pleases you to do so."

"And what if it does not?" I remembered doubts I had not felt since the night Tzigane had given me the ring, doubts about whether my desires were my own or Witch-sent. If I did choose to go inside the cave, would it really be my own free will? Or *theirs?* Had I really followed Tzigane because I wanted to? Or had the ring perhaps been intended to keep me from feeling my own doubts, rather than to shield me from occult attacks by agents of Satan's Enemy?

Knowing my thoughts, Tzigane said, "Vlad . . . please! I have never lied to you! Believe that if you believe nothing else! I . . . *love* you! And the feelings you have for me are your own as well. I . . . promise." She probed deeper into my thoughts. "You . . . think of your father and brother as soulless monsters? No, Vlad. No. They are not!"

"Nevertheless, I have no desire to see them ever again."

"Never? But . . . Vlad, they are your father and brother. Why would you say that . . ."

She probed deeper still. Deeper. Then suddenly surprise filled her eyes, followed by pain. "Oh, no. Vlad. Sweet Satan, no. . . . I should have looked deeper into your mind before, concerning this . . . but . . . perhaps I feared to find . . . this. I must have sensed it and veered away from knowing for certain. I—"

"Tzigane, what are you—"

"They disgust you, Vlad, in spite of all I have told you, all you have experienced and learned. The Undead, even your father and brother . . . repulse you, simply because they are Undead . . ."

She moaned low in her throat, looked at Lilitu, and said, "Oh, Sweet Satan . . . *simply because they are Undead!*"

I responded, *"Simply* because? They are cold-fleshed corpses, Tzigane! Who would *not* be repulsed? Surely even Witches cannot feel differently down deep where the truth hides. Look into the depths of your own mind, and I am certain you will find I am correct."

Looking at me, tears spilled from her eyes.

"Tzigane, please, there is no reason to cry. There—"

She suddenly turned with a sob and ran toward the cave.

"Tzigane!"

I was about to pursue her, but Lilitu placed a hand upon my arm. "I entreat you to be patient and understanding with her, Prince Dracula."

"But . . . why do my feelings about the Undead upset her so?"

"That is for her to tell. If you are ready, we can follow her inside."

The darkening forest remained silent, no night creatures stirred in its depths. The thought of remaining

105

outside in that black, dead silence was more disturbing than the thought of entering the cave and again seeing my father and brother. But Tzigane's tears were the most disturbing of all.

I stood in the growing dark among the Witches, in a place of Satanic legend. Fear stood there with me, but also love for a woman I had last seen in tears.

Tzigane. Not the wielder of occult powers. Not the Witch. But the woman who had become my friend and ally. The woman I loved. And trusted . . . hopefully of my own free will.

I had to find Tzigane and try to replace her tears with new smiles.

I inhaled a deep breath and said to Lilitu, ''Take me to Tzigane. I am ready to go inside.''

19
Scholomance

The entrance to the cave was large enough for several to walk abreast, but only Lilitu walked by my side as I entered the Scholomance. The other women followed silently behind, two of them leading the horses Tzigane and I had ridden.

Lilitu had assured me the animals would be cared for where their other beasts were kept. She said they had cattle and sheep and fowl. When I questioned how they fed sheep and cattle without grazing land, she smiled and replied that what the forest or lake did not provide, either Lord Satan or their own occult skills did.

The wide entrance gradually narrowed as we went deeper into the torchlit cave. Torches burned brightly in widely spaced wall brackets.

The stone walls of the passageway were smooth, showing no marks of tools and in that way reminding me of the deep passageway beneath the palace at Targoviste. But the stone here was a green so dark it was almost black, and in places it gleamed as if wet. When I touched it, however, it proved to be like the scales of reptiles that appear moist but are instead quite dry.

Soon, the passageway branched into three.

Lilitu indicated we were to continue down the center

path. I looked back to see the two who led the horses take the path to the left, the other women the one to the right.

With Lilitu by my side, we went farther into the heart of the cave. There was no longer room for more than two to walk abreast. But around a turn that sloped downward at a slight angle the passageway widened somewhat and we began passing dark openings, spaced irregularly on each side.

Some of the openings were large enough to allow a human to walk through without bending. Others were so small they could have only been useful to small beasts or birds, or snakes, if such there were in the cave.

As we passed some of the larger openings, I thought I heard, in our wake, vague rustlings and whisperings which left me feeling uneasy and urged me to look back more than once, sensing presences behind me that I could not see.

Would Tzigane have seen something with her well-developed Witch-sight that I could not with my beginner's skills, I wondered? If so, Lilitu no doubt could, too. But if she did, she made no sign, and I did not ask. Instead, I turned my thoughts again to Tzigane's tears.

"How much farther?" I asked.

"We are nearly there, Prince Dracula."

"And . . . my father and brother?"

"They, and your brother's wife, and others of Satan's Sacred Undead are elsewhere, down the path to the right where you saw most of the others go. At sunset they awaken and must be cared for."

"With . . . blood."

"At least once within each cycle of the Moon, yes. But we also use spellcraft to prepare for them certain herbal mixtures charged with vital energy, to help them stay strong and unaging."

"But when they do drink blood, it is . . . human blood?"

"The blood of animals lacks certain . . . qualities. It is the same with the milk of animals. Human infants grow strongest if fed the milk of a human mother."

"And the women who serve the Undead, it is *their* blood that feeds the Vampires?"

"When that honor befalls us, we each gladly—"

"You think it an honor to allow those monsters—"

"Prince Dracula, as Tzigane has told you, they are *not* monsters."

"They are to me. While Tzigane was living here, did she have to share her blood with . . . them?"

"Tzigane was a candidate in training to be your future mate. She was not required to serve the Honored Undead among us."

"Honored Undead. Perhaps they have used their mental powers to make you feel as you do. Perhaps they have woven spells of their own and have you in *their* power."

Lilitu responded, "When you have had time to learn more and . . . adjust your perceptions, perhaps you will see the Undead differently."

"I think not."

"For your own sake, and Tzigane's, I must hope that you will. But now, Prince Dracula, we have reached the heart of the Scholomance, and the one you seek."

The passageway opened into a large cavern. Around the walls, here and there, in the spaces between torches set in wall brackets, were many ornately carved wooden shelves and tables holding a multitude of books and scrolls, vials and earthenware jars, and other objects I could not identify from a distance.

The cavern was roughly circular. Its black-green walls gleamed in the flickering torchlight, but its ceiling was lost in shadows. And in the center rose a massive block of stone, a rectangle of what appeared to be white marble, stark against the darkness of its surroundings. And before the stone, her back to me, knelt Tzigane, head down. I saw no one else there but her.

"Tzigane?" I called.

"I have . . . duties, elsewhere," Lilitu said and gave a slight bow. She turned and walked back the way we had come.

Tzigane had not moved at the sound of my voice.

"Tzigane?" I called, louder, my voice echoing off the stone walls. I walked toward her. Still she did not turn. "Please, Tzigane, explain what is wrong. Why should my feelings about my father and brother, about the Undead, upset you so?"

I reached her. She still had not moved. Standing behind her, I said, "I do not want to see your tears, Tzigane. Only your smiles. Now, *please,* tell me what is wrong!"

She whispered, "There . . . is nothing you can do. You cannot change how you . . . feel, deep within. Your true feelings. And I cannot change what I must do."

I knelt beside her, turned her toward me, gently smoothed back the hair from her face, wiped at her tears.

"And what is that? Whatever it is, we shall do it together, as friends and allies and lovers should. Agreed?"

"No, Vlad. No."

"Tzigane, we have been so happy these last few days. I do, it seems, love you deeply. And you have said you love me."

"And I do, my Vlad, so very much . . ."

She pulled away and began weeping again.

"Tzigane. Stop. Please. You must talk to me! Explain—"

"There is nothing to explain!" she cried, facing me again. "You are repulsed by the Undead, and therefore, tonight at midnight, you will be repulsed . . . by me!"

20
Betrayal

Although her words were plain, my mind refused to accept them. "Tzigane? Tonight at midnight? What can you mean?"

"Exactly what I said! At the lake, at midnight, in a sacred ritual of Death and Resurrection, I will become Undead."

A deep coldness gripped me. A memory from that morning flashed through my mind. I saw her standing naked, facing the Sun, tears in her eyes when she turned to face me. I remembered her wanting to make love another time in the sunlight. And I remembered on the trail into the valley, when the Sun was about to sink below the rim, how she had looked up to catch one last glimpse.

One *last* glimpse . . .

Because the Undead could not bear the touch of the Sun. I had been blind. An idiot. I should have guessed! I could have stopped her from coming into the valley. "You should have told me, Tzigane. Why did you not tell me?"

"It was not . . . allowed, until we were here. I was going to tell you tonight, as soon as we—"

"It is still not too late. I will not allow you to—"

"Vlad, no. I have not come this far only to betray my sacred vows."

"What *vows*, Tzigane? Vows to Satan? And what about your vows to me? Never to tell me lies? And to be with me always, my friend and ally, teaching me occult secrets?"

Her eyes downcast, her voice a near whisper, she said, "I have not lied to you. I was not able to tell you all of the truth at times, but I never told you a lie. And from my view, nothing needs to change between us. Oh! How I have worried and prayed that it would not! But . . . I know now that you will be . . . repulsed by me, when I am Undead. I should have looked deeply enough into your mind sooner, but I see now that I was a coward where your true feelings about the Undead were concerned. I—"

"Tzigane! Listen to me. You are so young! When one is old and facing death, I can understand how, to some, the idea of becoming Undead to escape the grave might seem appealing. But not now! Not when a long life stretches before you. When our life *together* stretches before you."

"Becoming Undead is about more than escaping death, Vlad. It is about *power,* especially for someone with occult training. Vampires wield forces that a human, no matter how well trained, can never fully possess, because the Undead exist in more than one reality. When I am Undead, my knowledge and power will be increased many fold. And I will then be able to teach you more than ever I could before, to give you knowledge and power beyond anything you can dream. Don't you see? Only Undead can I help you prepare for your glory as Satan's King on Earth. Only Undead can I do that for which I have been destined and trained since

113

that night I conjured a vision of my future husband and learned that he was the Chosen One of Satan.''

Turning away from me she said, ''But it is a great joke, is it not? Satan's Enemies are no doubt laughing at we two this night. In fulfilling the Prophecies of Satan, the love between Satan's King and Queen will be destroyed! Please, Vlad. Leave me now. Leave me alone. And know this. Although I will still help you attain the Throne of the World as the prophecies ordain, I will never ask you to make me your wife, other than in name. I will not expect you to do anything you do not . . . want to do, or to conceal your repulsion. You need only learn what I have to teach.''

''Tzigane, is not the life we planned together more important than any prophecies, any vows? If you truly love me, you will come with me now, away from this place. Can you not understand? You, who can read my deepest thoughts? Even the Throne of the World means little to me when compared to what I feel for you!''

''I cannot forsake my vows to Satan! Would you ask me to betray my soul's honor? My destiny? All that has given my life meaning?''

''Our *love* is what gives our lives meaning. Come with me *now,* Tzigane. *Please.*''

Without hesitation she replied, anger in her eyes, ''If you truly loved me, you would not ask such a thing, and perhaps you would find a way to accept me as what I must become!''

''It is *because* I love you that I cannot condone this madness!''

''Madness? Do you think we few here in the Scholomance are Satan's only servants? He has worshippers everywhere! In Christendom. In Turk-land. In Cathay far to the east. Even in great lands across the western ocean about which those lacking Satan's secrets have yet to discover. And *all* of His followers know of the prophecies. All are awaiting them to be fulfilled. And I will not be the one to fail.

"You still do not fully understand, Vlad. You *are* Satan's Chosen King. And I have proven myself worthy to be His Queen. But Satan's King and Queen must reign through the centuries. *Immortals*. You must therefore yourself in time become immortal. Undead. And it is my destiny to be the one whose kiss makes you deathless, when you eventually request it of your own free will."

"Request it? Then your prophecies are false. I will *never* request it! From my thoughts you must know that this is true. Why, then, persist with—"

"You *will* request it. *You must.*"

"Only if you use spellcraft to force me. Is that what you have planned from the first, Tzigane? To alter my desires? To first make me lust for a Witch's flesh? And then, in time, to make me lust for Undeath?"

"You know that is not true! All must be according to your free will! I have told you, the prophecies—"

"Satan take your cursed prophecies! Knowing how I feel, you know I will never voluntarily become Undead. I must therefore *not* be the Chosen King after all."

"But you *are!*"

Feeling empty and dead inside, I forced a laugh. "You have failed, Tzigane. I have been your fool, but no more. This is not about prophecies or power. This is about betrayal."

"No, Vlad. I—"

I interrupted by quickly continuing, "Will I be allowed to leave this valley? Or must I cut my way out with my sword?"

"Of course you may leave the valley, leave . . . me, whenever it pleases you. But . . . for the sake of what

115

we have meant to each other, I ask of you just one more thing. Stand with me . . . tonight at the lake, at midnight, as the prophecies have foretold you would do.''

"You want me to *watch* you destroy our life together?''

"Will you be there, Vlad? Please? For what we meant to each other?''

"For the lie I believed to be true, you mean?'' I stood with my fists clenched at my sides, deadly emotions burning within me. "Perhaps I *will* be there, then, Gypsy girl. I have never before watched a beautiful woman throw away a life of happiness to become a monster. Or will this midnight ritual only reveal what has truly been there all along? So, yes, perhaps I will indeed be there. Such a pointless spectacle should prove most . . . entertaining, before I leave!''

Her voice was flat, dead, as she looked at the floor of the cavern and whispered, "Go now, Vlad. Please. Just . . . go.''

"Gladly!'' I pulled at the silver ring she had given to me. I had expected to have trouble removing it, as always I had before, but to my surprise it slid effortlessly from my finger.

I tossed the ring onto the cavern floor beside her. Then I turned and walked away and did not look back, not even when I heard her again begin to weep.

Chapter Six

21
Midnight

In spite of what I had said to Tzigane about being present at the midnight ritual, as I walked from the cavern I suddenly decided to leave the valley immediately. I would brave the dark and silent forest with a torch in my hand rather than stay in that cursed cave.

I could see now that after my mother's death, to protect myself from further emotional pain I had endeavored to crush strong emotions of affection for anyone or thing. The Turks had helped me perfect the defense. But then had come Tzigane, and I had foolishly allowed myself to care for her, only to be tricked and betrayed, and now left to feel more emotional pain than ever I had before.

I should never have allowed myself to become involved with her! *A Gypsy Woman* . . . how could I have been such a fool? I, who had survived unbroken all those years at the hands of the Turks, now felt well broken indeed.

But, I told myself, *the Turks had not used spellcraft on me.* And no matter all of Tzigane's talk about free will, that must be what she had used. Could I, a descendant of rulers, have so quickly fallen in love with a Gypsy if she had not also been a spell-wielding Witch?

Lilitu appeared in the passageway ahead of me. I wondered if she had listened to my conversation with Tzigane, but in truth I did not really care.

With a slight bow of her head, she said, "Prince Dracula. Your quarters are prepared, and a meal, when you so desire."

"Have my horse readied for riding at once. I am leaving."

Lilitu's face did not register surprise. Either she *had* been listening, or she had read my thoughts. Or both. She said, "The way from this valley is dangerous at night. It would be best, for your sake, if you delayed your departure until morning, at which time a guide could be provided to help you through the barrier of fog."

"I am leaving, now, and alone." The band of fog I would worry about when I reached it. Perhaps some of the occult skills I had learned from Tzigane would give me a chance of making it through. Or, more likely, without the Witch present there might not be any disorienting effects at all. It might be nothing but simple fog when she was not there to trick me with her spellcraft.

Lilitu said, "Your leaving will be a great disappointment for all of us . . . especially Tzigane. But it shall be as you wish. I will guide you to the stables at once."

We walked back the way we had come. As we passed the dark openings, again I heard rustlings and whisperings in our wake, and again I felt watched. But again I did not ask Lilitu about what I heard and felt. After Tzigane's trickery, I could not trust any explanation a Witch might give.

Witches and Witchcraft. Legends and superstitions. Would that I could forget all that had recently happened to me and again think all such things simple lies!

And what of my mother, screaming as she burned that

she was dying for a lie. I wondered now . . . had *she* been the one that was lying? Had she been, perhaps, a Witch? Tricking my father? Tricking me? I did not want to think so, but could I now be certain of anything I had once thought true? If, as Tzigane claimed, and I had dared to believe, I had been designated as Satan's Chosen King, who better to have given me life than a Witch? Had my mother, like Tzigane, once lived at the Scholomance?

And my father and brother. What was the truth of how and why they had become Undead? I could seek them out and ask them, but could I trust their answers? Did I really care enough to find out? I decided I did not.

My mind jumbled by conflicting thoughts, my emotions in turmoil, all I wanted was to leave the valley and live in the hard, physical world a man could readily understand. A world of life and true death, battles and victories, steel and blood.

When we came to the branching of the passageway, we turned in the direction I had earlier seen my horse led. "It is not much farther now, Prince Dracula," Lilitu said.

We emerged into a large cavern, though not as large as the one in which I had left Tzigane.

Tzigane. Curse the woman! When I thought of her I could still hear the sound of her sobbing as I walked away. And for a moment I had to fight an urge to go back to her and agree to whatever she wanted, just to see her smile once more, to hold her in my arms once again.

But I resisted the shaming urge by seeing to it that my horse was quickly prepared for riding.

Lilitu offered to bring provisions for my journey, but I refused. For all I knew they might give food to me that had been prepared with herbs and spells meant to weaken my resolve.

When I was ready, Lilitu said, "You will always be welcome here, Prince Dracula. But . . . won't you please reconsider leaving? Tzigane has worked hard for many long years in preparation for this night, and if you are not present at the ceremony, much of the ritual's meaning will be lost."

Without a word of reply I selected a torch from a wall bracket. Holding the flame so as not to make my horse shy away, I led the mare outside, mounted, and rode away in the general direction I felt would lead me to the path upon which I had arrived.

I did not look back even once, and I thought of Tzigane only twice more before the torch I held revealed the path and the dark forest into which it led.

The air was still and warm, unchilled by the night, but the total blackness overhead combined with the utter silence of the dark to produce a disheartening feeling of oppression.

As we neared the trees, my horse began to shy nervously, then suddenly cried out in fright and reared up. I tried to comfort her. But only when I allowed her to move away from the trees and back toward the cave was I able to again regain control.

I reined to a halt. The mare was trembling, her eyes were wild in the torchlight. Had she sensed danger in the forest? Or scented a hunting beast of some kind, a silent predator waiting to spring? Or was her reaction the result of more spellcraft?

I leaned down, patted her neck, talked soothingly to her, waited until she had settled down somewhat, then tried to enter the forest once more.

The beast reacted the same way again. If I left before dawn, it would obviously not be astride a horse's back.

I cursed this place. Lilitu must have known this would happen. Were she and the other Witches laughing at me even now? Perhaps Tzigane among them? Waiting to see me come shame-faced back to the cave?

Whether they were or not, I resolved not to enter the cave ever again. Instead, I would wait for the dawn there in the open. Should danger approach, surely either I or my horse would notice it in time to give me a warning.

I dismounted and stuck the shaft of the torch into the soft, sandy soil. Then, holding my horse's reins, I stood with her within the circle of torchlight and patted her neck.

After what seemed ages later, I was standing there still, the torch flickering fitfully, almost burned out, when the Witches began emerging from the cave for the midnight ritual at which Tzigane was to become Undead.

The thought was suddenly intolerable. I could not let it happen! No matter the cause, spellcraft or my own emotions, I did love her. I must not allow her to destroy the life we had planned! I could not let her harm herself so!

I slowly drew my sword then concealed the blade by holding it beneath my cloak, against my leg.

But what did I intend to do? Kill all of the Witches in the Scholomance? And destroy the Undead there, too?

Even if I could have hoped to accomplish such a thing, would it have made any difference to Tzigane? Would she be freed from some spell herself if those who had cast it were dead? Or would she attack me with the others?

I might have to slay her, too, which I doubted I could bear to do.

Or perhaps, if I could but keep her alive until dawn, keep her with me and hold the others at bay until the sky lightened overhead, might she then listen to reason and leave with me? Would she abandon the insanity in which she claimed to believe in order to share my life?

But which one of the emerging Witches was she? In the flickering shadows of the torches they carried, single file from the mouth of the cave, I did not see her face.

Then, behind the line of silent, black-clad Witches of the Scholomance came others walking two abreast, human in appearance save for eyes that glowed like hot coals, eyes such as I had seen before in the palace at Targoviste, the eyes of the Undead. But among them I did not see my father or brother.

One of the Witches veered from the line and came toward me where I stood far to one side. For a moment I hoped it would be Tzigane, but it proved to be Lilitu.

"You are staying, after all, Prince Dracula?"

"My horse would not enter the trees, as you no doubt well knew. I am merely keeping her company until she feels like traveling the forest path, I assume after dawn."

"Why, then, do you hold a drawn sword beneath your cloak?"

Curse their mind reading! "Pray you need not find out." I held in my thoughts an image of my sword shearing her head from her neck.

To my surprise, she smiled. "I do not fear for my head. You will not harm me. And none here mean you harm, our Chosen King, even if your fantasies of trickery and betrayal so greatly hurt our beloved Tzigane."

"It is not *I* who am hurting Tzigane! You have poisoned her with lies!"

With a look of sadness, Lilitu turned and walked away.

22
Monster

Still holding my sword beneath my cloak, I kept watching for Tzigane and my father and brother. Neither had I seen Varina, Mircea's wife.

I was surprised my horse did not shy with so many of the Undead nearby, but then I remembered Tzigane once saying that the Undead had power over beasts, as did Witches who knew the proper spells.

The Witches reached the edge of the lake, spread out into a semicircle facing the water, and stood silently, torches in their hands.

The Undead had stopped emerging from the cave. I noted that there were more Vampires than Witches who served them. They stood in two long lines stretching from the cave's entrance to the line of torch-bearing Witches on the shore.

Among the Undead I saw both men and women. All were clothed in black cloaks like the Witches. All were gaunt and pale. And none appeared too young nor too old. I wondered, however, with a shudder of disgust, how old they truly were.

They chilled me with deep fear. *And Tzigane wanted to become one of them!*

I tightened my grip on my sword, though after what

I had seen at the palace I doubted edged steel would prove of much use against their kind.

Then from the cave came two last figures. The Undead bowed their heads as the two began walking among them toward the shore.

One of the two was Tzigane, naked, looking more beautiful than ever I could remember, holding her head high with pride, though tears streaked her face.

The one who walked beside her, *holding her hand,* towered over her, a creature of nightmare, part woman, part beast, with leathery skin dark as night, taloned feet, clawed hands, fanged teeth, eyes burning with red fire, head crowned by a mane of hair long and silver, and wings, as of a monstrous bat, folded together behind.

As Tzigane and the thing with which she walked moved onward between the silent rows of Vampires, I knew that if I were going to act, it would have to be now. If I moved fast enough, perhaps with surprise on my side, I could pull her away and—

But I also knew that it was hopeless. I would have to slay the she-monster first, and even if I somehow managed that feat and was quick enough to escape the clutches of the Undead, I did not know enough occult skills to successfully resist mental attacks for long. The Undead could paralyze me with a glance of their eyes, and Witches could do the same with the proper words of power.

No, it was obvious that I would not succeed in taking Tzigane to safety, even if she were to change her mind and want to go, which I could not assume she would . . .

Unless she had changed her mind since my leaving.

Unless she had reconsidered and too late decided to depart with me.

I doubted that she had. But could I live with myself if I did not attempt to save her, even if from herself?

Yes, I would fail. *But I would at least have tried.*

Knowing myself a fool still in love with a woman who had betrayed me, I raised my sword and rushed forward to try and save Tzigane.

But suddenly my way was blocked by a tall man clad in black, red fire burning in his eyes. A Vampire. My father.

I had not seen him approach. My horse had not shied. Father had just suddenly blinked into existence to block my way.

"You will not hinder the ritual, my Son." In the torchlight I saw he now had a younger appearance than when he had died. "Put away your sword. Do not force us to restrain you."

"Good evening, Father," I said, standing my ground. I did not sheath my sword. "Do not try to stop me from doing what I must."

Two hands closed on my arms from behind. The fingers that pressed into my flesh felt like bands of steel, cold steel that almost instantly numbed my arms. But I stubbornly retained my grip on my sword.

"You will do nothing foolish, Brother," said Mircea behind me. "Relax and enjoy the beautiful . . . scenery. I can see why you came to care for her."

The idea of Mircea gazing upon Tzigane's naked flesh with his horrid burning eyes filled me with great anger. I struggled to escape his grip but might as well have struggled against iron manacles. Tzigane had told me the Undead possessed the physical strength of ten.

Tzigane! She and the she-monster had reached the Witches now. Two of them stepped aside, allowing Tzigane and her nightmare companion to pass through.

With the Witches now blocking my view, I could no

longer see what was happening to Tzigane. Might there still be a chance to try pulling her away?

"I want to go nearer," I said. "I can see nothing from here."

"And we want you nearer as well," said my father, "but without your sword." He pried my fingers from around the hilt and cast the blade aside. I turned just enough to see where the sword landed, in case I needed later to run back for it.

Father took my right arm, holding it fast with both of his hands. Mircea took hold of my left arm in a similar fashion.

They walked me forward to the Witches. Two of the women stepped aside without looking around.

We stopped when we were within arm's length of Tzigane and the monster. The air had a dry, acrid scent, I assumed from the monster.

Tzigane walked to me. She read my thoughts, learned I had hoped to rescue her. She wiped at her tears. And she said, in a near whisper, "My thanks for still caring what happens to me. Dare I hope that you will yet care afterward, after all?"

I thought of many things to say, but knowing she knew them without my speaking, I chose to remain silent.

She tentatively leaned nearer, for a kiss. For a moment I almost complied, but then I felt again my rage at her betrayal and my repulsion at what she was about to become.

I turned my head to one side, denying her my lips.

New tears gleamed in her eyes as she quickly pulled back and returned to the monster's side, rejecting me for a thing of nightmare.

The Witches knelt and bowed their heads. Tzigane knelt too. She bowed her head to the she-thing. And she said, "Ancient One, Sacred One, bestow upon me now the blessings of your Kiss of Undeath that I may become immortal by the power of Satan, and in Him ever strong!''

"Rise, Tzigane," spoke the creature with a voice low and harsh.

Tzigane rose to her feet. The Witches remained on their knees.

"Approach me," the thing commanded.

Tzigane stepped closer. It placed its leathery arms around her and held her tightly. Then, slowly, it leaned down and placed its befanged mouth against the soft flesh of her throat.

"No!" I cried out. "Tzigane! Please! No!"

Her eyes found mind. I saw in them pain, but also a kind of ecstasy and triumph, and unblinking she held my gaze as the monster began to feed.

23
Death

Tzigane continued to hold my gaze while I, held fast by the preternatural strength of my brother and father, could only watch as the monster slowly drained her of blood.

Eventually, Tzigane's eyelids began to lower as if she were growing drowsy. And though she fought to keep her eyes open, soon she closed them as if surrendering to sleep.

But the creature continued to drink from Tzigane's veins. The sound of its feasting sickened me. The horror of what it was doing overwhelmed me.

Finally, it raised its nightmare head, its befanged mouth stained and dripping with Tzigane's blood. Then it lifted its left arm, placed the wrist against its mouth, and bit down.

It lowered the arm, held its bleeding wrist near Tzigane's face. Dark blood oozed from the wound it had made with its own teeth.

"Drink now of my wine," it said.

Nausea clutched at me as without hesitation Tzigane placed her mouth upon the streaming wound. When she pulled back a moment later, her lips were dark with the she-beast's blood. Her tongue emerged and licked her lips clean. Then she stepped back from the monster.

Dizzy and horribly pale, struggling painfully for each breath because of the great amount of blood she had lost, Tzigane swayed unsteadily on her feet. None of the Witches, still on their knees with heads bowed, moved to aid her, and held as I was I could not help her myself.

The creature now stood as if of stone, gazing into the darkness over the lake.

It was terrible to see Tzigane weakened so. She who had always been so strong and full of life was now, by her own choice, hovering upon the border of Death, and I could do nothing to help her!

Her eyes closed, by force of will she stopped gasping for air and began taking slow, deep, shuddering breaths. I understood that she was concentrating, gathering her strength, as she had taught me to do in Targoviste . . .

Targoviste . . . in the palace, making love in secret with all the strength and passion of youth, making plans for a long life together, plans she had now betrayed . . .

Tzigane . . . Tzigane, I thought, hoping she would hear my thoughts, *how could you throw so much happiness away?* Surely no God, no Devil could bring joy as deep as the joy we had shared. *Tzigane!*

Tzigane opened her eyes, but she looked at Lilitu, not at me. Lilitu rose to her feet and stepped forward. She handed something I could not see to Tzigane. Then Lilitu returned to her place in the line of kneeling Witches and again went onto her knees.

Tzigane walked slowly, unsteadily toward me. As she reached me a shudder passed through her and she gasped for air, fighting to breathe just a little longer.

When she had steadied her breathing somewhat, she held her left hand out to me, palm up, to show me what was there.

131

Resting on her pale and trembling hand was the silver ring I had left in the cavern.

Struggling for each breath, she said, "Think of . . . me what you will . . . my Vlad, I will love you . . . always. I wanted you to . . . do what comes . . . next. But I know now you would . . . refuse."

She handed the ring to my father. "Prince Dracul, father of Satan's Chosen . . . King, cast now . . . into . . . the lake, this ring."

Father threw the ring into the darkness. It splashed into the water a great distance from the shore.

Holding my gaze, Tzigane said, "I . . . must go now, my Vlad. I must go . . . and find your ring."

I understood. The moment of her death had come. She would go into the lake a living woman and die there beneath the water. But she would find no peace in death, for she had been infected with Undeath by the bite and blood of the monstrous Vampire. I might see her again, *but never again alive.*

"Tzigane," I groaned. "Please! Denounce this horror! Come away with me instead!"

She smiled, sadly. "Wait for me here . . . Vlad, please, my love . . . and I . . . will bring back to you . . . your ring."

She leaned closer. Although the thought of kissing lips that had tasted the she-monster's blood repulsed me, I did not turn away this time from her kiss.

It would, indeed, be our last one.

Her lips were cool against mine, a hint of the coming chill of the grave. Tears streamed from her eyes when she stepped back. I wondered if the Undead could shed tears.

"Oh, yes . . . my Vlad," she said, knowing my thoughts, "and many . . . will flow from my eyes . . .

if you cannot find . . . it in your heart to . . . accept what I must now become.''

Then she turned and walked slowly into the lake, farther and farther from the shore, deeper and deeper, until only her shoulders and head remained above the water.

''No!'' I screamed. I struggled wildly to get free of the steel-fingered hold my father and brother had upon my arms, but I could not break loose.

''Tzigane! No!''

But she never once looked back. Then her head passed beneath the black surface of the lake, and she was gone.

Chapter Seven

24
Poet

After Tzigane vanished beneath the water, I fought shaming tears. I told myself I should not care about the death of a woman who had betrayed me. *I must not care.*

The Witches rose to their feet and began to whisper a rhythmic chant. Over and over they repeated the same guttural phrase in the Witch-language Tzigane had been teaching me.

Tzigane. Lost to me. Forever.

As they repeated the chanted phrase, the Witches' voices grew louder and the repetitions of the phrase faster, until soon I could not distinguish separate words, a chaos of sounds, shouting their chant into the night. Then, suddenly, the chant stopped, and all was silent save for the gentle lapping of water upon the shore.

My father and brother released my arms and walked away without a word. The line of Witches parted to let them through as they walked toward the other Undead from the cave. But the Vampires no longer stood in two lines. They had broken into a silent crowd.

One came forward from that crowd and embraced Mircea. It was Varina, his wife, now also Undead.

Then, as if the arrival of my father and brother had been a signal, *the Vampires began to change.*

Their forms grew hazy as mist suddenly blanketed the ground where they stood. Then, my brother and father included, they began vanishing beneath pillars of swirling fog, until there was *only* the fog where each had stood, swirling faster, faster, forming two interlocked spirals of whirling mist.

But the swirling spirals were only the beginning of the change. One by one, the twin spirals condensed into whirling spheres that quickly darkened, elongated horizontally, and began to solidify into shapes that were soon easily recognizable. The shapes of bats.

When the transformations were complete, upward they flew, vanishing into the darkness above.

Walking up to me, Lilitu said, "When they have passed through the layer of fog, they will be able to see the stars. I loved looking at the stars when I was a girl, before my parents brought me here, and someday I will see the stars again. One of our most beloved poets has written, 'And someday when has come, my own sweet time to die, I will, I know, join Night's fleet Children in the glorious midnight sky'." She smiled wistfully as she looked upward. "Your thoughts tell me you are surprised we have poets. Yet, you saw the poet tonight. One of our revered Ancient Ones. She who journeyed far from . . . elsewhere, to bestow upon Tzigane the Sacred Crimson Kiss of Undeath."

"That . . . *thing?*" Reminded of the creature, I looked for it. But it was gone. Remembering its wings, I wondered if it, too, was now soaring above the clouds.

"You have so very much yet to learn, Prince Dracula."

"But not here. I am even *more* determined to leave after what I witnessed, what I saw Tzigane do. I will go from this place of Evil and live my life as a *man,* a warrior, a ruler. I will do all I can to forget I ever knew

138

anyone named Tzigane. And when I die, it shall also be as a man, a clean death, a true death.''

Lilitu said nothing for a moment, then she looked toward the darkness of the lake. "She who loves you more than you know will soon return. Be the first she sees in her new life, I entreat you. Go to the shore and wait for her there. *Please*. For her sake.''

"Heard you nothing of what I said? And you will not confuse me with talk of Tzigane's having a new *life*. She will be a corpse, her flesh cold, her eyes dead! I will not wait for—''

"She is a *Witch*, Prince Dracula, trained in the ways of the Unseen. She will not be a hunger-driven predator like your father and brother were. They awoke unprepared for Undeath.''

"Nothing can make the woman I once knew live again. Undeath is not life!''

"In some ways, she will be more alive than ever before. Her senses will be heightened, her strength increased tenfold. And her emotions—''

"If someone must wait for her, let it be you, or that *poet* who drained her blood.''

I walked away from Lilitu. I went to my horse, waiting where I had left it. Holding the mare's reins, I led her where father had thrown my sword. I picked up the blade.

Hefting the weapon, I took comfort in the physical reality of the heavy length of steel. I decided not to sheathe it just yet.

I looked toward the shore to see if Lilitu had gone there to wait for Tzigane. But no one stood on the shore. Holding my horse's reins, I was alone once more.

The Witches had left their torches sticking in the soft ground near the water. But how had they returned to the cave without my noticing? Or perhaps they had *not* gone

139

anywhere. Perhaps they were standing near, watching me, cloaked by spells of invisibility.

I considered using the special way of seeing Tzigane had taught me, the occult vision by which I could see her when no one else could. But my mind veered away from the thought of using anything occult.

What did it matter if the Witches of the Scholomance were standing on all sides of me, watching in secret to see what I was going to do? Curse it all! Let them do what they wanted. For at dawn I would do as *I* wanted. I would ride away from the horrid valley, never to return.

25
Escape

Though I stood well back from the shoreline, holding the reins of my horse on the path by which I intended to leave at dawn, I had little doubt that long before sunrise Tzigane would see me standing there when she returned . . .

Undead . . .

And if she came toward me? And if Lilitu was wrong, or had lied, and Tzigane *was* like my father had been in the palace, attacking with paralyzing powers . . .

I had not yet mastered enough occult skills to control a Vampire, especially not one who had been trained as a Witch and was my teacher as well.

On a physical level, I still held my drawn sword, but I had learned that steel was of little use against a Vampire. And, even if my sword could have harmed Tzigane, I suddenly wondered if I could use it against the woman I had so recently loved.

But it would not be *that* woman who returned, I reminded myself. It would be a corpse, animated into an unnatural existence by the powers of Satan! A creature neither living nor dead.

There was, of course, one other option. Neither the forest nor cave offered any chance of escape. But I *could* escape by using my sword . . . on myself. Would it not be better to die cleanly and truly than to let Tzigane make me into a creature of Undeath?

The torch I had carried from the cave hours before had gone out. Some of the torches the Witches had left near the shore had also darkened. Behind me, the entrance to the cave was dark as well.

The starless sky showed no sign of brightening, and without stars or moon overhead by which to judge the time, it was impossible to know how long remained before dawn.

Eventually, when only two of the Witches' torches still burned near the shore and I felt several nights had had time to pass, I wondered if there were a chance Tzigane might *not* return before sunrise.

Was finding the ring before dawn, following her Undead resurrection beneath the water, perhaps another test of her worthiness? Or the phophecy? And if she failed, would she be allowed to return to the cave before sunrise? Or would she have to remain below until she found the ring?

And what of the beast the Witches called a dragon? Might it not attack Tzigane while she was within its domain?

Even if the beast did not attack her, though, could she survive the daylight hours beneath the water? Would the waters of the lake provide sufficient protection from the fog-cloaked sunlight overhead? Or would enough brightness penetrate to destroy Tzigane's Undead flesh?

To make her truly dead . . .

Surprise flashed through me at what that thought had unexpectedly made me feel.

It seemed impossible, and undoubtedly, infinitely foolish, *but I still cared what happened to her!*

The thought of losing her completely to true death

142

was suddenly more horrible than thinking of her as a Vampire.

My feelings toward the Undead had not changed. Thinking of them continued to inspire fear and revulsion. Why, then, if Tzigane had become one of them, should I still care—

Because you still love me!

Tzigane! I whirled around, sword held ready. But no one was there. I fought panic, the urge to run, and forced myself to stand my ground. Had mounting tension caused me to imagine her voice?

I can speak within your mind now, Vlad, when your desires invite me in, as they have now.

"Tzigane? You—"

Yes, Vlad! Your waiting is over. I will be with you again, now and for always, very soon!

26
Warmth

I faced the lake. One of the two remaining torches on the shoreline flickered its last and went out.

I spoke aloud, "Tzigane . . . come not near me when you return."

After a moment, within my mind came her reply.

There is no shame in the fear you feel. At the moment of my death I faced terror and found myself questioning everything in which I believed, except my love for you. But now—

"Tzigane, I will use my sword on myself to escape you, if I must."

Escape me! There is nothing to escape! I will not attack you as your father did in the palace. I will not bestow the kiss of immortality until you request it, whether now or many years from now.

"I will never ask."

And that is a fear I still have, my Vlad. I fear that you may foresake your destiny of glory and abandon me to loneliness, now that I have . . . changed. I fear that you will not acknowledge the love for me that still burns within you, a love I could not see beneath your fear of the Undead until Undeath itself strengthened my powers and let me see even deeper into your soul. Your love for me is strong enough to conquer your fear, Vlad! All you need do is allow it to rule your desires. Please, do not be ruled by your fear. Do not turn away from your destiny, and me, when I—

"I *cannot* love you now!"

But you do! I know it, and you will know it too, when you hold me in your arms once again. My flesh is still my flesh, even if no longer warm with mortal life.

"No, Tzigane. The emotions I am feeling . . . the love in which you want me to believe . . . it is spellcraft! You *died* in the lake, and now you are using your powers to make me feel—"

Vlad, I found your ring. I am going to return it to you now. Behold the glory of Satan! Behold Tzigane, Satan's Queen, immortal!

And the night began to change.

Crimson light flickered beneath the surface of the lake, then again, and again, as if a lightning storm raged within its depths.

Thunder rumbled, but from out of the dark void above.

The flickering beneath the water grew brighter and more frequent. The thunder from above grew louder.

Flashes of crimson revealed the canopy of fog to be swirling with the winds of a storm. Amid the thunder I soon heard the rushing of those winds as they came rapidly lower.

Gusts of wind buffeted me from first one direction then another, and from far out in the lake I suddenly heard the dragon bellow its terrifying cry.

My horse reared with fright and ran. The last torch on the shoreline went out.

I forced myself to stand my ground, clutching my sword, my black cloak flapping and billowing in the wind.

Streamers of fog reached the ground and covered me with a chaotic tempest of whirling mist, fitfully illuminated by the crimson lightning beneath the lake. Then, through the shifting curtains of mist I saw something rising out of the water.

At first I thought it to be the lake monster returning, but then I saw that it was instead a cloud-like pillar of swirling darkness shot through with streaks of crimson lightning, *like the one I had glimpsed in miniature in the vision beneath the crypt in Targoviste . . .*

The crashing thunder and roaring winds melded into the pulsating rumble of the looming, lightning-veined cloud.

Something cut through the misty air near my face. In the crimson flickering of the dark cloud I caught a glimpse of a large bat, then another and another until the air was filled with them, descending from above, the bat forms of the Vampires, swooping and diving on all sides around the hovering cloud of darkness.

The pulsing cloud moved in my direction, but it stopped when it reached the shore and . . . opened, revealing a glowing crimson womb, and within that womb a naked woman who stood proudly with her head held high.

Tzigane.

Her eyes shone with red fire.

Vampire.

The winds died. The mist vanished near the ground. The lake beast cried out once again, farther away, while the transformed Vampires circled and circled the rumbling cloud, their leathery wings propelling them through the air almost too swiftly for the eye to follow. And far in the distance, from above and on all sides, as if they encircled the valley beyond the fog, came the mournful howling of wolves.

146

I did not see Tzigane move from out of the cloud, but suddenly, as if in the blink of an eye, she was on the shore and walking slowly toward me, wreathed in swirling mist as I'd first seen her in my dream nine years before.

Silhouetted against the glowing crimson womb behind her, she drew ever nearer as I fought my panic, struggled with indecision. A scream of terror built within me. I struggled to keep silent.

The oval opening in the cloud behind Tzigane began to close, then suddenly, although I do not remember actually seeing it move, the pillar of darkness was hovering high over the center of the lake, illuminating the water and land below with its crimson lightning. The rumbling from within it pulsed with a deep throbbing sound now, as if it were the beating of a massive heart. Of the Vampires there was now no sign.

And still Tzigane came nearer, nearer, then stopped within arm's reach.

She smiled and held up my ring. "As the prophecy foretold, I have retrieved your ring from the Dragon's Lake." She looked at my drawn sword. "You have not used your sword on yourself. Will you use it now on me?"

Seeing her standing before me, still so very beautiful, weakened my resolve. Even her glowing eyes suddenly seemed beautiful, no longer like hot coals, but instead crimson stars captured from out of some magical midnight sky. I slowly lowered my sword.

"You *are* feeling desire for me, Vlad." It was not a question. "It is not spellcraft but your own emotions. And you *are* conquering your fear! I am so happy!"

"Tzigane . . . no matter what I feel, I . . . cannot—"

"You can!" She stepped closer. The air grew cold. She touched my left hand. Her cold touch made my heart race. She placed the ring, an ice-cold band of silver, on my finger once again. Then she said, "In the eyes of Satan, we are now wed!"

She put her arms around my waist and pressed against me. "The waters of the lake were so cold, my Vlad, but you are so very . . . very warm."

27
Ice

Tzigane touched my mouth with her cold lips. A chill of revulsion passed through me. But also a searing stab of desire. Still, I resisted.

"Warm me with your love," she whispered, her breath cool against my face. "Do not fight your desire. I have taught you how to release your passion. Do so now!"

"I . . . will not succumb to *your* desires."

"No. But to your own? Vlad! These are still the lips you long to kiss! Mine is still the flesh you hunger to possess! The warmth has left my body, but my soul still burns with love for you, as yours does for me, if you would but follow the true desires of your heart. Please, Vlad? Warm me with your passion!"

She kissed me again, and again I fought my desire to return her kiss.

"Remember the day atop the tower, my Vlad? When we made love in the snow? Was not my flesh cold then? And was not our passion wondrous even so? Warm me now as you warmed me then!"

And I did remember that day, my warm skin against her coldness, naked together in the snow . . .

I suddenly wished we were atop that tower where no one could see, instead of visible in the open.

She knew my thoughts. "Do you think I can no longer render us invisible, my Vlad?" She kissed me again. "That spell is even easier for me now. But if someone did see us, I would not care!" Again she pressed her cool lips against mine. "Would you?"

She was right. Just then I would not have cared. "No. But I—"

Another kiss, and this time I could not stop myself from returning it, tentatively at first, but then hungrily.

Cursing myself for giving in, I dropped my sword to the ground and crushed her to me. I kissed her, pressed my lips hard against hers.

Our tongues touched, fire and ice, and the wall of fear around my inmost core crumbled away, releasing the passions burning there.

Embracing and kissing, we sank slowly to our knees. Panting softly, she pulled at my clothes. I helped, suddenly wanting nothing to separate my flesh from hers.

When I was as naked as she, we embraced on the ground, my lips tracing patterns of desire upon her death-chilled skin.

Her nipples were cold between my teeth as I gently nibbled at first one, then the other. She gasped with pleasure and moaned with deeper needs, as did I.

I stroked her strong body, slowly moved my hands over her hips, buttocks, belly, thighs, until I reached her icy center.

"Tzigane," I whispered, "my love . . ."

"Yes, Vlad! Now, please . . ."

She guided me into her, sheathing my warmth within her death-cold flesh.

I clung to her, panting with pleasure as I began to move, thrusting slowly deeper, again and again, until I groaned with the pleasureful pain of my desire and moved faster, faster, climbing toward the fulfillment of my hunger, having mad thoughts that in this way I might return warm life to her flesh.

But suddenly she maneuvered me onto my back, then began to move atop me, slowly, teasingly, prolonging our pleasure until I cried out with passion and began moving too, bringing us to an explosion of shared ecstasy between our entwined bodies and souls.

A while later, resting in each others arms, I noticed that the crimson flickering overhead had stopped. All was now dark, and silent, save for Tzigane's star-like eyes and a tinge of gray that was beginning to show overhead.

I wanted the sun not to rise, because the dawn would drive Tzigane away, into the cave, to her . . . I did not want to think of it . . . to her *crypt*.

Knowing my thoughts, she touched my face and softly said, "There is a special place prepared for me, my Vlad."

I was surprised to find myself fighting tears. I had forgotten for a moment what had happened to her, and the thought of her crypt had brought deep feelings of mourning for a loved one no longer alive. Yet the passion we had just shared had been the strongest I had ever experienced. I was both confused and elated. Sad and ecstatically happy. I cleared my throat. "The . . . place they have prepared for you had best be a very special place indeed, for it is a Queen who will . . . sleep there."

She laughed, a wondrous sound I had greatly missed. "It is a very nice place to sleep. My sister Witches love and honor me too, Vlad. Though . . ." she reached down to stroke me with her cool fingers, "not in the same way as you."

151

I hardened beneath her touch, and soon we were making love again, taking a long, lingering time to fulfill our shared desires as the canopy of fog slowly brightened overhead with the approaching dawn.

Afterwards, I fell asleep in her cold arms.

And awakened after sunrise. Alone.

The overcast sky was bright. My cloak had been placed over me like a blanket. I looked for Tzigane and started to call her name, then remembered . . .

And everything changed.

Suddenly, thinking about what I had done in the dark, nausea possessed me. Tzigane's flesh, cold with death, beneath my hands, my lips . . . her cool lips touching mine, her chilled tongue inside my mouth . . .

I had not eaten since before arriving at the Scholomance, so there was little in my stomach to disgorge, but I heaved again and again and again, tasting death.

Shaken by the violence of my sickness, I sat back and breathed deeply, striving to regain control. When I felt I was again stable enough to move without becoming nauseous, I rose, collected my scattered clothes, and began to dress.

I felt unclean and craved a cleansing bath, but the thought of using the lake where Tzigane had died for that purpose was intolerable.

As I finished dressing, Lilitu emerged alone from the cave.

I picked up the sword I had cast aside during the night. I looked for my horse.

Reading my thoughts, Lilitu said, "Your mare returned to the stable. I am sorry you are not feeling well. Tzigane was so very happy when she returned before dawn. We are proud of her. And of you. I will take you to her now, if you wish." But she could tell by my thoughts that I had other plans.

With an expression of concern she said, "You are wrong, Prince Dracula. She used no spellcraft on you. The love you felt for her was as real as the ground upon which you stand. You were not tricked."

"I cannot believe anything a Witch says. Neither can I trust my own senses here in this place of the Devil. For a brief moment this morning, what I had done, or rather, what had been done to me, became clear, and I was sick to my soul. You and your kind will use me for your foul purposes no longer!"

"Foul purposes? Prince Dracula, please listen to me. Tzigane—"

"Never speak that name again. I know no one by that name. It was just a nightmare I once had. But now it is over."

I raised my sword. "Will you bring my horse to me? Or must I cut my way to the stables, killing as many Witches as I can in the process? I believe I would rather enjoy that, at the moment. Shall I start with you?"

It was a foolish thing to say to one such as Lilitu. She whispered three Witch-words and I found myself paralyzed, unable to move or speak.

"Certainly you may start with me, Prince Dracula, if you can break the simple spell by which I have now rendered you helpless."

I could not break the spell.

Lilitu looked at me a moment, then said, "Please listen to what I have to say. *Really listen,* Prince Dracula, I implore you. Lies you have been told and mental habits you have developed in your eighteen years of life have forged invisible chains of fear that bind your mind and soul. Your flesh knows the truth, and its desire for Tzigane last night overcame your fear. Today, standing in the light of dawn, let your *mind* also break its chains by the power of conscious thought and your desire for *knowledge.* And with knowledge, *power.*

"Your attitude this morning suggests you have forgotten why you came here with Tzigane. You came here *to learn!* To master occult powers so that you could read the minds of your enemies and more. Will you let your purpose, your ambition be thwarted for *any* reason? Least of all because of fears spawned by lies?

"Think on it! Last night you witnessed a miracle! The woman you love became immortal! Then she returned to you, loved you, and you loved her. Does the ring that you wear mean nothing to you now? Yes, she died! But she rose again, Satan's future Queen on Earth!

"You love Tzigane, but even if you did not, even if each thing you had to learn and do here proved to be terrifying ordeals, could you even then rationally refuse the occult knowledge and skill that alone can lead you to the Throne of the World?

"The false God of Light allows His most faithful servants to die and become food for worms. His promise of eternal life in Heaven is a lie! A monstrous joke! *Nothing more!*

"But those who serve Satan can live on and on, Undead in the flesh, feeding on the blood of those who serve Satan's Enemy. And when those upon whom we feed die, they rise again, freed of their false God's chains!

"We who are reviled as evil by the ignorant are the true saviors of humankind, Prince Dracula, not that crucified impostor our sheeplike enemies have been fooled into believing was their false God's son.

"If you feel a need to kill something this morning, kill the fear born of lies and misunderstanding that would have you throw away all that Tzigane and our Lord Satan offer you.

"So, then, if I release you now from the spell of paralysis, what will you do? Become a King? Or stay a man whose life is controlled by fear, a man who believes the lies about Life and Death told by Priests such as those who tortured and murdered his mother?"

She went down on her knees in front of me and bowed her head. "I shall release you now. For speaking so harshly to my future King, my head is yours to take, if you still wish it, my life yours to destroy."

She spoke the words of release.

I had indeed listened to all she had said, and the truth I felt in her words made the sword in my hand suddenly feel heavy and awkward, and foolish.

Since childhood I had angrily renounced the superstitious fears that had killed my mother and made otherwise intelligent people into weak fools. But I had been acting, and reacting, little better than one of the fearful, superstition-ridden people I professed to despise.

I would be ruled by fear no longer. I slipped my sword into its scabbard. I took a deep breath and let it slowly out. Then I said, "You are, of course, correct. I do not want your head, Witch woman. I want what is in it. Your wisdom. Your Knowledge. But most of all, just now, I want to be taken . . . to Tzigane."

28
Bride

As I walked with Lilitu toward the torchlit entrance to the Scholomance, the thought came to me that the way I was thinking and feeling now might yet be the work of spellcraft.

Reading my thoughts, Lilitu said, "Spellcraft! Prince Dracula, the sooner you learn more about the occult, the sooner you will have fewer doubts about such things."

"And would you really have let me behead you?"

"Well, perhaps I would have, or perhaps I would not."

"Tzigane answered me that way several times. I suppose she heard it from you while she was in training here."

"Maybe she did—"

"And maybe she did not?" I suddenly felt like laughing, but I resisted the impulse.

"Down this passageway, Prince Dracula."

We took the torch-lined passageway to the right, the one I had been told led to the honored Undead. It sloped downward into the Earth and twisted to the left, then back to the right. The air grew cooler.

Soon, the passage narrowed and torches were bracketed farther apart along the gleaming, black-green walls. Then came openings along the walls like those I had found disturbing in the central passageway. Again I heard whisperings and rustlings as we passed. Again I felt watched.

"Guardians," Lilitu said. "You were wondering about what watched you. They can read thoughts, too. No one may pass through here with harm to any of our number in mind. Do not ask me to describe the Guardians. You know not enough about the Unseen as of yet to fully comprehend them without doing your mind grievous harm."

A little way more and she said, "I must ask you not to speak aloud and to walk as quietly as you can when we reach the curtained alcoves of the Hall of Sleep."

We walked a way farther, then the openings of the Guardians stopped and regularly spaced openings large enough for a human to pass through appeared on each side. Each was covered by a thick black curtain, and when we passed I heard nothing, or no one, stirring beyond.

Monitoring my thoughts and knowing I was about to ask if my father and brother were in one of the alcoves, Lilitu raised a hand to remind me not to speak while in the Hall of Sleep.

I began counting the openings, but as the passageway twisted left, then right, and back again, on and on, I lost my count.

We came to the end of the curtained openings. The passageway, however, continued on, narrowing and running straight toward the entrance to a cavern. There were no torches now, and we walked, Lilitu's feet making no sound, my boots echoing hollowly on the stones, in darkness save for the faint flickering of candlelight emerging from the cavern.

Then we entered the cavern. It was smaller than the central cavern by at least half.

In the center rose a large, rectangular block of white marble, but unlike the one in the central cavern, this block's sides had been ornately and intricately carved, and its wide top surface was covered by a soft, thick pallet of quilted black cloth.

Massive silver candle holders cast in the guise of spiraling serpents stood at each corner of the white block of stone, each holding wrist-thick candles the color of blood.

The candles' flickering light softly illuminated rich tapestries covering the stone walls on all sides. And the gentle light also illuminated she who lay atop the cushioned marble.

She was clothed in the silver and black gown she had worn at our first meeting in her cottage. She lay with a peaceful expression on her beautiful face, her lips curved in a slight, secret smile. But her breasts did not rise and fall in her sleep, for she did not breathe nor move in any way.

My beautiful Tzigane. A Vampire, waiting for sunset. And for me.

Knowing my thoughts, Lilitu whispered, "You may go to her, if you wish."

I walked quietly forward until I stood next to the marble block. Her hands were folded on her chest, the fingers entwined in one of the occult patterns she had shown me.

I placed my hands atop hers. She was so cold. So lifeless.

Fear and revulsion suddenly stabbed through me, but I drove them back with angry thoughts and vowed never again to allow such weakness to drive me away from the woman that I loved.

I stood there gazing down at Tzigane, holding my hands over hers, wishing she could open her eyes. Then I began to feel so very tired. It was as if something deep within me had suddenly relaxed, the stress of all I had recently experienced fading away, leaving me weary to the bone. Everything was all right, now. Finally, everything was really all right.

Sleep with me, my husband, Tzigane's thoughts spoke within my mind. *You are surprised that I am aware of your presence, but it is only my flesh that requires sleep, during the daylight hours.*

I looked for Lilitu. She was gone. I was alone with my Undead bride.

There is sufficient room to rest beside me, is there not, my Vlad?

I leaned down and kissed her cold lips. "There is," I whispered, then I stretched out upon the pallet, pressed myself close against her, and almost at once fell asleep.

Chapter Eight

29
Immortal

You can feel Death when you touch a possession trea-sured by one newly dead, who will possess and touch it no more.

You can see Death when you look in a mirror and find someone older than you remember looking back.

Of course, if you are young enough, you may not worry overly much about your own Death. How could *you* ever die?

But if you are old enough, you may fear you will not see tomorrow.

And if you were physically immortal?

Can you imagine it? Knowing you will continue to exist through the ages? Not because of some faith you have in a religion that teaches an afterlife for your soul, but because your body does not age, does not sicken, remains young and strong while those around you stead-ily succumb to Death's creeping decay.

Tzigane was now Undead. Physically immortal.

I was eighteen, she slightly older. But in appearance she would remain the same while I aged. In time, I would appear old enough to be her father, or grandfa-ther. An amusing thought. But as yet it all seemed far from real. And as for asking Tzigane for the Crimson

Kiss of Undeath to become a Vampire myself, the thought remained something away from which my mind determinedly veered.

The first sunset following her death in the lake, Tzigane awoke me with a kiss.

I had meant to be awake before her, and several times during the afternoon I had awakened and tried to judge from the burning of the candles how much time remained before dark.

The first time I awoke, I had been so deeply asleep that I could not, for a moment, think where I was. And for a heartbeat, upon finding myself next to a corpse, fear and revulsion again strove to drive me away from the woman I loved. But I drove the ever-weakening emotions away instead and remained by her side, eventually returning to sleep.

The second time I awoke it was from a nightmare.

Tzigane had been screaming, being tortured in the burning depths of Hell. Again and again her bound nakedness was whip-seared by writhing streaks of crimson lightning shooting out of two oval, glowing clouds that hovered upright nearby.

One cloud was a gray so dark it was nearly black, the other light gray, all but white, and I knew Their names, Satan and God, physical manifestations of inhuman beings.

Deep laughter rumbled from the clouds as They tortured Tzigane, but I sensed They derived pleasure not so much from her pain as from making me watch, helpless to stop Them. And I felt for Them a vast, unbounded hatred. I vowed to destroy Them both for hurting Tzigane, which only increased Their laughter, and my hatred.

But upon awakening from that nightmare, I suddenly remembered the ceremony of the ring below the crypt in Targoviste. If I had failed the test set for me that night, Tzigane said she would have been punished for not preparing me properly. Would she have been punished if I had rejected her after her return from the lake? If I had left at dawn as I had planned, would she even now be screaming in Hell as in my dream?

The hatred I had felt for Satan and God in the dream returned, but now I also felt hatred for my blind self-concern, and I felt horror at the thought that I might again have nearly caused Tzigane untold agonies.

She must have known, reading thoughts as she could, that I had not remembered the possibility of her punishment, and that must have hurt her very deeply, I thought. I claimed I cared for her, loved her, and yet I had proven to be so self-centered that—

I do not doubt your love, Vlad, came Tzigane's thoughts into my mind, startling me.

"I . . . did not mean to awaken you," I whispered. "I suppose I must learn to think . . . quieter thoughts?"

Do not concern yourself with that. Your thoughts near me are a great comfort. The day-sleep of Undeath is not sleep as you understand it. And do not concern yourself about not remembering I could have been punished. Your decision means more to me because you did it out of a desire to stay with me, instead of from a motive of self-sacrifice.

"Still, I should have remembered. I will not forget again, my love." And I kissed her.

Forgive my not being able to . . . respond properly, to your kiss. I promise, however, to respond to even more, at sunset.

"You can feel me touching you?"

Of course. I am more sensitive now, in many ways, than before.

"Then, if I were to tease you by doing . . . this?" I

lightly stroked the black fabric of her gown where it stretched over the tips of her full breasts.

Vlad! Her laughter bubbled in my mind. *I will make you pay for . . . ah! . . . that! Now stop!''*

I stopped. "And how will you make me pay? Why, I could remove your gown and do anything I wished.''

And I could paralyze you with my powers and do the same to you.

"But not until sunset.''

I could paralyze you now.

"Even in your . . . sleep?''

Torment me further and you will have proof! Now sleep more, if you can. I need my rest, too.

"One other thing, if I might? Can you see in my thoughts what I saw in my dream?''

After a pause, her reply came, *Yes.*

"The clouds I saw, I felt they represented Satan and God. But the dark one was like the one I saw in my vision beneath the crypt in Targoviste, and like the one in which you rose out of the lake. Did you conjure the one in the lake? Or was it truly a manifestation of Satan?''

The cloud in which I returned was indeed one of the forms my Lord Satan can take upon the Earth. He would never harm me, though, as you saw Him and His Enemy doing in your dream. Only the false God of Light would take pleasure in making you watch my torture.

"Then . . . I saw Satan Himself last night?''

And made love to His Chosen Queen.

"I should be terrified. I think I am, a little. It is a terrifying thought, to have seen the Devil! But yet I—''

Rest, Vlad. There will be time for such discussions later, yes?

I kissed her again. "Yes.''

I quieted then and lay looking up into the shadows of

the cavern's ceiling for a while, striving to still my thoughts, until eventually I became drowsy and fell asleep once more, only to be awakened by Tzigane's cool lips touching mine. Sunset had come!

I kissed her back. "I had meant to awaken you with a kiss," I told her, "instead of the opposite."

She smiled and kissed me again. "I trust you had no more bad dreams, Vlad?"

"You've no doubt already read my thoughts and know I did not. And you? If your sleep is not as mine, did you have dreams?"

She laughed. "Of course."

After the daytime stillness of her body, seeing her move again, and again hearing her voice seemed as much a miracle as had her return from the lake in the cloud of Satan. The events of the night before already seemed more dreamlike than real. But now I was talking and laughing with her again, after having spent the day beside her lifeless corpse . . .

Again she laughed. "Shall I show you how much *life* this corpse has in it this evening, my love? And there is the matter of paying you back for cruelly teasing me while I slept. Perhaps I will paralyze you as I was this afternoon." She slowly slid her hands down my body. "And then, while you cannot move in any way, I will touch you . . . here!"

My laughter changed to moans of pleasure as she then did more than simply touch me.

And soon we were again making love.

30
Training

My training in matters occult at the Scholomance proceeded swiftly under Tzigane's guidance.

With her enhanced mental powers, she could now enter my mind and work directly with my thoughts and memories to make my efforts produce results more quickly than would otherwise have been the case.

I occasionally still wondered, though, if I were being the greatest of fools, trusting her so deeply, allowing her such intimate power over my very mind. But trust her I nonetheless did, and loved her more than before.

After only three nights of instruction and practice I mastered crude but effective empathic abilities, allowing me to sense the emotions of those near me, which Tzigane explained was a preliminary step in the process of learning to read thoughts.

The mind only knew what the heart told it, she said, and thoughts were nothing more than crystalized emotions.

She reminded me that my first pleasureful lesson in the cottage had dealt with the serious matter of learning to *release* my own emotions, which I would now learn to use as a source of magical power.

And while thoughts were powerful crystalized emotions, spells could be thought of as crystalized thoughts, forced into physical manifestation by the focused willpower of the magic worker.

Why, she asked me at one point, did I think the religion of the false God of Light taught that strong emotions, especially sexual passions, were a sin? It was, she assured me, to keep the false God's followers personally powerless, unthreatening sheep easy to control by priests who, in secret, used emotions forbidden to their flock to work evil magic against Satan and His passion-loving followers.

Tzigane claimed Satan's way was to help humans develop their full potential. She and her sister Witches of the Scholomance served Satan, but unlike the followers of the false God, they were not groveling slaves.

I questioned why, if that were the case, Satan would allow the false God to punish her if she failed in fulfilling her vows. Why did Satan not protect His own?

Her answer was that Satan was Himself bound by vows as part of treaties and agreements in His ongoing War Beyond Earth with the false God of Light.

But I could not forget my dream in which I had seen both Satan and God harming Tzigane, nor could I forget my feelings of hatred for Them. They had seemed more like allies to me than enemies.

She assured me that my dream had been formed from my own concerns and did not represent Satanic reality. On that point, however, I said I would reserve judgment until I knew from my own experience that Satan could be trusted. My suspicious skepticism suggested to me that a being so much more powerful than humankind might not be as bound by vows as Tzigane believed.

For all we knew, to Satan a sacred vow was no more than a calculated lie.

"That is simply not true, Vlad."

"It *might* be true. You cannot be absolutely certain."

"Just who is the Witch, here, and who the student? If you cannot trust and believe what I say, then—"

"It is not *your* word I mistrust, Tzigane. And if your Satan did not want me to be suspicious, He should have chosen someone else to be king."

She had no answer for that.

I suggested we could solve the conflict, or at least make it seem momentarily unimportant, by again practicing the sharing of passion.

She insisted we finish the night's lesson first.

And I learned that particular lesson more swiftly than any before it.

31
Hero

"We will be leaving soon, Vlad, you and I together. In three nights, when the Moon rises full beyond this valley, I will summon a Strigoi to take us elsewhere. Our destination is yours to choose. Where would you have gone when Vladislav returned, if not for me?"

I was struggling with the mental twistings of a new lesson when she said it. I did not hide my surprise. I had expected to continue learning at the Scholomance.

"I thought we would be staying here. I see no reason to leave until I have learned all I can. You were here for many years, were you not?"

"But I was not destined to become a hero of the living."

"And I am?"

She grinned. "Of course. You did not know?"

Already frustrated by the night's lesson, I said, with mild anger, "Tzigane, I do not enjoy the games that sometimes amuse you. I readily acknowledge that you know more than I do about certain things—"

"Certain *very important* things."

"So, why do you enjoy pretending you think I know things you know I do not?"

She leaned close and kissed me. "Because for a mo-

171

ment, just before you frown at me, a most endearing expression crosses your face."

"Endearing expression!"

"Rather like a newly hatched bird that, having just pecked its way through its shell, looks around and wonders if it should have stayed inside." She smiled sweetly.

"I will have to guard against such endearing expressions in the future."

"Why? I do so enjoy them." She looked genuinely disappointed.

I shook my head and laughed. I could not long remain angry with her. "So, I am to become a hero. And if I do not accomplish that feat?"

"You will. And your fame will spread far beyond your Carpathian homeland. You must be an inspiring king to the Undead and others of Satan's followers from many lands, not just to those of us from Wallachia and Transylvania. And thus will you unify Satan's Own into a great, nation-spanning force under a banner of freedom, breaking the chains of those enslaved by the false God of Light." She grinned again. "Will you not?"

I looked at her a moment, then I shrugged and said, "Such has, of course, been my ambition since birth."

She laughed. "So, Vlad, where are we going to go? We *could* have stayed here a while longer, but you have learned your basic lessons faster than anyone had predicted."

"In truth?" I felt a welling of pride. It had seemed to me that my progress was proceeding extremely slowly, but Tzigane had told me more than once that that was only because I was too impatient.

Another kiss. "In truth. We are very proud of you. Now, where to go?"

"I might have died fighting Vladislav."

"With your outnumbered Turks? You are not a stupid man."

"Or been assassinated."

"Possible, but unlikely. You are not an uncautious man."

"No. Well, I suppose I would have gone to Moldavia, to the court of Prince Stephen. He thinks himself my cousin, because he thinks my mother was the Moldavian Princess Cneajna. There would be refuge there for me, and allies."

"Then we will go to Moldavia. When you arrive, you will be thought to merely have been traveling from Wallachia after escaping Vladislav. Word will be sent to sister Witches in Moldavia, and they will have a horse readied for you to ride the last little way."

"But . . . my studies. I have not yet learned to read your mischievous thoughts, if you do not send them"

"We will, of course, continue your lessons, in Moldavia, but in secret."

I groaned. "I suppose, then, I can look forward to more of your wicked tricks?"

She assumed a most innocent expression. "Wicked tricks?"

"Walking naked into a room filled with men when I am the only one who can see you is a trick of vast wickedness. Or, invisible to others, whispering erotic suggestions in my ear while I try to carry on a serious conversation with someone. Or—"

"Oh. Those kinds of things. I see. Well, I promise, then, never to do those kinds of things to you again," she laughed, "during the daylight hours."

I had for a moment forgotten she would no longer be able to be with me while the sun was above the horizon. There, in the caves of the Scholomance, I had adjusted myself to the hours that Tzigane was awake. Food was brought to me when she and I awoke, then again at midnight, and before she slipped into her day-sleep. Food, in the form of Witches giving willingly a small portion of their blood, was also brought to Tzigane at those times.

But once we were in the outside world again, the differences between the requirements of her Undead existence and the world of the living would form a sharp contrast that would spawn numerous problems.

I would have to sleep, but I could not sleep during the day without being thought mad by the living. Any sleep I obtained at night, however, would mean less time spent with Tzigane.

It would have all been so much simpler to have simply stayed at the Scholomance where I could concentrate on my studies, free of distracting mundane concerns.

"Tzigane, I foresee many . . . problems, because of the difference between your waking hours and the time I will have to be awake among the living. If only we could stay here, such problems would not even exist."

She paused a moment before answering. She took my hands. "Vlad, I would prefer staying here, too. But for the reasons I have told you, and which you must recognize the truth of yourself, you must return to the outside world. And waiting any longer would arouse suspicions, would it not? However, to avoid problems, would you prefer me to . . . stay here? It would make your life less complicated, and—"

"No, Tzigane. That is not what I meant." Tears had begun to glisten in her eyes. "I want you with me. And I want you to continue my lessons. We will work out the problems. And, with you involved, I am certain the challenge will prove very . . . exciting."

She kissed me. And I kissed her back.

"I love you so, Vlad."

"We must stay together, Tzigane. Not only as lovers, but as friends and allies. With your help, I will strive to become what you say I must. Being a hero does not sound like a bad thing, if my victories bring the proper . . . rewards."

As we kissed yet again, I slowly slipped her black and silver gown from her cool, pale shoulders and pulled it down to her slender waist.

"Vlad, your . . . lesson . . ."

"We can finish it later." I bent down to kiss her breasts.

And we did complete that night's lesson, but *much* later, and in a hurry, finishing only just before dawn.

32

Lilith

On the day before the night of the full moon, when we were to depart for Moldavia, I awoke well before sunset and was unable to return to sleep.

I recognized a feeling similar to that which I had felt the night before leaving Turk-land to return to Wallachia. Anticipation. Excitement. An impatience to get under way. And of course concern for what the future might hold.

Considering my initial reluctance to stay, I had come to think of the Scholomance as a kind of home remarkably quickly. I might not miss the setting, but I would miss the lack of distractions and the absence of a need for the constant wariness that had previously filled my life.

But as I thought more about the Scholomance, I suddenly saw one aspect of it differently.

Why had it not seemed unusual to me that, except for a number of the Undead, my father and brother included, I was the only man there.

The fact that all of the Witches should be women was not the curious thing, though, for at that time I supposed *only* women could be Witches. No, what was curious was that, until that moment, living among a society of

176

women had not seemed unusual to me. Indeed, I had missed the company of men not at all!

It had been a relief to be free from the presence of men and the threats they could represent. I had spent eighteen years watching, and experiencing, male cruelty and violence, eighteen years striving not only to be a part of their dangerous world, but to become a master of it, a victim no longer but someone they feared, and therefore respected.

When sunset came and Tzigane awoke, I spoke with her about it. She readily agreed with my assessment of the world of men. But when I asked her why there were only women serving Satan among the living at the Scholomance, her answer was that it was as Satan wished it to be. My not having found it unusual only further proved, to her mind, that I was indeed one of Satan's Own.

She added that there were theological speculations about whether or not their all-women culture involved being descended from the First Woman, not the Eve of the false God, but the most ancient Lilitu, known as Lilith and a Demoness to followers of the false God of Light, but an inspirational demi-Goddess to followers of Satan.

This seemed logical, many learned Witches agreed, because the leader of the Scholomance had, upon ascension to leadership, taken the name Lilitu for as long as anyone remembered. But the sacred Scrolls of Satan contained nothing to either confirm or deny the theory.

I was interested in further discussing the matter, but Tzigane changed the subject.

"Vlad, there are two things of which I must speak before our departure at midnight. The first has to do with your father and brother. Won't you talk with them before we leave? Do you still refuse to see them?"

177

I paused, then said, "I have thought about them a number of times in the last few nights. My feelings toward the Undead have changed, somewhat, at least where you are concerned. And I . . . believe I would not mind seeing them."

She smiled and squeezed my hands with her strong, cool fingers. "I am glad. I will take you to them, as soon as we speak of the other matter."

"Which is?"

Tzigane walked a few paces away then turned back to face me. "As I promised, so shall it be. I will not give you the Crimson kiss of Immortality until you request it. But have you at least considered it, Vlad? You know you need not become Undead immediately. Indeed, becoming a hero of the living would be very difficult if you were not of the living yourself. But if I were to give you the Kiss, and share a taste of my blood with you, you would obtain many important advantages."

"Tzigane, I—"

"Please, let me have my say. Please?"

I nodded for her to continue.

"The Kiss would strengthen you in many ways, physically, mentally, and magically, making the learning of difficult future lessons in matters occult somewhat easier. You would not have to worry at all about suffering sicknesses. And, if you were wounded in a battle, your flesh would quickly heal. Or, should you . . . die, be killed in battle or otherwise, you would then rise Undead.

"Please, Vlad. Consider it seriously. I would worry so much less, knowing I had given you great strength for living and protection from death."

She held my gaze but said no more.

"Tzigane, I am simply not yet ready. What you say has great sense to it. But you also said the prophecy required the request to be of my own desire, and that I do not yet have. Although I love you and want to be with you, and while I want you to be happy and to worry as little as possible, a desire for the Kiss is simply not yet in my heart."

"It would also draw us . . . closer, Vlad. During your lessons, during normal conversations, and when we make love, your mind and mine, our thoughts and emotions would be even more intimately linked than they already are, if that makes any difference to your . . . desire?"

I did not answer at once. "It may well, Tzigane. I will think more about it, I promise. And I am certain that in time I will truly desire it. Are you not certain of that, too?"

Her deep disappointment was obvious, but she forced a smile, kissed me, and embracing me tightly said, "Yes, of course, my love. Of course. In time . . ."

Another quick kiss, then she said, "I will take you to your father and brother now, if you are ready?"

And I said that I was.

33
Kin

They were waiting in one of the larger chambers along the Hall of Sleep.

Tzigane pulled back the thick black curtain and I entered.

On each side of the opening was a cushioned sleeping stone, similar in size to the one upon which Tzigane and I slept, save that while ours was white marble, these were of the same black-green stone that comprised the walls.

Father, Mircea, and Varina stood within the chamber. Varina wore a simple black gown. The two men wore black boots and black trousers and tunics.

Now that I was there, I had nothing to say to them, and neither, it seemed, did they to me. For a long and awkward moment everyone was silent. Then Tzigane said, "Should I introduce you one to the other? Was I mistaken that you have previously met?"

We still said nothing. I regretted coming.

Tzigane gave a short laugh. "Very well, then. Vlad, allow me to present your father, Voivode Dracul, your brother, Prince Mircea, and the Princess Varina. And this," she gave me a slight bow, "is your future king, Prince Vlad Dracula. Perhaps I should also mention that the object burning with a soft light over there is called a candle, and—"

"Enough, Tzigane. Your humor is not needed just now."

"I rather thought it was. Well, at least it made Varina smile. Varina, come with me. We will leave these three to frown at each other without distractions."

Varina and Tzigane left the chamber.

Taking a deep breath, I held out my hand and said, "Father."

He nodded stiffly and shook my hand, his touch cold. "Son. I . . . should not have . . . attacked you in the palace." It was as close to an apology as I'd ever heard father make.

"Tzigane has explained that you were not prepared beforehand for your . . . awakening." And that was as close as I intended to come to saying I forgave him. There was, to my mind, a great deal more for me to forgive than his succumbing to an instinctual Vampiric hunger. This was the man responsible for my mother's death. Responsible for so many childhood horrors. And for abandoning Radu and me to the Turks.

Mircea extended his hand. "Brother."

"Mircea." I shook his hand. I held his spying responsible for my mother's death as well, plus many other childhood wrongs. I looked at their sleeping stones. "You are both . . . comfortable here? The Witches are providing for you well?"

"They are," replied Dracul.

"Yes," Mircea agreed. "Varina misses the sun. But it is a small matter to me, an insignificant price to pay for immortality, do you not agree?"

I did not, but I did not say so. I wondered if they could also read my mind and decided they probably could.

181

"And so," I continued, "you harbor no ill feelings for those who made you Undead?"

Dracul said, "If given the choice, I would not have chosen to remain dead after Vladislav killed me."

"No. Of course not."

"Brother, I suppose we should *thank* you for your role in our new . . . existence. If you were not Satan's Chosen King, father and I would now be nothing more than food for worms in unmarked graves."

Mircea's eyes were glassy, unreadable. I tried to use the empathic abilities Tzigane had taught to me, but I sensed no emotions at all radiating from Mircea and Dracul. The Undead could have emotions, I knew, because Tzigane's were if anything stronger now than before. So, either her Undead existence was of a different order than theirs, or they were both skillfully masking their feelings from me, which could mean they felt they had something to hide. But what? Hatred? Simple jealousy and envy, perhaps? Or plots and plans for my demise?

"I am leaving tonight, with Tzigane."

"Yes," Dracul replied. "I would ask you to give Prince Stephen our regards, but of course to him we are no longer alive. A fortunate thing for you, though, to have ties to the Moldavian throne."

Did he expect my thanks for killing my mother to preserve an illusion I was now about to exploit? I began to regret choosing Moldavia as our destination. But it still made the greatest sense. Others who also believed the lie of my mother's identity would have expected me to go there, too.

"It will be my first journey in the talons of a Strigoi. Did you find your journey here by that method interesting?"

Mircea shrugged. "It was, but you may find it less

182

comforting than did we." He grinned, showing his sharp white teeth. "The cold of the upper air did not bother father and I, but Varina, who was then among the living, as you still are, suffered greatly."

I returned his shrug. "Tzigane's Witchcraft will shield my *warm* flesh from the cold. She possesses powerful spellcraft. A worthy ally. I would not envy anyone who became her enemy."

"It is fortunate for us, then," Dracul said, "that we are all working for the same prize, to see you seated upon the Throne of the World, my son."

"Yes," Mircea added, "we are fortunate indeed."

There was again a long silence. I saw no point in prolonging the confrontation.

"I must help Tzigane prepare for our departure." It was not entirely untrue. "I am glad we had this . . . talk."

"As are we," Dracul agreed.

"Yes, brother. As are we."

I nodded to them, turned, and left their chamber. But as I walked away, I thought I heard a muffled laugh and then whispers coming from behind their curtain.

34
Beauty

Though I knew this time what to expect, it was still a terrifying sight when the Strigoi appeared above the lake, a vast dark shape emerging through the moon-silvered canopy of fog above the Scholomance.

Tzigane and I stood near the shore of the lake. She again wore the clothing which she had worn that first night in Targoviste, black leather boots and trousers and a tunic with a black cloak over it all, her pale flesh a stark contrast to the dark clothing.

The Witches, bearing torches, were assembled nearby, as too were the Undead, their eyes glowing red with the night vision that revealed to them much more than the flickering torches revealed to the living. Tzigane's eyes, of course, were also aglow.

I saw no sign of the she-monster who had bestowed upon Tzigane the sacred Kiss.

Dracul, Mircea, and Varina stood in the front ranks of the Vampires. I saw father whisper something to Mircea. My brother looked at me and grinned.

I returned my attention to the Strigoi.

Tzigane, arms upraised, continued chanting powerful words of occult power, controlling the descending beast she had summoned from beyond Earth. The cold, stench-laden wind from its wings buffetted the shoreline. The urge to draw my sword was strong, but so was my confidence in Tzigane's abilities. So, I clutched my black cloak tightly about me and stood my ground.

Tzigane turned. Lilitu came forward. They embraced and kissed. Lilitu came to me. I allowed her to embrace and kiss me as well.

Lilitu stepped back and bowed to us both. "Satan's blessings be upon you." In the torchlight her eyes glistened with tears. "I am so very proud of you both. You will be greatly missed."

Tzigane embraced the elder Witch again and held her tightly. Tzigane's glowing eyes dimmed with tears. "I will miss you, too. My own mother could not mean more."

Lilitu wiped her tears. "Go safely, now," she whispered.

I nodded to her. "My thanks, for caring for Tzigane, and for me."

"It was our honor. Fare you well, Prince Dracula, until next we meet."

I stepped nearer to her and kept my voice low as I said, "One more thing, if I might. My father and brother, be wary of them. They were dangerous and cunning while alive, and I do not believe becoming Undead has changed their nature. Trusting them would not be wise. Probing their thoughts, though, might be."

A frown creased Lilitu's brow. "Surely they would not try to harm anyone here. But you know them far better than I. Your warning will be heeded, Prince Dracula. My thanks for your concern."

The frown gone, she smiled again at Tzigane and me and said, "Go now, and go safely."

Tzigane turned back to face the hovering monster. She shouted words of command in her Witch-language, a few words of which I was finally beginning to understand.

The Strigoi came closer to the shoreline and opened its massive talons.

I forced myself to do as Tzigane had instructed and walk within the talon's deadly grasp. When I touched one, it was as if I had touched ice. I shivered, suddenly chilled within and without by a cold unlike any I had ever felt before.

Tzigane followed and pressed closely against me. I put my arms around her and held her tightly. Sensing my discomfort, she quickly shielded me with a spell of warmth. "The cold you felt is not entirely of the Earth," she told me.

She then commanded the Strigoi to gently close its talons to support us, and when it had, she ordered it to lift us into the sky.

It happened quickly, then, a dizzying ascent, the figures on the shoreline swiftly became smaller and smaller, the ground, lake, and forest rapidly receding beneath us. I half-expected to see the Vampires transform to bats and escort us upward, but they did not. I did, however, hear the cry of the dragon from somewhere out in the dark lake far below. Then we reached the fog and for several moments the world was reduced to a swirling silver-gray mist.

Moments later, the wings of the Strigoi beating faster, moving us more and more swiftly through the cold night air, we broke through the fog.

Above us burned stars in a midnight sky. Above the rim of the circular valley the full moon shone down with its brilliant light. The fog below us was a bright, moonlit silver-white. And suddenly, from all around the valley came the howling of wolves.

"The beauty!" Tzigane cried. "Oh, Vlad! You cannot see what I do with my night vision! The stars! And the Moon! It is as if I had never seen them before, and indeed I have not. Not like this!''

"What do you see that I do not?"

"The colors are unlike any the eyes of the living can see. And . . . they are alive, Vlad! Each star is aware!''

"Of . . . us?''

"No. I think not. I think they are too far away. Of themselves they are aware, though. Oh, yes. Of themselves. But the Moon is . . . oh! . . . *very* aware of us.''

I looked at the Moon. "I do not believe I care for that notion, Tzigane.''

She laughed. "No? Oh Vlad! The beauty!''

And onward we flew through the night.

35
Castle

We flew east at first and then, following the mountains, curved to the north, leaving Wallachia behind, heading north over Transylvania toward Moldavia.

As the snow-shrouded Carpathians passed slowly beneath us, the bright moonlight made of their peaks and valleys a majestic, hauntingly beautiful sight. "There is much to recommend this method of travel, Tzigane, if something could be done about the stench of the beast and the wind cutting into my eyes."

"I wish you could see what my eyes see, Vlad, below as well as above. I wish you could see how *alive* everything is. Everything!"

"Tzigane, even . . . rocks?"

"It seems so, Vlad, to my night eyes."

I thought about that, but it seemed unlikely to me. Perhaps Tzigane was misinterpreting the things her night vision was revealing. Or perhaps not. Things far stranger than living rocks had been proven true to me in the last few weeks.

The moon descended slowly toward the western horizon as the night wore on and the Strigoi flew steadily northward above the mountains.

At times, so unreal was the scene, that I felt I had

fallen asleep and must be dreaming. But at other times my thoughts came excruciatingly clear, especially about what lay ahead for me and what it meant to my relationship with Tzigane.

My life was about to become two lives, the one in which I could be with Tzigane, but only at night, and the other which I would have to live without her during the day.

Certainly, there would be nights when I did not see her at all, perhaps many nights in a row when I was involved in such things as military campaigns. Or would she try to follow, perhaps cared for by Witches along the way? Follow to watch over me? To try and protect me from death, lest I die without receiving the Crimson Kiss and thereby pass beyond her reach.

How she would worry if I went into battle without first requesting the Kiss! But the only way to prevent her worry was to do that which I did not yet desire. Yet, perhaps I did desire it, since I desired to keep Tzigane from worrying. And I certainly did not want to be killed without chance of rising to walk with her throughout the nights of time.

So then, I wondered, why did I still hesitate to request the Kiss?

My thoughts went first one way then another, and if Tzigane was aware of my mental struggle, she gave no sign.

"How much longer will our journey take, Tzigane? You must find shelter from the Sun before dawn."

"All has been arranged. The Witches who are waiting for us in Moldavia have prepared a proper place. Do not worry about the sunrise. We will be there before dawn, even after taking time to visit a . . . special place."

"And that is?"

"Our future home, Vlad. The Castle of Satan's Throne on Earth."

"About which I have never heard, until this moment!"

"For good reason. The castle is a great secret, and had I told you about it at the Scholomance, someone not meant to know might have read your thoughts."

"Someone such as my father or brother?"

"Possibly, if your suspicions about them are true. But there are also Witches who covet knowledge they have not earned. All was not as harmonious at the Scholomance as it may have seemed."

"In a way, that is a comfort to know. So, Witches have their equivalent of court intrigue too, do they?"

"Of course."

"And Satan tolerates their disobedience?"

"In His wisdom, He may even encourage it, to keep those of us faithful to Him alert and strong of spirit. And we must always—"

She broke off the sentence. "Look, Vlad! There it is!"

And far below I saw for the first time the castle that was to be our future home.

36
Always

My first sight of the extraordinary castle filled me with a sudden dread. But Tzigane was so excited!

She shouted words of command and the Strigoi began to descend toward the massive edifice.

The extensive stone fortress was perched like a bird of prey atop a dizzying column of rock. Its towers and battlements were arranged without any clearly discernible pattern, a chaos of spires and archways and steeply slanting rooftops, edged in ghostly, moon-silvered snow.

No light burned in any of the myriad windows, and nothing moved in the empty courtyards that lay mazelike among the jutting towers and strangely angled walls.

From my vantage point above, I saw that the castle could be easily defended. The only access was by a single, dangerously narrow road that twisted back and forth like a serpent ascending the one side of the mountain that was less than a sheer vertical wall. Tracing the road back through the forests lower down, I saw that some distance away it joined a larger road cutting through a mountain pass.

"The castle was built here, near the Borgo Pass, by Satan's Own many centuries ago, Vlad. It is spell-cloaked to render it unseen from a distance, and the road is always guarded by packs of wolves who prevent any but those who know the proper words of power from passing through.''

"A rather . . . safe place to sleep, I should think.''

"So should I! Do you like it, Vlad? Our future home?''

"It is a most impressive sight, Tzigane. Any king would find it a worthy palace.''

"But . . . do you *like* it?''

The more I looked at it, the more I was surprised to find that I actually did like it. Surely there could not be another of its kind anywhere in the world. "Yes. A grim place, but wonderful, I think.''

"There is enough time to stop and feel its stones beneath our feet. Shall we, Vlad? Would you like that?''

"Of course, if you are certain we will still reach your place of sleep before dawn.''

She commanded the Strigoi to lower us onto the roof of the highest tower. The beast opened its talons. The stones were covered by a soft layer of snow.

Tzigane rushed ahead of me and, smiling back, laughed and whirled herself around once, twice, three times, arms outstretched, dancing her way to the edge. Watching her, I could not help but smile. It was wonderful to see her so happy.

When I too reached the edge, but of course by merely walking, she slipped an arm around my waist and we gazed down at the castle spread out below us.

Tzigane said, "When we hold court here, this will become known to the high initiates of Satan around the world as Castle Dracula, where reigns Satan's King and Queen. So say the Prophecies of Satan, and so it shall be, if we but remain strong and wary through the years to come, you and I, and avoid the Evil that Satan's enemies would do to us to prevent our assuming our rightful thrones.''

"Years, while I become a hero to the living, as you have said.''

"Yes. First you must survive many dangers . . . battles, avoiding death.''

"If I did not know your faith and devotion to your beliefs to be unshakeable, Tzigane, I would even now try to convince you to come with me anywhere but where I am known. A simple life together—''

"With me as I now am? And with what you know of the occult? The skills you have already mastered and the powers yet to be obtained? Vlad, you would not truly be content to abandon the glory awaiting you.''

"We could *make our own* destiny, Tzigane. Curse all prophecies and occult powers! Do we not deserve lives of our own?''

She smiled sadly and touched my cheek. "No, Vlad. We do not. Not as you mean it. We are who we are and what we will become. My poor Vlad! A king that longs to be a common man.''

"If you were with me, my life would be far from common.''

"Your destiny is in your blood. True happiness will only come when you have become what the Prophecy of Satan has decreed.''

I paused, then I said, holding the gaze of her glowing eyes, "If we could stay here longer, I would show you my idea of true happiness, Tzigane, as I did in the snow atop that tower in Targoviste.'' I kissed her, then I looked back down at the dark castle. "When was this fortress last occupied? Or has it ever been?''

"Not as you mean the term. But neither has it ever been entirely deserted. Not even now, to my eyes.''

"But what lives here I cannot see?''

"Not yet. The basic occult skills you have learned are not enough. You have, however, encountered similar beings before. The helpers of whom I spoke at the forest cottage and the watchers in the walls of the passageways in the Scholomance are of the same race as those who guard and care for our future home."

I glanced up at the Strigoi. Tzigane had sent it to circle overhead to await her next command. And there in the sky it flew, a monstrous dragon of a beast from beyond the realm of Earth, circling a moonlit castle where dwelt inhuman things I could not see, a castle that was to be my future home. And by my side, a woman neither living nor dead, her pale flesh cold, her eyes burning like ruby stars. A Vampire. Whom I loved.

"Perhaps I am still a child, Tzigane. A child asleep and dreaming of impossible things. Perhaps it is even the same dream in which I first saw you, a dream that seems to have taken years to happen but is really only a few moments out of one night in my childhood."

"If so, would you want to awaken, Vlad?"

"And find you were not real? No! Curse me for a fool, but no. If this is a dream, let it never end."

"It does not have to end, Vlad. Not ever. As you know."

I inhaled the cold mountain air deeply into my lungs and then slowly exhaled. "I have been thinking about that during our journey, Tzigane. Perhaps you heard the thoughts I was having?"

"I did, but . . . I forced myself to remain silent, and after a while I stopped listening. I feared your decision would again be other than I hoped."

I smiled at her. "I thank you for letting me struggle with myself in private. But here are the thoughts to which I kept returning.

"You have said that the Kiss would give me added

physical strengths as well as making occult skills more easily mastered. And those things would give me a greater chance of surviving among the living and aid me in achieving the worldly ambitions I would have had even if you had not entered my life. The Kiss of Undeath would therefore help me to retake the Wallachian throne and hold my power there. And it would help me obtain revenge against the Turks, as well as Vladislav and the conspirators who helped him kill my father and brother."

"Yes. It would help you . . . survive becoming the hero your destiny demands."

I nodded. "And I would be lying to myself if I claimed I did not hunger to possess the occult powers I have seen you wield. So, I should be convinced of the logic of requesting the Kiss, even if eventual immortality were not part of the bargain."

"It . . . would seem so, to me."

"But what I found in my thinking to be of greater importance to me, Tzigane, was neither logic nor worldly ambition, but emotion.

"Without the Kiss, if I died of sickness, at an assassin's hand, or in a battle, Death would separate me from you forever. And I do not desire that, Tzigane. *Never*.

"So, is that, perhaps, enough? A desire not to be separated from you would mean a desire for the Kiss of Undeath, would it not? If that were the only way for us to be together always? And it is, is it not?"

"It is." She whispered so softly I could barely hear. "And you know that nothing would make me happier."

One last flare of doubt and fear made me hesitate another moment, the terrifying enormity of what I was about to do giving me pause. But both ambition and emotion urged me on, and after a moment I quietly said, "Make certain, then, that if death comes to me, I will rise to be with you always. Do it now, here, atop our future home. But quickly. For your sake we must yet race the Sun." The eastern horizon was beginning to gray with the first hints of dawn.

Tears glistened in Tzigane's glowing eyes. "I love you so, my dear Vlad," she whispered.

We embraced. We kissed, long and deep. Then she moved her cool mouth down my pulsing throat, found the jugular, and slowly pressed her icy teeth into my flesh.

There was but a moment of pain, then a flood of pleasure rushed through me. I felt my manhood harden. I longed to be making love to her. I moaned with desire.

She drew back. "Your blood is my ecstasy," she breathed. "Oh, Vlad, my love . . ."

She kissed me again. I tasted my blood on her lips.

"And now, you must taste of mine," she said.

I saw her extend the tip of her tongue from her mouth and bite down. Her blood welled forth.

I hesitated but a moment, then pressed my lips against hers and drew her tongue into my mouth.

I swallowed the thick coldness of her blood, felt it slide down my throat, and for a moment it seemed to coil in my stomach like a living serpent, writhing to be free.

Nausea twisted within me. But almost as soon as it came, it passed, and I was shocked to feel . . . almost frighteningly, *alive*. My senses felt predator sharp. Alert. Intensely aware.

And Tzigane, her mind, emotions, soul, felt so close to me now, so much a part of my awareness, linked intimately to my existence, as if we had been but two halves of a whole, now combined into one entity.

I embraced her tightly, glorying in the feel of her strong body beneath my hands. I buried my face in her wild mane of dark, cool hair and breathed deeply of its scent. I kissed her again, my senses roaring with her taste. And I whispered, "Even Death cannot part us now, my love."

"No, Vlad," she answered, clutching me to her with her Undead arms, "not even Death."

Chapter Nine

37
Weavers

"Would you like to *enter* the castle now, Vlad?"

I was still adjusting to the effects of the Kiss. Her question was a total surprise. "But, I thought—"

"I could not be certain you were going to request the sacred Kiss, and you could not safely enter the castle until after you did. Before the Kiss, the occult forces permeating the interior would have strained your grasp on sanity. But now, the Kiss and my blood have altered your body and mind so that you can endure the castle's effects. And I can sleep within the castle even more safely than in the place prepared for me in Moldavia."

"But, we are expected in Moldavia."

"Only by the Witches with whom I have been in mental contact. You can, therefore, if you wish, not only enter the castle but remain with me here for a time, studying in seclusion. The effects of the castle and your Undeath-enhanced blood will make it possible for your mastery of occult skills to proceed at an even more rapid pace. You can complete your journey to Moldavia later, if you still wish to go there."

I thought a moment. "But being absent from the outer world for an extended period of time would still bring suspicions on me, would it not?"

"Not if the Weavers help. I have not spoken of them to you before. Their existence is another closely guarded secret. The Weavers of Memory are three elder Witches skilled in a form of paranormal trickery by which events that have not happened *but might well have happened* are remembered as having actually taken place.

"Memory Weaving cannot actually *change* history, of course, but it can, and has, been used on special occasions to alter the way history is *recorded*.

"So, the Weavers could create the illusion, after the fact, that you have been somewhere you have not. Witnesses will swear that they have seen you in places you have not been and remember your doing things you have not done, as long as nothing you are remembered doing affects major events.

"So, if you choose to use the Weavers, Vlad, where would be a good place for them to make it seem you have been?"

I reminded myself that after all I had seen and experienced, being skeptical of something Tzigane said was a foolish thing to do. So, no matter how fantastic the idea of Memory Weavers initially struck me, after a slight pause I replied, "Had I not fled northward when Vladislav returned, the only other option open to me would have been to return to Turk-land."

"A deception easily accomplished."

"But I would have stayed there only until I could have found a means to slip away and journey to Moldavia."

"Which could coincide with your actual arrival there."

"Yes. If I decide to stay here in the castle for a while."

I saw her glance with a slight anxiousness at the brightening eastern sky. "We must leave now, Vlad, if we are not going to stay."

202

"You said it would be safer for you here than in Moldavia. And I would feel no disappointment at the prospect of spending more time with you alone." I hesitated a moment more, then said, "Very well, Tzigane. I do indeed choose to stay with you here, for a time. Let us enter quickly our new home and find you a place to sleep!"

She kissed me. "I am so glad, Vlad!"

I laughed and held her tightly. "As am I." My senses and emotions, enhanced by the Kiss of Undeath and Tzigane's blood, spawned a deep hunger for her. But I felt a hunger for other things as well, for the knowledge I was soon to acquire, and for the power that I would use that knowledge to wield in the future.

I was possessed by a sense of a victory won and felt an excited happiness stronger than I could remember ever having felt before.

Tzigane commanded the Strigoi to take us below, into the main courtyard.

When the winged beast released us and my feet touched the ground, a spear of coldness stabbed through me, but the chill quickly passed.

I stood with Tzigane and watched the Strigoi ascend into the graying, pre-dawn sky.

Wolves howled in the distance.

"The wolves know we are here, of course," Tzigane said. "They know their future King and Queen have come to the great house they guard."

I laughed. "Am I now to be Satan's King of Wolves as well?"

Tzigane frowned at me. "You are to sit the Throne of the World. Are not wolves part of the world? Sometimes, Vlad, I think you still do not really *believe* all I have told you is true."

"What I find *more* remarkable, Tzigane, is that sometimes I *do.*"

She glanced at the graying eastern sky. "I must sleep soon. I can feel the heavy approach of the Sun. But how I wish I could watch the sunrise with you!"

"Tonight is the second night of the full Moon. Its rising should be a fine sight from the battlements, I believe."

She smiled and kissed me. "Yes. Of course. Tonight we will watch the moonrise together. And together we can enter our castle, right now!"

38
Gateway

Before entering the castle, I quickly examined the courtyard.

On three sides loomed towering walls with tall, narrow windows from which, like all the other windows I had seen, no light gleamed. At ground level, several dark passageways led away beneath rounded arches. In one wall was a great door, studded with large iron nails and set in a projecting doorway of massive stones. I assumed it led into the castle proper.

I suddenly had the uncomfortable feeling of being watched. Was one or all of the invisible residents Tzigane had mentioned watching us? From the dark archways? From the lightless windows? Would it matter if they were? I decided it might as well not, since there was nothing I could do about it. But perhaps soon that would change. Perhaps my enhanced blood would soon help me learn how to see them.

The fourth side of the courtyard, which by the stars and the brightening eastern sky I judged to be the north one, contained the gate to the outside and the castle's drawbridge. During our approach to the castle, I had noticed that the drawbridge was raised, effectively isolating the castle on its pinnacle of rock across a deep, steep-walled ravine.

I returned my attention to the nail-studded door, then became distracted by the sudden realization that I was seeing far too well in the shadowed courtyard. The bright Moon was below the top of the castle walls, and the pre-dawn sky was not yet bright enough to account for the sharpness of my vision in the darkness.

If *all* of my senses were sharper under the influence of my Undeath-enhanced blood, it would explain having better than human vision, I decided. I wondered if my eyes were glowing like Tzigane's.

She was listening to my thoughts. "No, Vlad. Your eyes do not yet glow with the full night vision of the Undead. You possess but a hint of what I can now see."

Together we walked to the nail-studded door. The carvings in the wooden door's massive, projecting stonework intrigued me. For no apparent cause, I found the carvings slightly disturbing. They seemed a bit like writing, but in no script I had ever seen before. Detecting my thoughts, Tzigane said, "Yes. A most ancient script in the tongue of the Old Ones who ruled the Earth in Satan's name long before the dawn of humankind."

"*Before* humankind? Then I am not to be Satan's *first* King on Earth?"

"You will be His first *human* King on Earth."

"And was this their castle? These . . . what did you call them? Old Ones?"

"No. But this, the stonework in which the door is set, not the door itself, is one of their gateways into our realm of reality."

"*Is* one of their gateways? They use it still?"

"Occasionally."

"But they no longer rule here."

"No. Their time has passed. Though some say they

are not dead, but dreaming, and will one day rule again.''

"Then I will have to learn as much about them as I can. If they try to usurp my throne, I would have to become their enemy.''

"I do not believe that would happen.''

"Why not, Tzigane?''

"There is so much for you to learn, Vlad.'' She looked again at the brightening sky, "But later, please?''

"Of course.'' I tried to open the door. It would not open. I kept trying. Tzigane had to get inside!

Tzigane placed a hand on my arm. "There are protective spells, Vlad.'' She whispered a sequence of Witch-words. "Try now.''

The door opened smoothly and silently. Cold air from inside washed over me. The black silence of a deep cave waited beyond the threshold, but only for a moment, then flickering torches flared to life within. "And did the ones I cannot yet see light those torches?'' I asked.

"Yes.''

I stood aside for Tzigane to enter.

"No.'' She took my hand. "Together. The portal is wide, is it not?''

And, side by side, we entered our future home.

39
Tomb

I closed the door behind us and looked for a means to secure it. There was a massive iron lock but no key, and there were no bolts to slide closed. But then I thought about the isolation of the castle. Surely no invader could hope to reach the castle across the ravine while the drawbridge was raised.

"No *human* invader, Vlad," Tzigane said, knowing my thoughts, "and most of Satan's nonhuman enemies are not strong enough to penetrate the protective spells that surround this mountain."

"Most, but not all?"

"Other spells protect the castle itself, as you saw outside when first you tried to open the door, and I have been told that even more powerful spellcraft protects my place of sleep."

"And the key?" I asked, motioning to the empty lock. "Is there no need for one, then?"

"It is more than a mere physical key. When you are ready, it will be given to you."

"You have it, then?"

"No. It is kept by one of those you cannot as yet see."

"And the place of sleep you mentioned. I would have

thought perhaps anyplace within these walls would do. Surely the sunlight cannot harm you here.''

"No. But I will sleep best where protective spellcraft is strongest. And sleep I must, as well you know, while the Sun is above the horizon. One who serves here is even now waiting to lead me to my special place."

She spoke to the empty air before us. "We are ready."

We walked down a narrow hallway and came to a great, winding staircase. Passageways led away on each side. At the top of the stairs I thought I saw a shadowy shape move within the other shadows there.

"A shadow from another reality, Vlad. You will see more of such things while you are here, and learn to tell much about other realms of existence by interpreting the sightings. That particular . . . vision was of something called a shadow-thin."

"And did it see us, too?"

"Perhaps."

I was not unhappy when we did not ascend the steps. Instead, we went down the passageway that opened to the left. Soft candlelight illuminated the hallway.

We turned right down a short flight of stairs, then walked along another passageway lined with doors on each side. Small, gilt-framed paintings adorned the wall between the doors, paintings of scenes that seemed to shift and change as we passed.

Ahead of us, one of the doors slowly opened, revealing darkness.

As we went into the room through the opened door, the darkness gave way to flickering candlelight. The door closed behind us.

It was a small room, bare of furnishings or wall hangings of any kind, but in one wall, a window showed a vista of forests and distant, snow-capped mountains revealed in the brightening, pre-dawn light.

Tzigane shielded her eyes from the light as we crossed the room and exited through a door in the left-hand wall.

We went down a stone passageway with a low ceiling. Soon, we came to a spiral stairway that descended steeply.

Down and down the winding stairs we went. At the bottom was a tunnel-like passageway. At its end was an iron-banded door. It did not open.

Tzigane spoke Witch-words of command to allow us entrance. The door opened. We went through into a large chamber that reminded me of the caverns of the Scholomance, except that this one was rectangular, not circular, and there seemed to be a kind of altar at the far end. In fact, in spite of the fact that there was no cross above the altar, no icons on the walls, no churchlike trappings of any kind, I *felt* the chamber to be a kind of chapel. Vague whisperings and rustlings drifted down from the shadowed ceiling above, I assumed from more of the invisible ones.

The iron-banded door closed behind us. Along the left-hand wall of the chamber were two dark archways with steps leading down into vaults.

We went through the nearest archway and down the steps into a vaulted crypt where other archways led away on all sides. We went through one, turned, went through another, turned again, and then went through yet another, walking on and on, following the guide that only Tzigane could see through an intricate maze of passageways, until finally we emerged into a crypt of vast proportions.

Around the crypt several torches burned. Arched, shadowy recesses were cut into the walls, but no other passageways led away from that place, there were no other steps leading down. We must therefore, I reasoned, be in the deepest part of the castle, and with that thought came a sense of the crushing heaviness of the structure above.

In the center of the cavern-like crypt was a dais, and upon it an open tomb carved from a single, massive block of black stone. Thick candles held in intricately carved golden stands burned at each corner.

We walked to the dais. On the side of the tomb a name was carved in lordly letters. My name.

DRACULA.

I did not care for seeing it there!

Tzigane slid her arm around my waist. "And look at the other side, Vlad."

We walked around the dais. A different name was carved on that side of the tomb.

TZIGANE.

"Many female babies in my tribe have been given the name of Tzigane over the years, in the hopes that the honor of one day becoming Satan's Queen on Earth might be theirs, for the prophecies foretold that Tzigane would be the name of King Dracula's mate."

We stepped onto the dais and looked down. A recessed area, the length of a tall man and twice a man's width, was cut into the top of the stone to a depth of about two feet. The bottom was covered with bare soil.

"You need not sleep here with me, Vlad."

"There is room."

"Yes. But there are more . . . comfortable places for you to sleep."

"Near you? Down here?"

"No. Above, in the castle."

"I prefer to sleep with you."

"It will be cold for you, once I am asleep and no longer project the spell of warmth, though the cold will bother you less now than before you received the Kiss."

"My cloak will keep me warm enough."

"One of the helpers will bring you wine to warm you, and food if you hunger. You need but request it."

"Perhaps I shall. And you? Your . . . hunger? You took so little of my blood . . ."

"And I will take no more, Vlad."

"I . . . would not mind."

She kissed me. "My needs will be provided for here, as in the Scholomance. Those who serve here are not bloodless, as you will see when you learn other enhanced vision skills."

Her eyelids were growing heavy with her coming sleep. I helped her into the tomb. She lay back and arranged her black cloak around her. I stretched out beside her. She smiled at me.

"Sleep well, Tzigane."

"I am so happy, Vlad. We are together in our future home! There is so much to do, now. So much we will soon share as you learn more and more of the occult."

"I, too, am happy, my love."

We kissed.

Soon, she fell asleep. And stopped breathing.

The torchlight that had been illuminating the crypt began to dim. I suddenly could not bear the thought of being in that deep place in total darkness.

"Do not extinguish the light," I said loudly, wondering if the unseen one who tended the flames would hear and obey. After a moment, the flickering light brightened again. I smiled with satisfaction. Then, to my surprise, my stomach rumbled its emptiness, and I realized I was ravenous. I remembered what Tzigane had said about the wine and food.

"Bring food to me," I ordered, "and wine."

Not feeling sleepy, I rose from the tomb and stood on the dais. All was silent. I stepped down and walked about, exploring the immediate area but careful not to lose sight of the tomb.

The passageway by which we had entered was now completely dark. Did the helpers, like the Undead, have no need of light? Were they, too, Vampires? Or, since they were servants of Satan, might the term of *demon* apply?

In the dark recesses around the walls I found other open tombs, smaller than the one bearing my name and all of them empty, I was glad to see, unless those I could not see slept inside, a thought I did not find comforting.

As I explored, I heard no sounds save those I made myself, but when I next looked at the dais, food and wine awaited me there. Upon a golden platter had been placed a loaf of black bread and goat cheese and a chicken seasoned with peppers. There was also a flagon of golden wine and a slim-stemmed golden goblet of elegant design.

I poured wine into the goblet, then sat down, leaned back against Tzigane's place of sleep, and leisurely ate my meal.

The wine was strong and delicious, and never had food tasted so wonderful. My senses, sharpened by the Kiss of Undeath, treated me to pleasureful flavors more vivid than had been possible before.

After I had eaten, I drank more wine until I began to feel warm and relaxed and drowsy. Then I stretched out beside Tzigane again and lay looking up into the shadows above the tomb.

While the caverns of the Scholomance had made me feel well-protected, the deep crypt where I now lay made me feel even more secure. Gone now was the feeling of crushing heaviness I had earlier experienced.

I let my mind wander back over all that had happened to me since leaving Turk-land. I thought about how much

I had changed, my beliefs, attitudes, expectations, ambitions. And now also my body.

I made a fist and clenched it tightly before my face, feeling its iron strength.

I had been strong before, the result of long years of practice with weapons and exercise designed to strengthen my muscles for battle, but I felt a different kind of strength in my body now, a strength that somehow made the strength I had known before seem weak and childlike. And, in time, when I had joined Tzigane in Undeath, I would be stronger still! As strong as ten men, she had said. The thought was very appealing.

I could not help but acknowledge that I was feeling intensely superior to the man I had been, and a kind of pity for any man limited by mere human strength came over me . . . and I was feeling great pride in what I had become and was becoming, and pride for the woman I loved. *More than woman!* An Undead Goddess! Superior to all others! As I was now superior to merely human men.

I reached over and took Tzigane's hand in mine. I lifted it to my lips and kissed its cool flesh. And then I lay on my side, gazing at her beautiful profile until I fell asleep.

Chapter Ten

40
Routine

I stayed in Castle Dracula for nearly a year, acquiring occult knowledge, gaining occult skills and powers.

Sleeping during the day beside Tzigane and awakening with her each sunset, it was a year in which I rarely saw the Sun.

Our routine varied but little over the months. After awakening and, perhaps, making love, we would arise and ascend into the castle to be fed by those who served us there. Blood, of course, for Tzigane, a variety of food and wine for me.

Afterward, Tzigane would begin that night's lesson. We usually went to the castle's library for my studies, a large room at the end of a narrow hallway on the second level, to the left of the head of the main staircase.

In the library, three of the walls, save for the doorway and a large fireplace, were covered from floor to shadowed ceiling with crowded shelves holding books, scrolls, and less conventional tools of knowledge such as crystals and stones charged with occult energy of various kinds, or perhaps peculiar bones inscribed with occult symbols and formulae, or vials containing occasionally noxious and usually unidentifiable substances.

Over the fireplace hung a large mirror, its frame intricately carved with symbols similar to those on the portal of the main doorway. And, like the carven portal, the mirror too was a kind of gateway, capable of providing misty glimpses of things not always pleasant to see, but fascinating to learn.

The first time Tzigane stood with me before the mirror, however, proved a shock, for the mirror showed only my reflection, not hers.

The Undead, she explained, do not cast a reflection that can be seen by mortal eyes. To her eyes, however, she was as visible as always, and in time, she promised, I would learn how to see her reflection, too.

Into the fourth wall of the library, opposite the doorway, was set a large window made up of many small panes in the manor of stained glass, save that there was no color in them. All were clear.

The window looked out over the vast expanse of space beyond the sheer vertical wall of rock upon which the castle sat. The view, of course, was spectacular, particularly during the appropriate time of the Moon's cycle when we would watch the silver orb rise above the distant eastern horizon.

Mountain thunderstorms were also magnificent when viewed from the library, and if we wished to see one when the sky was clear, there was spellcraft that could bring rain before dawn, that Tzigane, and later I myself, made use of more than once during my sojurn with her there.

Sometimes, however, for my studies Tzigane would take me to one of several different rooms, none of which could have been even remotely termed *normal,* as I had once, in more unenlightened days, understood that knowledge-hampering term.

One of the first she showed me had windows that

looked out onto another world. Twin moons hung in the sky amidst stars whose patterns I could not recognize. And on the ground below that unfamiliar sky crept glowing things like monstrous snakes making high-pitched piping sounds that, within moments, became distressingly disturbing. We stayed there, nevertheless, for most of that night, listening to a Teacher not even Tzigane could see.

Before each sunrise, before eating a light meal in preparation for our return to the crypt to sleep, we exercised to keep our bodies strong. Although at first I supposed occult work would require only mental strength, I soon discovered it to be extremely taxing physically, requiring great physical endurance in order to maintain concentration and force of will.

I performed weapons' practice and strengthening exercises much like those I had used in my cell in Turkland, but Tzigane began her exercise with dancing, slow and relaxed at first, then quickly progressing to patterns of strenuous swirling and leaping, all the while humming and singing traditional melodies of her Gypsy tribe, sometimes punctuated by the clapping of her hands.

After completing her dance, she then practiced her transformational powers, taking the forms of a bat, a wolf, or glowing mist, and the sight never failed to fascinate me. At first, however, it made her difference from me so obvious that her transformation also caused me to feel fear, but that soon passed.

She eventually asked me if I would teach her the basics of weapons' use. Neither of us could anticipate her ever needing to use a physical weapon to defend herself, but for the pleasure of learning a new skill she felt it would be well worth her time. I agreed, of course, and for a few weeks felt a satisfying superiority at being able to do something better than my Gypsy Witch! But her Undead strength and dancer's coordination soon made her my equal, after which we accomplished some interesting exercise, indeed.

But many times the most interesting exercise came afterwards, when we put our weapons aside, and our clothing, to make sometimes violent, sometimes gentle, but always quite wonderful love in our extraordinary home high in the beautiful Carpathians near the Borgo Pass.

41
Progress

As my studies progressed and I learned ever more about the Unseen, the world I had known seemed ever less significant.

The more my knowledge of the totality of existence broadened, the less important became the affairs of mere humans.

Even the great struggle between Christendom and Turk-land at times seemed trivial, a squabble between humans blinded by the same false God of Light, Who, I speculated, might not truly care which side prevailed, but only that the battles and the suffering they caused be entertaining.

By the end of the first month I had learned to grasp fragments of Tzigane's thoughts when she was *not* intentionally projecting them into my head. Shortly thereafter, I became skilled enough with occult vision to glimpse the hazy outlines of the invisible ones who served us.

My ability to detect Tzigane's unprojected thoughts and to see our servants progressed rapidly, and within another month I could, when concentrating properly, read Tzigane's thoughts at will . . . when she was not deliberately shielding them from me, a protective privacy technique she promised to teach to me next. And I could soon clearly see our servants.

They were not what I had expected. I had wondered if they might be Satan's demons, sporting horns and monstrous faces, as portrayed by artists of that time. Instead, some could have almost passed for human, especially one fiery-haired female, save for her catlike manners and sharp-clawed hands and feet.

Some, though, at first glance could not be distinguished from simple beasts, but not always beasts with which I was familiar on Earth.

Many of the servants, however, could scarcely be described with human language, so otherworldly and impossible did their appearances strike me.

Another month passed before I began to hear the sounds the servants made, sounds Tzigane said I was not hearing with my *physical* ears, but with occult hearing that was a kind of extension to my occult seeing.

And so did the spring and summer and autumn pass in Castle Dracula, as my studies continued and my knowledge and skill grew, until finally came again the first snows of winter and the season of the Winter Solstice, near which occurred the longest night of the year.

We made that longest night a festive one, dressed in the most fashionable of clothing and I with my never-empty flagon of golden wine, Tzigane with sips of the wine-laced blood of the more human of the willing servants, for whom it was also a festive night.

Others of our servants, whom by then I could now see almost without making the effort, provided music and entertainment, and at midnight Tzigane performed a dance of joy and desire that left both of us hungry for the other's arms, a hunger we then fed, in private, while elsewhere in the castle the servants from beyond Earth continued to dance and celebrate until came the dawn.

We had discussed inviting guests to the festivities, perhaps the Undead from the Scholomance, as well as Lilitu and other Witches there who had received the Kiss of Undeath and tasted of Undead blood, so that they could endure the occult emanations of the castle without going mad. But we had decided to selfishly keep this night for ourselves and our servants, because the time was fast approaching when we would no longer have the luxury of being alone, the knowledge of which at times made our festive mood feel slightly forced.

We had decided that soon after the beginning of the new year I would return to the world beyond the castle's walls.

Tzigane would be coming with me, of course, but no longer would we be able to devote ourselves to each other during all the hours of darkness.

Continuing to stay in Castle Dracula was a most appealing notion, but there was still the matter of my becoming a hero to my homeland and Christendom, and thereby fulfilling the prophecies that would convince all of Satan's folk I was indeed His chosen King on Earth.

I once voiced a question as to why Satan, if He had chosen me, did not simply command His followers all over the world to accept me as their king. But Tzigane said Satan did not employ the tyrannical methods of His Enemy, and she reminded me that even the false God of Light had taken pains to see that His Son and chosen King, Who had also risen from a tomb as I was eventually to do, and whose rituals included the changing of wine into blood, had also fulfilled prophecies to convince followers of His identity.

No, I must still fulfill Satan's prophecies, partly for understandable reasons, partly for reasons understandable only to Satan and His Enemy in the context of Their wagers and treaties in Their ongoing War Beyond Earth.

Too soon, then, came the new year and with it the night we had chosen to leave for Moldavia, completing the journey we had begun nearly twelve months before.

In the courtyard, Tzigane summoned a Strigoi, and as it lifted us into the cold, moonless sky, we held each other tightly, and watched as our castle receded rapidly into the distance, disappearing into the darkness of the night and the unretrievable past.

Neither of us guessed it would be twenty-seven long years before we returned.

42
History

History records that I died in my forty-sixth year after twice recapturing the Wallachian throne, a hero to many, a monster to some.

You, who are living your short span of mortal years in this closing decade of the twentieth century, can read books written by historical scholars about those forty-six years, books that detail the violent life of a fifteenth-century Knight of Christendom, a Wallachian Voivode who came to be called Vlad the Impaler by his terrorized enemies, with good cause.

But historians tell you nothing of what was always most important to me, my secret life with Tzigane, the unknown history that often shaped the known, about which you have already learned a great deal.

Seek out those books of history nonetheless, if those forty-six years of my mortal existence hold interest to you. I myself have often found amusement in such books, and most of what they tell you is true, save of course for the parts woven by the Weavers of Memory to conceal and confuse, or the things I simply kept secret. But with the knowledge you are gaining here, I trust you can detect the most obvious of those historical errors and glean the truth behind the fiction.

You will find, for example, in the pages of some history books that more than once I evaded assassination, or other danger, by seemingly being forewarned. After reading what you have of *this* book, you will no doubt speculate that either I or Tzigane had discovered those assassination plots by using occult skills, and in most cases you will be correct.

However, on the chance that you care little for books written by historians, I will briefly recount something of those heroic, historic years.

While most of my eighteenth year was spent in the castle with Tzigane, the Weavers of Memory arranged to have history say I had been in Turk-land.

My nineteenth year was then spent, both in history and in fact, in Moldavia at the court of Prince Bogdan II. Prince Stephen Bathory, his son, was nearly my age, though slightly younger. During that year, Stephen and I fought together in a battle at Crasna to repel a Polish invasion of Moldavia.

In October of my twentieth year, forewarned by Tzigane, I fled Moldavia with Stephen after his father was assassinated.

Stephen was later to become known as Stephen the Great. He was an ancestor of another famous Bathory, by the way, the Countess Erzebet, about whose life in sixteenth- and seventeenth-century Hungary many of you are no doubt well aware. She became known as the Blood Countess who, it was claimed, delighted in torturing young women and, occasionally, bathing in their blood. About Erzebet, as about myself, however, many lies have been told. Perhaps a time will come in which I will share with you the truth about her. But this is not that time.

So, after his father's death Stephen and I journeyed to

Transylvania over the Borgo Pass, from which ran the narrow road leading to my unseen castle.

I asked Stephen if he had ever heard legends about Satan's Castle being located somewhere in that area, and he said of course he had, since childhood, but that it was best not to speak about it aloud in that part of the mountains for fear the Devil might hear us. I had to struggle mightily to keep from laughing.

The man in power in Transylvania at that time was John Hunyadi. He had backed Vladislav's usurpation of my father's throne and was, therefore, indirectly responsible for Dracul's and Mircea's deaths. He therefore assumed I was his enemy and hired assassins who tried, but failed, to kill me. But two years later, with Constantinople falling to the Turks and all of European Christendom in danger, Hunyadi needed all the experienced warriors he could find, and made of me his ally.

In my twenty-fifth year a bright comet appeared in the sky, a comet known to you today as Halley's.

Tzigane was overjoyed. Part of the prophecy was that in the year I ascended the Wallachian throne for the second time, a fiery comet would appear, and I was already making my plans to bring this part of the prophesy to fruition.

In the summer of 1456, then, I captured again the Wallachian throne, caught Vladislav, and personally saw to his long and lingering death, proper repayment for the manner in which he had killed my brother and father, and would, had he caught me eight years before, have also killed me.

I also executed many of the nobles who had conspired against my father to help Vladislav. I did this to save myself the trouble of dealing with the intrigues and plots for having me slain.

It was, of course, during the nearly six years of my

second reign that I gained the title of the Impaler from my enemies.

All who opposed me soon learned to fear the thought of a lingering death by impalement. There were times when it was necessary to erect virtual forests of agony, soaking the soil with the blood of my enemies.

In truth, though, such executions were not inventions of my own. As in the New World, whose so-called discovery was then still several decades in the future, and where the natives would become feared by the white invaders for their practice of scalping, learned from whites who had first done it to the natives, so too had the Turks taught we Christians the delights of executing human men and women by slowly impaling them upon tall and pointed wooden stakes.

And what of my vowed revenge upon the Turks? After all I had learned of existence from Tzigane, my revenge upon such misguided mortals seemed a trivial matter. But they were the enemy of Christendom, and I was supposedly a Soldier of the Cross. Having my revenge, therefore, became a matter of political policy, a matter of armies and battles.

And so, in my thirtieth year I launched a campaign against the Turks in the name of my beleaguered homeland and all of Christendom.

It was a glorious time of victories as I drove the Turks from the borders of Wallachia and swept them eastward along the Danube toward the Black Sea, forcing those who survived to flee the shores of my country in terror.

Had I been sent the help other Christian nations, my supposed allies, had promised, I could have continued my victories into Turk-land itself. But I was betrayed by broken vows.

Help did not arrive, not even that promised by Prince

Stephen, whom I counted as my best and oldest friend among mortal men.

How I would have loved to have continued that campaign and driven the Turks from Constantinople as well! Not because Christendom or even Wallachia by then mattered all that much to me, but simply because the posturing leaders of Christendom had deemed the recapturing of Constantinople an all but impossible thing to do, and I would have relished showing those fearful fools that it was not impossible at all. For me.

After wintering near the Black Sea, waiting for the help that never came, in the spring of my thirty-first year, I looked out over the water and watched the massed warships of Turk-land making their way toward shore and my greatly outnumbered warriors.

The Turks were being led by my own brother, Radu the Spineless, as I called him, with whom I had been sent to Turk-land so many years before. Radu, the Sultan's Toy.

Their counterattack pushed my army back into Wallachia.

As we retreated northward, I burnt the land and poisoned the wells so that my enemies would be hard pressed to survive. And then I escaped over the mountains. A woman I had made, for political purposes, my wife in name only, was killed at that time by her own fears, taking her own life and, conveniently, leaving me again unencumbered by mortalities.

I considered slipping away from those who escaped with me in order to visit the Scholomance and rest there with Tzigane for a while, but we decided against it. Instead, we made other plans that would allow us more time together in the years to come, time in which I could master yet more occult skills before joining Tzigane in the immortality of Undeath.

Tzigane agreed that the prophecies about my becoming a hero had been more than adequately fulfilled.

I then secretly prepared a letter indicating I had traitorous intentions and made certain it reached the proper hands.

Historians have speculated that the letter was a forgery arranged by Christian leaders whom my exploits had made look less than heroic, the same leaders who had broken their promises to aid me, thereby ensuring my defeat. Leaders who knew that if I became known as a traitor instead of a hero, few could blame them for having been suspicious of me and failing to send the promised aid. Indeed, they might even be thought clever for having suspected a trap and avoided it.

I, Christendom's greatest hero, was therefore, as I secretly desired, soon taken west into Hungary to be imprisoned as a traitor.

Then, locked away in isolation, each night after sunset a swirling cloud of glowing mist entered my cell, seeping either through a barred window or beneath the locked door, mist that spun into a column of two entwined spirals and became a beautiful Gypsy Witch with glowing red eyes. My beloved Tzigane.

We sometimes recited a chant to open the door locks and left my cell to stroll about unseen, cloaked by a spell of invisibility, to do mischief for our amusement. But usually we stayed in the cell and worked to improve and increase my occult knowledge and skills.

Always, however, whether in my cell or invisible in other parts of the castle, or out of doors, we found time and ever more interesting and entertaining ways to make love.

We could have retreated back to our castle in the Carpathians, of course, and allowed the Weavers to make it seem I had been elsewhere. But we both felt it was wise to learn more about the Earth we were destined to rule in Satan's name.

Save for my time in Turk-land as a prisoner, neither of us had ever traveled far from Transylvania, where we were both born. And while Hungary bordered Transylvania on the west, its ties with the rest of Europe made it a fine place to taste the Earth's delights, and learn more about the world beyond our native land.

After a time, then, we arranged for me less harsh conditions and much finer quarters . . . in the palace of the Hungarian king, a wealthy center of the Hungarian Renaissance, where I soon became a fascinating curiosity for the court and their guests. Vlad Dracula, the heroic warrior, the monstrous impaler, told of in story and song, appearing now, in person, at the court of the Hungarian king!

During my stay as a pampered prisoner in the palace, I allowed a portrait of myself to be painted. A copy of it, for I possess the original that is now deemed lost, was later hung in Castle Ambras near Innsbrook in a so-called Gallery of Monsters. An amusing thing.

Shortly after my thirty-fifth birthday, I was freed completely, because Tzigane and I wished it to be so and manipulated matters to arrange it. The prophecies said I would sit the Wallachian throne three times, and it was time to begin working toward that goal, while continuing my studies with Tzigane in secret.

The Hungarian king agreed to free me when I agreed to marry his cousin, the Countess Helen, but before the marriage I also had to agree to convert to the Catholic faith.

To Orthodox Wallachians, such as I had been raised, Catholics were heretics. However, no longer did either version of Christianity have meaning for me, except as a tool of Satan's Enemy.

I had some slight apprehensions, however, about the effect a Catholic ceremony might have on me, with my body and blood enhanced by Tzigane's blood and her Kiss. But, as Tzigane had predicted, her spells of protection kept me safe from experiencing any adverse effects from the symbols and rituals of Satan's Enemy.

Tzigane and I went to live in the Countess Helen's house in Pesth across the Danube from Buda, and Helen, a young and not unattractive woman, proved more than a little interested in sexual matters. For example, she had the irritating desire to call making love to me being impaled by my passion, in honor of my reputation.

Rather than being upset by Helen's amorous intents, Tzigane, to my annoyance, found the warm-fleshed woman's pursuit of me immensely amusing.

Fortunately, by using the occult skills I had by then mastered, and because I no longer cared for the thought of making love to anyone save Tzigane, I was able to make Helen fall asleep and dream of wonderful sexual encounters so vivid that she treated them as memories the following day.

Another problem arose concerning my patterns of sleeping.

In order to be with Tzigane as much as possible at night, I slept more than Helen thought wise during the day. So, more than once I had to remind her that I needed my rest if I was to provide her with prolonged pleasure after dark.

History records that Helen gave me two sons, Mihnea and Mircea, but of course they were not truly *mine*. Mental spellcraft was used to provide a father to the children that Helen was made to think was me . . . not a difficult spell, if the room is kept sufficiently dark.

Having mortal heirs no longer held any appeal for me. Thinking of my future, I did not care to have ties with the world of the living when the time came for me to leave it.

As the years passed and Tzigane remained young while I slowly aged, and my appearance became that of a man old enough to be her father, I lost my last lingering reluctance to join her in Undeath.

My health and strength, because of the Kiss of Undeath and Tzigane's blood, was still quite excellent. But age was preying on me in other ways, and I was growing tired of the pretense of appearing as inferior and mortal as those with whom I spent my days.

In my forty-fifty year, then, I began making plans to do two things, retake the Wallachian throne one third and final time, and shortly thereafter, fake my death and exit the stage of mortal history.

Just before my forty-sixth birthday, aided by the Hungarian King and Prince Stephen, now ruler of Moldavia, I succeeded in driving a Turkish puppet name Laiota from the Wallachian throne and once more took power for myself. But by then the seat of power had moved south of Targoviste to a city I had founded and fortified during my second reign nearly twenty years before. Perhaps you have heard of it? It is even today the capital of that country, the city of Bucharest.

On my way south to Bucharest, however, my army made camp at Targoviste, and that night Tzigane and I slipped away, concealed by a spell of invisibility, for a sentimental visit to the forest hut in which we had first made love.

We found it fallen into ruins, but we spread our cloaks upon the ground and made love there anyway.

Not long after arriving in Bucharest, my occult skills discovered a plot by Wallachian conspirators who opposed my return to power. They planned to lure me into a marsh in the nearby forest of Vlasie to be killed.

The opportunity was just what I needed.

And so, shortly after my forty-sixth birthday, I faked my death in that marsh using a headless corpse of my size and general build, dressed in my clothing.

Then I rode away from the world I had known to await the coming of sunset, and Tzigane, and my own immortality. My Undeath.

Chapter Eleven

43
Return

I reached the agreed upon place of rendezvous deep in the forest well before sunset. The Gypsies were already there, and with them Tzigane, asleep in an ornately carved and gilded coffin inside the heavily curtained and colorfully painted wagon of the leader.

You should be aware that not all Gypsies were then, or are now, as were those waiting for me in that camp. For one thing, most Gypsies are not, neither then nor now, counted among Satan's Own. Indeed, Tzigane's tribe was far from accepted by other tribes. But her people cared little what other Gypsies thought of them, for they proudly counted among their number the family of Satan's future Queen on Earth.

I had met the Gypsies waiting for me in the camp before, of course, during the other times over the years when they had tended to Tzigane's needs while traveling. And with them were three Witches from the Scholomance who had been caring for and protecting her during the daylight hours, as well as shielding the Gypsy caravan with spells of invisibility.

One of the Witches was Tzigane's younger sister, a woman who now, still mortal, looked old enough to be Tzigane's mother. Their real mother had passed into Undeath three years before and was an honored guest at the Scholomance.

Largely because of the honor Tzigane had brought to her tribe, her father had become leader many years ago, and her brother was next in line.

Witches and Gypsies alike greeted me with all the courtesies and respect due their future king.

I was offered food but I declined. I had fasted since the night before, having taken my last meal of crude mortal food with Tzigane at my side. Neither did I accept wine, but drank only water to ease my thirst.

Though the day had been cold and overcast, threatening snow, I did not mourn the lack of sunlight on that last day of my mortal life. Tzigane had long since told me all of the prophecy that was known to her, and part of it said that the final proof of Satan's Own that I was their rightful king would be when I found a way to do what no Vampire had ever down before, to defy the sunlight and walk forth unharmed during the day, an unchallengable demonstration of Satan's power to protect His chosen King on Earth.

The prophecy said nothing, however, about the same being true for Satan's Queen, who missed the Sun dearly even twenty-eight years after seeing it for the last time. But if there were a way for us to one day stand together in the sunlight as of old, I had vowed to find it.

When at last the Sun slipped below the horizon, and twilight descended upon the Gypsy camp, Tzigane stirred in her coffin and arose.

After being with her for over half my life, I was no stranger to her beauty, but each time she awoke, each time I saw her again moving with life, looked into her eyes, heard the sound of her voice, it was almost as if I were seeing her again for the first time, her beauty as stunning and fresh to me as it had been when a young man of only eighteen years was falling deeply in love with a Witch who had already long haunted his dreams.

I loved her so very much. I *owed* her so very much!

In the fifteenth century, forty-six years was a long time for a warlord to have survived, and if not for Tzigane, I would have been weakened by battle wounds and age, nearing death, or perhaps long-since dead. Instead, I now stood ready to embark upon a new existence, strong and immortal. Power and glory awaited me that would soon, I assumed, make all the years of my mortal life seem but the pale dream of a sleeping man who had theretofore only imagined himself to be awake.

You own much to yourself, too, my Vlad, Tzigane said with her thoughts. *There were many times when you could have turned away from your destiny, and me, but you did not.*

But you told me of that destiny, I answered with my thoughts, for I had long since become skilled enough to allow us to carry on secret conversations. *And you gave me a reason to desire it beyond my own ambitions and hunger for power, and a way to defy the fate of death that would otherwise have eventually parted us.*

She kissed me and said, "I am so very proud of you, Vlad."

I laughed. "And I of you! Shall I summon the Strigoi?"

It was not the first time I had summoned one of the winged beasts from beyond Earth, but the effort was taxing and the experience of touching that netherworld always a bit sickening to my as yet still largely mortal flesh. Summoning a Strigoi would, of course, like so many other occult skills, be easier after Undeath.

"I summoned the Strigoi that first took us to our castle," she answered. "I would be honored to also summon the one that takes us there when we return."

And so, she summoned a Strigoi and soon we were high above the twilight-shadowed Earth, flying above the snowcapped Carpathian Mountains toward the Borgo Pass and Castle Dracula, returning at last to our home.

44

Vortex

As we flew northward, it began to snow.

Tzigane or I were both more than capable of using spellcraft to control the weather and stop the snow, but there was no need to expend the effort. Instead, we had the Strigoi fly above the clouds.

Stars glittered above us in a black, moonless sky. Below stretched the cloudtops in all directions for as far as we could see, a dreamlike journey, the only sound that of the Strigoi's wings rhythmically cutting the air.

The beast needed no landmarks by which to find its way. Its otherworldly senses could feel the occult power vortex of Castle Dracula drawing it toward the north.

We were both tense with excitement, anxious to reach our home, and yet not. We were fast approaching the fulfillment of the shared destinies for which we had so long planned and trained. But the challenges and dangers and responsibilities that lay ahead would demand much of our time, leaving fewer opportunities for us to simply be together.

Indeed, there would be little privacy for us when we reached our home. Satan's Own from all over the world had secretly gathered there to witness my ascension to the Throne of the World, during which I was to lead a

Grand Conjuration, as part of which I would invite Satan Himself to appear.

Satan's coming to my call was another part of the prophecy that had yet to be fulfilled, but I was confident of my part in the ritual, and had little choice but to believe that Satan would do His part to give His followers the proof of my kinghood the prophecy required.

On and on we flew above the clouds, the slow wheeling of the stars overhead marking the passage of time, until at last there appeared ahead a circular break in the clouds, and beneath that patch of spell-cleared sky Castle Dracula waited atop its pinnacle of rock.

Many of the castle's windows glowed with light, and by the flickering of a dozen torches we saw that the main courtyard was crowded with Satan's Own. Having sensed our approach, they had gathered outside to greet their future King and Queen.

As the Strigoi lowered us to the courtyard, a cheer of greeting rose to meet us. I saw many I recognized in the crowd, among them Lilitu and others from the Scholomance.

Standing near Lilitu were my father and brother, whom I had last seen at a secret gathering on one of Satan's sacred nights the year before. Although on cordial terms, and although they had never done anything to give flesh to my suspicions, I had never entirely conquered my feelings of mistrust about them. And while I could now read the minds of others, neither Dracul nor Mircea ever dropped their mental shields when I was near, suggesting to me that they did indeed harbor thoughts of which they did not want me to know. Of course I likewise kept mental shields in place when I was near them.

Also with Lilitu was Tzigane's mother, a strikingly beautiful woman made young again by Undeath. She looked so like her honored daughter that one who did not know might well have assumed them twins.

But many who awaited us in the courtyard were strangers, some mortal, protected by spells from the castle's occult emanations. Of course there were also many Undead, and a few visitors from elsewhere that were visible only to my occult vision.

Still mortal, and therefore having aged twenty-eight years since first I had met her, Lilitu yet remained a strong and capable woman who had taken charge of the gathering at the castle. Having discussed with her a few days past who would be attending, I knew that our human visitors from foreign lands included warlord leaders and other members of nobility, but also occult scholars, alchemists, Witches, wizards, poets, blacksmiths, and on and on.

There were people from far to the east, their skin tinged golden yellow, and people with richly dark skin from the distant south. There were also tall, pale-skinned descendants of Vikings from northern lands and fiery-haired sons and daughters of Erin. And from across the great ocean to the west had journeyed red- and brown-skinned guests, their lands as yet unknown to most people, for at that time the first voyage of Columbus, whom history would incorrectly deem to have discovered a New World, was still more than a decade away.

When at last we stood in the courtyard, Lilitu came forward to formally greet us. The assembled guests all paid us the courtesy of bows, save those from the north, who I had heard did not believe anyone should bow to another, not even to a God or a Devil. Those heirs of Vikings did, however, salute me with their weapons. They had respect for proven leaders and warriors such as myself, but unlike their Christianized countrymen, they had little use for kings or queens. After my experiences with the intrigues and betrayals of royal courts, I found their northern arrogance quite admirable.

When Lilitu had finished her speech of greeting, Tzigane and I led the way inside the castle. Torches, candles, and lamps burning scented oil flickered everywhere. Servants invisible to the untrained eye hurried and bustled to and fro.

The aroma of freshly cooked food grew stronger as we neared the great hall of the castle. The long table had been set for a sumptuous feast. Sustenance for mortals and Undead alike had been provided.

Having fasted since the previous night, my stomach rumbled its hunger, but when we sat down and our guests began to eat, I resisted temptation and continued my fast. The many toasts that various visitors proposed I answered only with sips of water from a golden goblet.

When dawn drew near, those who did not have to flee the sunlight were encouraged to continue feasting for as long as they wished, then Tzigane and I led the Undead, including my father and brother, below.

After making certain our Undead guests were comfortable in the areas prepared for them in the upper levels of the crypt, Tzigane and I descended into the castle's lowest reaches and through the maze of passageways to our tomb.

At last we had privacy, and as we lay embracing, Tzigane said, "If you wish to leave me during the day today, Vlad, to go above, I will understand."

I kissed her. "No, Tzigane. I will stay with you. When next I see the Sun, perhaps I will have found a way for you to see it too, at my side."

Then we shared passion and with the rising of the Sun fell asleep in each other's arms.

45
Satan

When the last glow of twilight had faded from the sky and full darkness had fallen outside Castle Dracula, Tzigane and I and the castle's guests assembled in the throne room. Then I began the Grand Conjuration which at midnight would culminate in my call to Satan.

When He appeared, before Him and His assembled followers, I would then plunge a consecrated dagger into my heart, sacrificing myself to Satan, then rising Undead, His chosen king.

As I began the ritual, the tension that had been building in me since sunset vanished. My concentration upon the task I had long trained to do forced all else from my mind.

I moved expertly from one degree of the conjuration to the next, carefully pronouncing each Witch-word of power in exactly the correct way while, like a veteran warrior wielding the weapons of battle, I confidently commanded the forces of the Unseen with a black-bladed conjuring dagger, a silver chalice of chilled blood set with thirteen rubies around its rim, and other powerful spell-tools as required for the Grand Conjuration.

While I worked, I often had cause to glance at the ring Tzigane had given to me so very long ago. I had learned well how to use it in the years since she had placed it on my left hand. Charged by the gathering energies of the ongoing conjuration, it glowed with pulsating occult power, its writhing runes no longer mysteries to me but indispensable aids to help me properly execute the task at hand.

As the hours before midnight wore on, Tzigane assisted me when required, and at appropriate times the throng repeated the words of power I intoned. Had I not possessed the enhanced strength given to me by Tzigane's Kiss of Undeath, I would not have had the endurance needed to continue the physically, mentally, and emotionally tasking conjuration to its end.

Incantations, invocations, summonings, banishings, on and on went the ritual, until finally came the Witching Hour halfway between sunset and sunrise, true midnight, that magical borderland between Darkness and Light when, as at true mid-day, the vibratory veil separating the Seen and Unseen is at its thinnest.

Without hesitation, filled with a deep exultation because the moment had finally arrived, I charged my will with the occult energies the hours-long ritual had brought forth, then channeled those energies into my voice and shouted the Incantation of Calling, inviting Satan to appear.

The room fell silent.

Almost at once a deep rumbling began. It grew rapidly louder until the throne room vibrated with its thunder. Then, in the space about the intricately carved twin thrones, a boiling black cloud appeared, its seething darkness shot through with veins of writhing crimson lightning.

Like the cloud I had seen in my vision in the crypt in Targoviste, and again at the lake on the night Tzigane became Undead, and in my nightmare about Tzigane being punished, the black cloud of Satan's physical manifestation on Earth was oval in shape, oriented vertically.

The ritual had worked as planned! And Satan had answered my call.

"Hail, Lord Satan!" I shouted. The crowd repeated my hail, then all of them went onto their knees except for Tzigane and I and the blond-haired northerners, who lifted their weapons in salute while glaring defiantly upward at the thundering cloud.

I lifted the consecrated iron dagger with which I was to sacrifice myself and held it high, offering it for Satan's approval and blessing.

Thoughts of suicide had never been mine, not even as a terrified child in the Turkish dungeons of Egrigoz. The thought of driving the blade into my heart was repugnant to me. But I *would* do it, because like many other things I had been required to do in the course of my life, it was necessary to obtain a greater goal.

When I had held the blade toward Satan for nine heartbeats, I held the dagger toward the crowd and repeated my hail to Satan, which the crowd again echoed. Then I placed the blade on the throne of Satan's King on Earth and turned to face Tzigane.

We were dressed, she and I, in flowing black robes that covered us from our necks to our ankles. Witches chanting incantations had sewn occult designs in silver and crimson into the fabric of those robes. Beneath them we were both naked.

The most powerful, and therefore dangerous, spellcraft Tzigane had taught me over the years involved the use of the occult energies generated from great passion, either the hatred of an enemy, or the love and lust for a sexual partner. It was not surprising, then, that the prophecy required me to die at the moment sexual lust was fulfilled.

The Grand Conjuration had prepared me for that moment. Dying while infused with ecstasy I would pass from mortal life to the realm of Undeath with sufficient spell-woven energy to communicate directly with Satan and learn the secret of how the Undead might walk forth in sunlight unharmed.

Facing each other, Tzigane and I held each other's gaze. Then we removed our robes and stood naked beneath the rumbling Cloud of Satan and before His assembled host.

The stone floor leading to our thrones had been strewn with the furs of thirteen wolves, sacrificed on Satanic festivals and consecrated for this night of nights.

We stepped toward each other, the furs soft beneath our bare feet. We embraced. Kissed. Went onto our knees still embracing. Then Tzigane lay back upon the furs, looked up at me, and to my amazement gave me a mischievous wink! Surely the desperately serious thing we were about to do could tolerate no frivolity. But a moment later a distracting frivolity of my own intruded upon my concentration as a flicker of embarrassment flashed through me. The thought of making love to Tzigane with so many watching suddenly caused my face to redden.

This is no time for blushing, my Vlad, her thoughts spoke within my mind. *Love me, my only one,* she added, then pulled me down onto her and locked her legs tightly around my hips. *I do not care if the world witnesses our passion! I want them to see, so that I may hear them weep with envy!*

"Tzigane," I whispered and kissed her, plunging my tongue deeply into her mouth, accepting the thrust of hers into mine even as she guided my hardened manhood into her coldness and clenched me tightly with her inner strength.

We made love, then, concentrating in our shared thoughts upon occult formulae and potent symbolic visualizations that would allow us to guide the sexual fire burning within us to a point of focused passion at the moment of our dual climax.

As we continued to slowly allow our desires to build, from time to time we used varied positions as required to release all of the subtly different types of energies that would together create the needed effect.

Finally, as the ritual rapidly approached its culmination, I lay back on the furs and Tzigane sat astride me, riding my erect manhood with focused desire. Then, whispering an incantation together, our voices and minds and bodies in perfect occult alignment, her heart and mine literally beating as one, our breathing in unison, she reached to the throne of the king and handed to me the instrument of my death.

Our eyes locked. Still whispering our incantations, I raised the dagger and prepared to plunge it into my chest. I was careful to angle it properly so that it would avoid my ribs and breast bone and enter my heart. Long ago I had learned to kill others in this fashion, but killing oneself was, needless to say, a far different thing.

Tzigane continued to move atop me while I moved my own body as well, timing my thrusts with hers so that they in turn matched our unified heartbeats and breathing, on and on, building toward our shared goal of passion.

Moments before the climax came, in spite of all my training and determination, doubt suddenly entered my mind, spawned by thoughts of the precious mortal life I was about to destroy, memories stretching back to my childhood, my mother, her horrible death . . .

I ruthlessly crushed the weakening doubts, casting them away from my consciousness, just as at long last we both cried out with release, exploding with shared ecstasy. And at that moment I drove the dagger deep into my flesh.

Agony blended with ecstasy, supreme pleasure with searing pain as the iron blade pierced my heart.

I arched upward for a moment, then collapsed back onto the furs, thinking how little blood there was and then telling myself there would be more if the dagger were removed.

I could sense a curtain of suffocating blackness descending upon me as I gasped with pain and suffering, feeling my life draining away. I would have already been dead save for the extra strength given to my flesh by the Undeath in my veins. Even so, I had not expected prolonged pain. But I did not give voice to my agony. Instead, I stoically waited in silence for death to end my discomfort.

My vision darkened. I could no longer see. But I felt Tzigane's cool fingers stroking my face.

Only a moment more, my Vlad, she said with her thoughts. *I . . . will miss your warmth. Awaken soon, my dearest love.*

She gripped my hands in hers and I tried to squeeze hers in return. But I discovered I could not. And then I died.

46
Heaven

Enclosed fleshless in total darkness, I felt my consciousness falling-rising, between-within reality.

I fought sudden panic, forced myself to recall all I had learned, tried to become an attentive observer that I might learn even more.

The feelings of panic did not go away, but they became controllable.

As my darkness continued, I began to sense time as once I had sensed space, a measurable quantity understandable to me in that disembodied state not as distance and shape but rather as duration and direction.

And time stretched, slowed, stopped, until suddenly I was *There,* hovering above yet below and within yet without a vast sphere of time-frozen darkness that did not move, yet whirled madly upon an axis oriented in all directions yet none, a pit of annihilation around which curved all Space and Time.

I understood it completely, grappled hopelessly with comprehension, balanced on the edge of insanity for an eternity, a moment. Then suddenly, though I had no voice, I inexplicably felt like laughing, because while what I was experiencing was infinitely terrifying, there was nothing *Else* to fear, which seemed infinitely humorous.

A voice in my mind thundered, *Take care you mock Me not, lest I cast you from this Heaven into the false God's Hell!*

Satan's voice!

My conscious mind knew I should have been afraid, but I did not *feel* afraid. Instead, my good humor increased at the thought of Satan calling what I was experiencing Heaven. But I struggled against the dangerous humor that had possessed me and reminded myself that if I angered Satan He might not share with me the secret of how I, though Undead, could walk in sunlight . . . and how Tzigane might do the same.

Tzigane. The thought of her brought purpose and direction to my journey through chaos. I must learn the secret and return to Tzigane!

I disciplined my thoughts and projected the words, *I do not mock you, Lord Satan. Your chosen King on Earth has come into Your presence to learn that which was prophesied, the secret of how the Undead might walk unharmed in sunlight.*

There was a pause that stretched on and on or perhaps lasted but a moment, then, *The secret is only for my King, but in your soul I see treachery. You wish to share the secret with a woman!*

His reaction surprised me, but I quickly replied, *Only with Your chosen Queen, Lord Satan! With Tzigane, surely the most faithful of all Your followers. Without her, I would not be here now to fulfill Your will, Your prophecy. Without her—*

You love this woman more than you love me!

I did not know what to reply. Could this Being truly be jealous? Or was it somehow a test of my loyalties?

Your chosen King awaits Your commands, I finally

answered. *As You must know from my life, I have dem-onstrated dedication and fierceness in battle many times, nearly defeating the Turks when all others thought their defeat impossible. And I will be no less dedicated and fierce as Your Earthly leader. As for love, surely by lov-ing Tzigane, Your most faithful servant, I am thereby also loving You. But in my experience, wars are not won with weapons of love, but with leadership, terror, and death, so that my feelings for her in no way compromise by dedication to Your Earthly battles. If, however, my thinking on this matter is in error, I trust You will in-struct me in Your truth.*

Another pause. *Your response is acceptable to Me. Love the woman as you will and walk in sunlight with her if you wish, but share the secret with no others. Learn now what you seek, then return and lead My forces in conquest of the Earth! Let the Undead spread My blessings of freedom and physical immortality by feasting upon the blood of My Enemy's slaves. And let the still mortal amongst My subjects continue to convert My Ene-my's sheep with My truth!*

Into my mind came a vivid image of a Being of Light, winged, arms outstretched in greeting, a face and body so radiant I could not see any distinguishing features.

The inner image became an outer vision that rushed toward me, engulfed me in its Light, penetrated my mind, my soul, touched my memories, implanted new ones. Implanted new knowledge. Secrets. Then cast me out into darkness once more.

Tzigane! I silently shouted with my thoughts. *The se-cret is ours!*

I felt something stir in the darkness, and I knew with-out knowing how I knew that it was my physical body awakening to Undeath.

Tzigane! I called. And my darkness was gone.

Light flooded my slowly opening eyes. My vision focused and I saw Tzigane looking down at me as she cradled me in her arms, whispering incantations of protection and strength to help me safely return.

We kissed hungrily, lovers reunited.

I have the secret, Tzigane. But now you must decide a very important thing. From where do you wish to watch the next sunrise?

Tears moistened her eyes.

We rose to our feet and faced the assembled throng.

"Hail your Undead King!" Tzigane shouted. "King Dracula!"

And the crowd raised their voices as one.

47
Sunrise

Tzigane chose the highest tower, the one upon which we had stood during our first visit to Castle Dracula twenty-eight years before.

The spellcraft that had cleared the sky for our arrival had been withdrawn after the Strigoi's departure, allowing new snow more than ankle deep to blanket the castle as even deeper snow had covered the surrounding countryside. But the snow had been brushed away atop Tzigane's Tower, as I had decided it would thereafter be called, by servants after she had decided to watch the sunrise from there.

In the day and night since our arrival, the weather had cleared, and of clouds in the sky that morning there were none. Had it not been clear, we who had power over the weather would have made it so for that most special of occasions.

I was still adjusting to the sensations associated with possessing Undead flesh, but I gloried in those sensations.

My strength was now that of ten, and the predatory sharpness of my mind and senses and occult powers had all been raised to a vastly superior level. But I had not foreseen the greater wonder. Now that I was also Undead, Tzigane's flesh was no longer cold to my touch and no longer seemed other than normal.

We stood alone atop the tower, arms around each other, awaiting the sun. Beneath her black cloak she wore her black leather, boots, trousers, tunic, gloves. Similar clothes had been made for me, and I wore them now for the first time, so that we looked like hunters ready to stalk our prey.

It was amusing to me, however, that any hunting *we* might do would be for prey that walked on two legs, not four.

The thought of hunting the false God's human followers with Tzigane, and through the kiss of Undeath freeing them from their religious bondage seemed deeply satisfying and exciting, even sexually arousing.

We should, I decided, try just such a hunt very soon, perhaps even that night, if we could find a way to slip free of our guests, and if Tzigane desired to do so.

I was a bit surprised that hunting humans seemed so appealing. Although I was now more than human, an immortal, I had been mortal and human less than one day before.

But then, had I not been a predator of one sort or another most of my life? I thought about all the times I had hunted humans, in a fashion, as a warlord during the waging of wars, as a ruler discovering and punishing traitorous threats to the throne. So, perhaps only my weapons and motives had changed.

Or had my motive always, then and now, been a desire for power? For what else was the sport, the *art* of hunting if not an exercise of the power of life and death, whether over a member of one's own species or another?

As a small child, I was powerless as I watched my mother die, and I had longed for the power to save her and punish her murderers.

As a hostage at the mercy of the Turks I had longed for the power to take revenge upon my tormentors.

Then, as a young ruler I had longed for the power to keep my first throne but had been offered instead the Throne of the World by a Witch, who also taught me the power of the mind and emotions, the power of knowledge, passion, and love.

And now, as Satan's King on Earth, I *had* power, and I could, if I wished, wield my power to free the souls of mortals enslaved to the false God. Or perhaps I would do so simply for the pleasure of controlling the fate of others, deciding how long they would be permitted to live, or die, and perhaps, on my whim, rise Undead.

I wondered if Tzigane had ever felt a desire to hunt human prey? To my knowledge she had never taken any but the blood of the willing, including my own when she had bestowed upon me the sacred kiss atop the very tower where we now stood.

How would she feel about hunting with me in the night, choosing our victims then invading their homes while they slept, our occult skills ensuring that they remained asleep and helpless as we tasted of their rich, warm blood?

Would Tzigane find the prospect of such a hunt as exciting as I? Was it something all Vampires felt? An instinctual need? Perhaps awakened by their first taste of human blood? Indeed, my thoughts of hunting human prey had begun after my first sweet draught of mortal blood.

Before ascending the tower, Lilitu had presented to me three Witches who had earned the honor of being the first to ease my newborn thirst. Tzigane teasingly called them my *brides*, and then watched while I, feeling as if I were somehow being unfaithful to her, tentatively placed my mouth upon the smooth, warm throat of the first Witch, a woman named Florinda.

Instinct washed away the awkwardness I was experiencing when against my lips I felt Florinda's heartbeat pulsing beneath her flesh. Almost without thinking I pressed my cold teeth through the soft barrier of her skin and plunged into the river of warm life streaming through her veins. And although I did not become sexually aroused, the feelings I experienced were quite similar, feelings of posessing another while yet being possessed oneself, feelings of deep intimacy and sharing, feelings of being made complete.

But I took only a small portion of blood from Florinda before moving to the next of the three Witches, a young woman named Dorottya, and then the third, a Gypsy named Ezmeralda who was honored to be of Tzigane's tribe.

Tzigane suddenly brought my thoughts back to the tower and the forbidden thing we were about to do. She leaned close and whispered, "Vlad, I believe that . . . I am very afraid."

The mortals among our guests were watching us from the courtyards or windows or the other towers, anxious to witness the prophesied miracle. The Undead guests of Castle Dracula were also watching, but from the safety of the crypt, their minds linked to the minds of mortals so that they too could see their king and queen do what had always been deemed impossible.

I pressed Tzigane to me. "You have nothing to fear."

"Yet all of my instincts urge me to flee to safety!"

"Tzigane, the Undeath that now animates my flesh urges me to seek darkness, too. But we must not. We cannot break faith now, not after all the years of study and work leading to this moment."

I paused. I smiled and kissed her. "It should be you

saying such words of encouragement, as always you have before."

She managed a quick smile. "That is true. But to think of remaining here until the warmth of the Sun bathes my flesh as of old . . . it not only terrifies the Undeath in me, but also what remains of the mortal woman I once was, because again seeing the Sun would make me so happy! And if my hopes of doing so could not be realized—"

"They *will* be. If Satan lied to me, it would defeat His own purposes, would it not? You have long trusted Him. You have long trusted me. Trust us both just a little longer."

"You know I will. But, oh! How bright it is in the east!" She shielded her eyes with a pale, trembling hand. "So much light!"

The eastern sky was indeed dangerously bright. The appearance of the Sun over the horizon could be but moments away, and the coming of that burning orb was like silent thunder vibrating my Undead flesh from within, swiftly approaching, rapidly increasing. Unendurable. Impossible to survive. And yet I willed myself to stand my ground and hold Tzigane as she held me.

"Now, Tzigane. It is time."

As I had instructed her to do on our way to the tower, she linked her mind with me as I began the spell of protection Satan had implanted in my memories. And as the spell-shield took form around my Undead flesh, Tzigane likewise began to cast one about herself.

Because of the effort required to maintain the spell, if we chose to venture forth during the daylight hours we would be no stronger than mortals. Our occult powers would also be greatly limited while the Sun was in the sky, because most of our occult resources would be required to keep the unseen shield strong. And we could only transform into one of our other forms at the moment of exact noon, midway between sunrise and sunset when Light and Darkness were balanced, as at true midnight. But there would be times when such limitations were acceptable, such as the moment now at hand.

At the core of the spell was my remembrance of the paradoxical sphere of darkness I had experienced, the nothingness around which everything somehow curved.

From that central visualization then, I mentally pushed the stationary-whirling darkness-light of the sphere below-above within-without outward until it surrounded my body and stood ready to deflect-absorb the invisible occult essence of the Sun's rays before they could harm my Undead flesh.

I knew the spell was working when the threatening inner vibrations I had been feeling heralding the Sun's approach faded away. And because our minds were linked, I knew that the same had happened to Tzigane.

Our fear was gone.

And in glory the Sun, Burning Eye of Day, Destroyer of Night, blazing with terrifying beauty *then did rise!*

Chapter Twelve

48
Miracles

Miracles can be dulled by the weight of repetition and familiarity, for example the miracle of *existence*.

Life is too often taken for granted by mortals, Undeath by Vampires.

There is, however, one miracle *never* deemed commonplace by the Undead, the miracle that makes possible the life on Earth off of whose blood we feed. The miracle that can destroy us, yet indirectly gives us much of our strength and power.

The Sun.

The link between moonlight and Witchcraft is well known. The Moon has been called the Transformer by occultists, because moonlight is a vital and vitalizing ingredient in many spells. And moonlight is especially useful to the Undead. It can even provide a mode of travel.

One night when I was yet mortal, Tzigane had demonstrated how the Undead could ride upon moonbeams when the Moon was full and strong.

I had watched as she first transformed herself into swirling mist, then shaped the Moon's power with her disembodied consciousness, ascended into the sky as if a small cloud, and in that form she had *ridden the moonlight*.

If you dare, some night when the Moon is full go outside and watch for small clouds sailing the moon-silvered skies. Might not some of those clouds be more than they seem? Might not some of them be looking back at you? Indeed!

The Secret of Moonlight, however, is that it is Sun's light reflected by the Moon and by the Moon's essence transformed.

Direct sunlight destroys us, but sunlight transformed by the Moon strengthens us, as does the blood of human mortals, carrying as it does the Sun's energy by Life transformed into yet another useful form.

But now, standing in direct sunlight atop Tzigane's Tower, protected only by spell-shields, Tzigane and I experienced with our Undead senses the Sun's terrifyingly majestic *presence* full force, and as those who are about to die sometimes remember their lives in a few fleeting moments, the beautiful terror of the rising Sun awakened the memories that mattered most in my life . . .

And suddenly I was four years old again, smelling the flower-scent of Katiasa's apron as she held me to her and told me she was my real mother and loved me so very, very much . . . and I was a young man making love to Tzigane for the very first time . . . and again at the lake after her Undeath . . . and in the throne room of Castle Dracula at the moment of my death . . .

I looked then at Tzigane and she was looking at me, tears glistening in the sunlight.

We embraced and held each other tightly as if seeking to become one being, one love, and only when the initial shock of the Sun's effects began to pass did I become aware that the mortals who had been watching were cheering the miracle atop Tzigane's Tower.

Satan's Undead King and Queen were standing in sunlight, unharmed.

It was time to do what Satan wanted done next.

Satan had implanted within my mind more than the spell to defy sunlight. I also possessed His plans for His conquest of the Earth.

From atop Tzigane's Tower, then, I told the assembled throng what Satan wanted them to do in His war to free the souls of humankind from the false God's seductive chains. Together, with Satan's power on our side, we would win the Earth so that He, and they, would in time inherit the world upon which I was King and Tzigane Queen.

In the crypt below, the Undead also heard and received their assignments through mind-links with mortals above.

The Sun slowly rose higher in the sky while I talked. Then, when finally I finished telling Satan's Own what He required of them, they raised another cheer. But when I turned and looked for Tzigane, I found her standing no more, but lying upon her black cloak, bathed in sunlight, her clothing strewn by her in a pile.

No one could see her on the stone floor behind the battlements on that tallest of towers, but in her case I doubted privacy had been a consideration.

She stretched luxuriously in the warmth of the sun's rays, sighed with infinite contentment, and beckoned me down beside her. She was so very beautiful there, her pale skin excitingly, dangerously bared to the destroying sun, protected only by the spell-shield of Satan.

"Make love to me, Vlad, in the sunlight as of old."

And I gladly obeyed the command of Satan's Queen.

49
Hunt

By midmorning, the rigors of maintaining the spell that protected us from the Sun had begun to tire us both. With practice, we expected to be able to sustain the spell-shield all day if desired. But there was no need to unduly tire ourselves that first day.

That first *day*.

How wonderful it had been for Tzigane! After nearly three decades, she had again seen the Sun.

We retired to our tomb and there ended the sun-shield spell.

Immediately I felt the weight of Day that compels the Undead to sleep.

Slipping into the Daysleep of the Undead felt little different to me than ordinary sleep.

Vivid dreams came to me then and were pleasant enough at first, but toward sunset they darkened, and I dreamed again of my mother being burned alive at the stake. Then the sound of her screams changed and it was Tzigane screaming, bound to a monstrous Cross while a glowing white, laughing giant lashed her again and again with a thick black whip, slowly stripping away her skin.

I fought to save her, but a throng of smiling people

held me back, among them my father and brother, laughing loudly as I struggled in vain to reach the woman I loved.

When we awoke at sunset I told Tzigane of the dream. It reminded me of the dream I had had years before in which she had been punished for my failure. And of course it also reminded me of the vision of punishment I had experienced in the crypt beneath the palace at Targoviste.

She reminded me then how intent I had been that I not fail to perfectly perform the ceremony of the night before, and then again at the dawn. Now that all had gone well, perhaps it was only to be expected that as my unsubstantiated worries of failing departed, bad dreams had been spawned in their wake. She predicted that when next I slept my dreams would be more pleasant.

To be certain the dream was not necessarily a foreshadowing of danger, but, we used our occult skills to search the immediate future. However we found nothing about which to worry.

Relieved and reassured, it seemed a good time to discuss my thoughts concerning hunting. To my surprise and delight, she told me she had felt similar urges over the years. But her sense of duty had prevented her from giving in to those feelings. Hunting had been a luxury she felt she could not afford while watching over me and teaching me occult secrets in preparation for my kingship.

As with me, she traced her desire to hunt human prey to her first taste of human blood after becoming Undead. The first taste had awakened the survival instincts of a predator, or perhaps only strengthened ones that were already there.

So it was that we decided we would indeed hunt together that night.

After midnight we slipped away from the ongoing festivities and ascended Tzigane's Tower alone.

The night was cold and clear. Stars burned brightly. No Moon lightened the sky. The vast forests around the castle were silent.

It was not necessary to remove our clothing before changing to other forms. The transformative force that allowed us to change our shapes altered matter at the most basic of levels, where the only difference between one physical form and another was the degree and direction of vibratory essences. Our powers could therefore, within a limited range, transform the basic essences of any cloth or leather covering our flesh as easily as it could the flesh itself.

Controlling a transformation was a simple matter for me, because I had long since mastered the art of occult visualization that triggered the change in form.

"Shall I guide you through the process this first time, Vlad?"

"I think you need not."

I closed my eyes and concentrated my mind and will. I visualized the proper occult forms and formulae. I manifested the needed occult force. And I began to change.

The experience was not at all what I had expected. I had assumed there would be at least a moment of disorientation while between forms, but as the matter that composed my flesh and blood and bones began to break down into the essences out of which all things were made, I was left only with my consciousness, my soul, and suddenly never had I felt *more* myself. Never had I felt more powerful.

And the things I sensed, experienced, the potentialities and probabilities and forces I interpenetrated, the breathtaking wonders of the infinitely small in that realm of invisible essences . . . unnameable mysteries, unutterable secrets, unimaginable colors, sounds, delights.

The temptation was strong to stay between forms and never return to the heavy confines of limiting flesh, but I fought the desire and focused my will in order to shape my new form.

To Tzigane, watching, I had become a column of swirling mist that then began to split into twin spirals entwined and whirling about a common axis that soon condensed into the form of a large bat that flew up and over the side of the tower, swooping with ease through the night air, eyes glowing with red fire.

The act of flying seemed completely natural to me. It was as if I had *always* flown the night on the wings of a bat! Because, as I later learned, a form, once adopted, brings with it all the instincts and skills inherent in that form.

From aloft I watched Tzigane transform herself as well, and within moments two bats with burning eyes flew together through the night.

We did not need to rely on the limited communication skills of bats, however. Our minds were still our own, and with them we could communicate as before.

This is glorious! Tzigane said with her thoughts. *But where shall we go on our hunt?*

Have you not caught the scent of our prey? To the west? I had detected the scent of blood by instinct without so much as a conscious thought.

Tzigane hesitated, then responded, *Yes! To the west.*

We flew westward over the nighted forests. From time to time wolves on the hunt would sense our presence and pause to howl greetings to the winged predators far above.

Soon, we found a small hut in a snow-covered clearing near a deeply rutted forest trail.

Smoke curled lazily from the hut's chimney. Outside, all was dark and silent, but the scent of blood from within was strong, four distinct scents, now that we were near, two of them sweeter than the others, the sweet smell of children's blood.

As silent as snow falling upon snow, we glided down.

50
Children

We touched the minds of the humans within the hut and confirmed that a family slept within. The father was a woodcutter, the woman a midwife.

We transformed from bats to mist outside the door.

Because I wanted to test my personal reactions to some of the ancient Rules of Undeath, I first attempted to violate the Rule of Invitation by slipping in mist-form through a slight crack where the door had become slightly warped, but enter I could not!

So, it was true that only after being invited into a dwelling could a Vampire cross the threshold. It angered me. *Why must this be so?* I asked Tzigane.

It has always been this way, according to ancient lore, as you well know.

But why, Tzigane? Why?

Perhaps we who can walk in sunlight will find out, in time, but not tonight. I hunger. May I obtain the invitation?

The honor is yours.

While our physical forms were not permitted to enter without invitation, the same was not true of the force of our minds. Occult barriers could have prevented it, but those who slept within had no knowledge of the occult.

The religion of the false God of Light intentionally kept them ignorant of such things by claiming occult knowledge was Evil while secretly reserving those secrets for their priests.

While I used my mental powers to ensure that the father and children would remain asleep, Tzigane entered the mind of the mother and caused her to think she heard her children calling from outside in the snow.

A few moments passed, then the mother opened the door. Under Tzigane's control, she saw her children instead of two columns of swirling mist.

"What do you there, outside in the cold?" We sensed terror. She beckoned us within. "Hurry, lest we wake father and anger him again."

She was terrified not of us but of her husband. We now noticed bruises on her face, and dipping into her mind we found memories of many beatings, and not just of herself. Her children, too, had been beaten, and often, by her husband.

We drifted over the threshold. The woman closed the door and barred it. Then Tzigane caused her to go back to sleep.

We transformed to our human forms. We looked at the sleeping humans, illuminated by the crackling flames in the fireplace. *This is so exciting, Vlad!*

Yes.

And what is even more wonderful, when we have tasted of their life streams, they will, after death, become Undead, free of the false God's bondage. We must hunt often, Vlad. Often!

It was a delight to see her so happy. *The son is the youngest, barely more than an infant. If you wish it, he is yours.*

She eagerly knelt beside the sleeping boy. She stroked

his hair. *He is so beautiful, Vlad. Would that he were ours.*

We had talked in the past about children. We would both have enjoyed having children of our own. But our destinies decreed otherwise, for though Undeath bestowed many miraculous powers, it took away perhaps the most miraculous power of all, the ability of men to fertilize and women to bear new life.

We must always remember to be gentle with the children we hunt, Vlad. She pressed her lips lightly to the small throat. *No more than a pinprick with our teeth . . .*

She moaned with pleasure as the first taste of the boy's sweet blood flooded her mouth.

I knelt beside the small bed wherein the daughter slept and placed my lips against her throat. The scent of her blood was a pleasure nearly intoxicating in its intensity. My teeth broke gently through the sleeping child's flesh.

The pleasure of her blood coursed through me, filling me with the warmth of her young life. But when I had tasted but a small portion of her rich elixir, I drew back.

Tzigane had already finished with the boy, who under our continuing mental influence slept on, as did the rest of his family. Tzigane moved to stand over the father. *He even beats his young son, Vlad! Would that I could rip his throat and watch him die.*

As he no doubt deserves. I remembered my father beating me. *But what then would become of this woman and her children?*

I wish they could live at the castle with us. We would have to make some alterations in their minds, to their memories, and give them knowledge so that they did not fear us, and protection from the castle's occult emanations.

Tzigane, I don't—

But perhaps we should take only the children? Or just

273

the boy? To protect him. I cannot allow his monstrous father to harm him again!

He is the boy's father, Tzigane, whether a good one or bad. But, do you suppose a deep nightmare might make him think twice before again harming his family? Could you not enter his mind and make him dream of what you will return and do to him if he ever again strikes them? You could make him believe it down deep where reason cannot reach, could you not?

She hesitated. *You are correct, of course.* She looked wistfully back at the small boy.

Perhaps we will find a child to steal some other night, Tzigane, and some good reason for doing it.

But not tonight. I . . . agree. I will begin now to pull this evil monster's claws.

So, while I drank my fill from the mother's veins, Tzigane took the father's blood into her body and placed her thoughts into his mind, making him moan in horror and struggle unsuccessfully to awaken as she created nightmares intended to ever after haunt his soul.

51
Abducted

I took enough blood from the mother to strengthen and satisfy me but not enough to unduly weaken her. Then, while Tzigane was finishing with the father, I searched the hut for items to test my reaction to other Rules of Undeath.

Garlic repelled Vampires, said one rule. I found garlic, and though its smell disgusted me and caused a burning sensation inside my nostrils, I was not repelled beyond my strength to resist. Perhaps my reaction to it now was largely due to the greater sensitivity of my Undead senses, and the fact that I had never cared for garlic while a mortal.

Symbols of the false God's religion repelled Vampires, said another rule. A simple wooden cross, crudely carved, hung on one wall. Seeing it had no effect on me at all. I reached out and cautiously touched it without experiencing anything unusual. Perhaps the effect such symbols had on the Undead was related to the faith of the one who wielded it. Or perhaps the effect it had on the Undead mirrored the effect it had had over them while they were mortal. If so, my lack of reverence for the cross since the day a priest wearing one helped murder my mother probably went far to explain my immunity to its power now.

Tzigane came to stand by me as I continued to stare thoughtfully at the cross. She asked, "Are you considering repenting, Vlad?"

I laughed loudly. The mother and children moved in their sleep at the sound, but they were still under our control and could not awaken. "You pulled the husband's claws, did you?"

She grinned unpleasantly and glanced back at the man, whom she had left weakened from loss of blood, some of which still stained her lips. "Oh, yes. I did indeed."

"Good." I motioned to the cross. "It affects me not at all, not even when I touch it." I touched it again to demonstrate.

"But the sight of it, Vlad, it disgusts me so. The hypocrisy! Torture and tyranny pretending to be love!"

"Exactly what one would expect of a *false* God of Light."

"Yes, but at least here are four who will escape His chains after death. And so very many more will be freed all over the world when our guests depart for their homes. That was a most inspiring speech you gave them today."

"Merely what Satan wanted me to say."

"But you said it so well."

I took her in my arms. "I am surprised that you heard. You were very busy shedding your clothes behind my back, as I recall."

She laughed wickedly. "A pleasant surprise when you turned, was it not?"

I kissed her.

"Make love to me here, Vlad, with our prey sleeping nearby!"

"Is your appetite for passion endless?"

"No more than yours."

After we shared our passion in the hut, we left and transformed back to bats for our return journey to Castle Dracula.

As we flew eastward above the treetops toward our home, the horizon ahead slowly began to brighten with the coming of the Sun. But there was more than sufficient time in which to reach the castle before dawn. And even should we be caught outside when the Destroying Eye of Fire broke the horizon, we could always summon our spell-shields to keep us safe from harm.

And then, as I flew silently through the night with Tzigane at my side, glorying in my Undead strength and powers, and the satisfaction of a most pleasurable hunt, without warning danger suddenly fell upon us.

One moment the way ahead was clear. The next moment two boiling clouds towered rumbling with terrifying thunder before us. One was black and shot through with crackling crimson lightning, the other white and riddled with crawling black veins of hissing energy.

I had not even time to veer away before a bolt of crimson lightning shot out from the black cloud and engulfed my bat form in a sphere of pulsing energy.

From the white cloud a bolt of hissing blackness whipped around Tzigane, binding her with ebony strands, pinning her wings to her body. Then suddenly she was back in human form and writhing in agony.

Vlad! her thoughts screamed to me.

Imprisoned in the crimson sphere, I too was suddenly thrust back into my human form as through my mental link with Tzigane I felt agony course through her, the black bands eating like acid into her flesh. Then her clothing, her hair, her skin, erupted in flames and the

277

white cloud began to vanish from the realm of Earth, taking her with it.

Her screams filled my consciousness, her agony tore at my soul. But then, as if a door had been shut, her cries and pain were suddenly gone, along with all signs of the seething white cloud.

Tzigane! I shouted with my mind, but I could no longer reach her. She had been abducted from the Earth!

I struggled wildly to free myself from the sphere of crimson energy.

Struggle against me not! Satan's rumbling thoughts exploded in my mind. *Much glory awaits you. You have pleased me well.*

I struggled harder to break free. *Tzigane! Bring her back!*

Think of her not. She is beyond help now, an amusement for my Enemy, in return for certain . . . concessions.

You betrayed her? The most faithful of Your followers? Betrayed her to Your Enemy? The vision in the crypt at Targoviste came crashing back into my mind, as did the dream I had twice experienced of her being punished, endlessly made to scream by torture without end.

Panic and terror such as I had never known possessed me then. *She is your Queen!* I cried with my thoughts. *Bring her back! You must bring her back!*

I have no further need of her, and you risk much for a mere female. But I will take pity. I will quiet your mind, alter your memories, make you forget.

No! Bring Tzigane back, or I vow to be Your enemy instead of Your King!

The Cloud of Satan rumbled with laughter. *Tzigane? A woman who never existed. A woman no one shall henceforth remember. I will now make it so.*

No!

Crimson tendrils penetrated my mind, broke easily through my hastily erected mental shields, began to bury my memories of Tzigane, of our love, our plans, our dreams.

Curse you! Stop! You must . . . stop . . .

But then I could not remember why. And I slept. In darkness. Without dreams.

Chapter Thirteen

52
Alone

I awoke alone in my tomb.

I thought for a moment someone was with me, beside me, but there was no one.

Had there been someone? Long ago? A woman? A trusted . . . friend?

No. Only a dream. A fantasy. Nothing more.

Friendship with a woman! A fantasy indeed. With my mental powers and Undead strength I could *make* a woman want me, or fear me, as I pleased. I could give them great pleasure or, if it amused me, great pain. And I could raise them to immortality or kill them on a whim. I most definitely did *not* need their friendship to obtain what I desired!

To obey, to serve, to entertain, these were the tasks I would allow to a woman. To be hunted, taken in lust, and rewarded with passion if obedient, but punished if they disobeyed, these were what women could expect of me, their Master!

Their King!

And men? If they followed me, they would be rewarded. If they tried to stand against me, I would send to Satan their souls.

Alone I was, but content. Alone I was, but complete.

I smiled and rose from my tomb.

I saw my name carved on the stone side of the tomb.

Suddenly it seemed there once had been another name carved there. But . . . no. That was also part of the dream. As was fitting, there had *never* been any name but mine on the tomb. I walked to the other side and looked down at the single, lordly word that was also carved there.

Dracula.

An image flashed through my mind, lying in the tomb with a woman, possessing her with passion . . .

The idea of bringing an unwilling mortal there suddenly excited me. Imagining the terror she would experience, I felt passion rise within me.

I laughed aloud. The sound echoed hollowly through the darkness.

My night vision showed me the way through the dark as I navigated the maze of passageways into the upper reaches of the crypt. Many of the Undead among my guests who were sleeping there were already awake, while others were only now awakening. I noticed that my father and brother had already risen and were gone.

Those who saw me bowed to their king, but I ignored them and made my way upstairs.

Three Witches waited for me in my private chambers to share with me their blood. My three *brides,* I suddenly remembered someone saying, and I smiled as if at a private joke, but I could not remember the author of the jest. Perhaps I had said it myself.

Yes. They *were* my brides, and after I had tasted of their blood they would be, if I chose, my wives, or if I preferred, my *slaves,* to do with as I pleased.

Their blood warmed me. Strengthened me. Aroused my lust.

I ordered them to remove their clothing that I might

see who was the most pleasing. They hesitated, then obeyed. For that hesitation, I decided, they should be punished. Perhaps later. A diversion for my guests. An example to others who might see fit to question my commands.

When they were naked, I chose the most beautiful and sent the other two away. The victor in my contest of beauty was a Gypsy. She reminded me, strangely, of sunshine.

I sated my lust with her. But when I was done, the sight of her suddenly disturbed me, reminded me of some great hatred I could not name. I commanded her from my sight.

Shortly thereafter, a servant announced that my father and brother wished to see me. I had no desire to see them, but I bade them enter.

They were laughing as they came into my presence but fell silent upon seeing me. They gave slight bows, then Mircea said, "I trust you . . . slept well, your majesty?"

I said nothing. As always, their mental shields repelled my attempts to read their thoughts. I was, of course, also shielding my thoughts from them.

"Is not your tomb rather lonely, at times, majesty?" asked Dracul.

I still said nothing.

"Surely," Dracul continued, "companionship is something even a king occasionally desires, and there are those of us among your court who are concerned for your happiness."

I thought of the Gypsy I had just taken. I smiled unpleasantly. "Your concern is misplaced."

"As you wish, majesty," Dracul said, giving another slight bow. "But should you wish it, we will gladly apply ourselves to the task of securing proper companions for you. Perhaps companions from beyond the castle walls, *unwilling* companions . . .''

''I hunt and take what I need. You will now leave. This audience is at an end.''

Mircea said, ''We were thinking only of your happiness.''

''You will now leave!''

Giving new bows, they obeyed, but just before the door closed I heard their laughter resume.

I sat alone in my private chamber, seeking control over my anger, wishing all of my guests were gone so that I could have solitude. Then, if I desired, I could bring different *guests* to the castle, beautiful and unwilling ones, with which to amuse myself.

I thought again of having passion with a terrified woman in my tomb, and into my mind came a memory of a pleasant interlude that had occurred during my second reign in Targoviste.

A young woman from a good family was brought before me, accused by her husband of being unfaithful.

A woman with spirit, she counteraccused him of the same.

I personally supervised her public flogging. The crowd cheered each stroke that marred her naked flesh. Then I impaled her atop a tall wooden stake outside the palace walls so that all who wished to witness her agony and shame might do so.

Her husband I also had stripped, flogged, and impaled upon a stake of equal size facing her, nearly touching, as if they were still lovers about to kiss.

If both were guilty, for one to have had a shorter stake than the other would have been unjust. If either, or both, were innocent, then either or both had wasted my time with lies.

It took them an admirably long time to die, but the

woman outlived the man by nearly half a day. She was not as weighty, you see, allowing the stake to penetrate her body at a much more leisurely, and satisfying, pace.

Smiling at the memory, I decided to dismiss my guests that night, then I walked to the throne room alone, and only for one brief moment did I feel that someone should be walking with me . . . not a pace behind as was fitting, but at my side . . . a woman . . . at my side . . . *as an equal!*

I wondered why I had imagined such a ridiculous thing, and I laughed, but the sound was not a pleasant one, and those who heard bowed low as I strode past.

53
Brides

At my command, Castle Dracula's guests began departing for their homelands the next night, to do there as Satan wished.

Further, I commanded them to report their progress to me each full Moon when the forces that enabled occult communication were the strongest. I, in turn, from Castle Dracula would be judging them. All knew I would have servants from beyond Earth, beings even occult's highest members could not detect, watch in secret and report to me what they found.

Finally, I told Satan's Own to expect to receive new commands from time to time as I, or Satan, deemed necessary.

My father and brother and the others from the Scholomance I sent away, too. I wanted no one near save the servants who had tended the castle since long before I arrived.

But solitude did not bring peace. Beneath the surface of my consciousness seethed a great anger, I knew not why.

The first night I was alone, I felt a need to climb the tallest tower and look out over the nighted land, but something about the tower made my anger flare anew.

And when I thought of using my spell-shield to watch the sunrise, I became possessed by an unreasoning rage, during which I transformed into my bat-form and hastily made my way to a woodcutter's cottage that I hazily remembered visiting sometime before.

And there I vented my rage, slaking well my thirst first on the sweet blood of the woodcutter's two children, then on his blood and the blood of his wife.

But afterward, I found myself fighting a shaming remorse, and in anger over my feelings of regret, I burned the remains of the four within their home so that none would rise Undead.

Night after night, in solitary thought I strove to find the source of my underlying distress, but nothing helpful did I find. And during my Daysleep I had no dreams from which I might discern a reason for my dissatisfaction.

But what more could I want than what I had? I was Satan's King on Earth! Occult powers that to mortals seemed miraculous were mine, as was the Throne of the World!

Why, then, in my throne room was I vaguely troubled that only one throne sat in the empty hall? Surely one throne was sufficient even for the Earth's supreme king!

My nightly hunts brought but slight relief from my brooding anger. Other than the distances I had to travel to obtain the blood I required, there was little challenge in preying upon sleeping mortals, including, I discovered, servants of the false God.

To amuse myself, I then had seven winged servants bring to my castle seven entertainingly unwilling virgin Brides of Christ.

After tasting their blood, but otherwise touching them not, I had the seven terrified women taken down into the dark and damp of the dungeon. There, chained to walls tapestried by the webs of black spiders and hungrily watched by the bright eyes of rats, I left my brides until the following sunset.

After again sampling their crimson warmth, the three whose appearances I found the most pleasing I left unharmed to watch the fate of the other four.

I wished to discover if those three possessed the wisdom to pay homage to me without the influence of my occult powers, and they did not disappoint me. After the other four had screamed their last, the three witnesses had indeed found wisdom.

Released from their chains, they went onto their knees and with bowed heads renounced the false God's Son, tearfully begging me to make of them my wives.

I did not answer at once, but left them chained there until the next sunset, at which time I mercifully granted their wish.

I gave my wives suitable names. One I named Gold for her golden hair. The tall one with dark hair and brown eyes I called Topaz. The thin one, whose hair was also dark but her eyes green, I chose to call Emerald.

With my help, all three discovered a taste for passion, and I saw fit to bless them with immortality when loss of blood finally ended their mortal lives.

The admirable servitude of my wives eased, but did not rid me of my deep anger and melancholy. The simplest of things could often throw me into a rage, at which time the three quickly learned not to come near unless I ordered them to do so.

A routine soon developed. Each night I would hunt. The idea of allowing one of my wives to accompany me on a hunt occured to me once, but I grew angry at the thought and immediately rejected the notion.

Now and then I brought my wives a gift in the form

of an infant or small child. Usually, however, the three fed on the blood of guests that had either been lured there by trickery or brought there unwillingly by my unseen servants.

Each night after I and my wives had, in our own fashions, strengthened ourselves with life's crimson stream, I would occupy myself until dawn with the teaching of occult skills to my companions.

Undeath gave them the instincts to use their Undead powers, of course, but there was so much more that I could teach them, just as Satan had once taught me in the long years leading to my Undeath.

Yes, Satan had taught me His secrets, but it sometimes strangely seemed to me, as I was instructing my wives in their lessons, as if I had been taught those secrets by someone else. By a woman. Whose voice I could not remember but that I longed to hear again. Whose eyes I could not remember but into which I longed to gaze once more. And whose laughter always seemed, in moments of unguarded fantasy, to change into endless screams.

54
Lightning

The year slowly turned, until once again winter covered the Carpathians with snow.

Reports from Satan's Own around the world indicated that His plans were going forward as desired. Only twice in the year had my unseen watchers reported violations of my commands, and those violations I quickly punished.

Once, during the summer, I accepted guests, a group from the Scholomance that included my father and brother. I allowed them to stay a fortnight, but could abide them no longer and sent them on their way so that I could again be alone with my wives.

Topaz worked the hardest on her studies. She had a keen intelligence I found disturbing, because it reminded me of someone I could not name. And now and then I found myself regretting the name I had chosen for her, because it occasionally reminded me of something, or someone, I wanted to remember but, to my continued frustration and anger, could not.

Gold also did well at her studies, though often with less work. She had excellent occult instincts and often surpassed Topaz's successes with seemingly little effort.

But Emerald's accomplishments, no matter how hard

she worked, always lagged behind the others', except for one lesson, which happened to be one of the most important.

Emerald swiftly became more than competent at the arousing and fulfilling of passion, and when we studied the use of focused lust to power spellcraft, she easily mastered what took the others many lessons to perfect . . . though I never found the repeating of those lessons for the others too great a chore.

But then came the night that ended the routine existence we four had come to know.

It happened on the night after the first anniversary of my becoming Undead.

After taking nourishment, we retired to the castle's library as usual for that night's lesson.

The library was a place I cared for but little. Like the tallest tower, it had the power to arouse the nameless anger that still seethed below the surface of my consciousness. But the library was the logical place in which to conduct lessons.

Had not the library been where Satan had come each night to teach me His secrets? So, surely it was only fitting that my wives also be taught there amongst the books and scrolls and other arcane tools of instruction.

I began that night's lesson as I began each, by stating its purpose. Then, as was often helpful, I gave a demonstration.

The lesson concerned the controlling of weather, and the thunderstorm I conjured was a spectacular sight from the eastern-looking window of the library, the flashes of lightning doubly bright because the snow-covered forests reflected the light back from below.

Then, as we were all watching with avid attention, from seemingly *within* a flash of lightning, I suddenly saw something other than the storm.

As if the lightning had broken down a wall that concealed another world, before the accompanying crash of thunder reached my ears, I saw a prolonged vision of horror.

At first I saw only a woman's eyes, half-closed with pain or ecstasy, I could not initially tell. Then I saw the whole of her face.

Lines of agony marred her beauty, and bruises, and blood.

Her hair, black as a raven's wing, was filthy and matted.

Her body, naked, was chained to an iron table from which protruded short spikes that dug into her bare back and buttocks and thighs as she lay painfully stretched, her joints racked nearly to dislocation.

Her skin was covered by wounds, her nakedness streaked with blood, glistening with sweat. Blood also oozed from beneath the iron manacles that clamped her slender wrists and ankles.

Then into the scene came a man, naked save for a filthy loincloth and a black mask that covered his head.

He stood beside her iron bed of pain and held up for her inspection an ugly device covered with jagged blades.

Her mouth distended in a scream I could not hear as the torturer began to use the ripper to destroy what remained of her beauty until soon, from face to knees she had become a raw and mutilated thing that spasmed helplessly upon the spikes.

But the torturer was not done. He had left her eyes intact, and she helplessly watched as he slowly pulled a bed of hot coals beneath the iron bed.

The spikes upon which she lay began to heat red hot.

And as she spasmed with new vigor, inspired by new

pain, he placed hot coals upon her bloodied torso, then one on each eye, and finally a small one in her mouth.

But her pain was still not enough for him, and a moment later he began to lash her raw flesh with an iron-barbed whip . . . until finally it mercifully ended . . . when she moved no more. Breathed no more.

Death had released her at last from her agony.

And yet not. Because a moment later the full horror of the scene was revealed to me . . . as she began to heal!

Within moments she was again whole, her beauty unmarred.

And she awoke.

And the torture began again . . . but I saw no more, for the flash of lightning that had brought the vision then faded away.

Thunder crashed about the castle.

A moment later came another streak of lightning, but it showed me only the storm.

The emotions roused by what I had seen, however, still remained, emotions that told me one desperate and impossible thing.

I had to save the woman. I had to find her and stop her pain. Because I suddenly felt certain beyond all reasoning that what I had seen *was real* and had been happening, on and on . . . for how long? *For how unmercifully long?*

I had to stop it. *I had to stop it now!*

Why, though, I asked myself, was I concerned? Why did I care what happened to a woman whose name I did not even know?

Because, I decided, even if I could remember nothing about her, she was obviously special to me. The severity of the torture in and of itself was certainly not what had caused me to feel the way I was feeling. I had seen much worse done to women and men, often at my command. But to see it happening to *her* . . . the thought was intolerable! It must not happen to her! *Not to her!*

But it *was* happening to her, and how could I stop it when I knew not who or where she was? In spite of all my occult powers and knowledge, I was helpless with ignorance, consumed by frustration, my anger fueled by desperation, the rage that had gone unnamed for a year burning deeper and deeper into my consciousness . . .

For a year! Yes . . . a year . . .

Had something happened a year ago that I could not remember? Was tonight an anniversary of some forgotten horror? But why forgotten?

The questions . . . *questions!* Without answers.

My rage was now amplified by the fresh memories of the vision I had seen, and my anger burned deeper than ever it had before, as if lightning were striking not into the Earth, but into my soul, deeper and deeper . . . until suddenly I felt within my mind a slight *movement,* as if a thick black curtain hanging in darkness had been disturbed, a barrier that had once been solid but was now soft, weakened by the unrelenting heat of the hidden anger that had been burning in me without pause for a year.

And then I felt the thickness of the black curtain move again, and behind it I sensed a haunting presence . . . a woman . . . and suddenly I saw a glimpse of her face . . . the tortured woman's face . . . but so much younger, hardly more than a child, smiling and happy . . . a Gypsy girl . . . *whose name I could almost recall* . . .

Using my occult skills, I concentrated my will and focused my rage against the softening barrier deep within my consciousness. And the curtain of darkness flared with light, with fire.

But even as the curtain was consumed by the flames of my anger, I saw the Gypsy being pulled by streamers of darkness behind yet another barrier even deeper within my consciousness.

No! I cried out with my thoughts. I tried to go forward, but was held back by invisible chains.

Within my mind I screamed in anger and frustration. I had been so close, only to lose her . . . *again.* Until without warning out of despair came wonder. *Hope.* For the first barrier had now burned completely away, and with its passing came an inner flash of light that suddenly revealed to me her name.

Tzigane.

Her name is Tzigane! My thoughts shouted at the barrier behind which the Gypsy girl had been pulled.

Her name is Tzigane! I repeated, and I saw the barrier tremble, soften, allowing another piece of the memory to flash into my mind.

Her name is Tzigane! And she is a Witch!

The barrier shook and another flash of memory returned, striking my consciousness with the force of a raging storm, dissolving the invisible chains that had held me back.

Her name is Tzigane! She is a Witch! And she is my wife!

The barrier became tattered and decayed, and through its disintegrating fabric I saw her again, older now, a beautiful woman, smiling at me, dressed in black leather as if ready for a hunt . . . *a hunt* . . . with Tzigane . . . returning to the castle . . . dawn drawing near . . . one year ago that night . . . but she never reached the castle . . . she—

Searing flashes crashed through my mind as the memories Satan had kept from me returned, staggering me with the pain of suddenly remembering . . . all of it . . . *all* . . .

And then it was over. The pleasant lie that I had lived for a year.

And then it began. The horror of the truth. But also the freedom. *And the rage.*

In the library, Topaz, Gold, and Emerald were still watching the storm, unaware of all that had happened within my mind. Indeed, only a few brief moments had passed in the outer world while I was waging my inner war for the truth.

I told the three women to stay there and watch the storm. Then I left. I dared not tell them more. The servants would take care of them. But the servants were Satan's Own and were also certain to question my brides, to probe their thoughts, as others who served Satan's lies would also no doubt come to the castle and do.

Because Satan would soon know, perhaps already did, that I had remembered that which He had forbidden. And He would try to stop me from doing what I knew without question I had to do.

I did not take time to climb to the tallest tower, *Tzigane's Tower,* as I now remembered I had named it when we had thought the future was ours. Instead, I hurried from the library and down the staircase then swiftly made my way out of the castle into the main courtyard.

The storm raged around me, whipping my black cloak about me. But moments later I soared upward into the crashing storm on the wings of a bat and away from my home, already feeling myself no longer the hunter, but the hunted, as I flew from Satan's Castle, away from His betrayals, away from His lies! But toward, I vowed, somehow, somewhere, the friend, the ally, *the woman* that I loved.

Chapter Fourteen

55
Prey

As I flew through the storm, fighting my way through gusting winds and pouring rain, I was careful to keep my thoughts shielded and a spell of invisibility about me. None but Satan could penetrate my mental shield, but the spell of invisibility would not thwart those of His followers who possessed occult vision. However, not all of Satan's Own had mastered that skill.

In addition to shielding my thoughts, I sought to control them and my emotions, to think not about what I was doing or why, lest Satan use my thoughts to locate me. And each time I remembered that last flight with Tzigane and how Satan and His Enemy had suddenly appeared without warning in our paths, I willed the image away, to prevent it and the emotions attached to it from attracting Satan's attention.

As I traveled farther from the castle, I began to pass beyond the limits of the storm I had earlier, in a different life it now seemed, conjured. And with the storm went a good deal of my protection.

Because spellcraft bears the occult vibrations of the one who casts the spell, the storm had concealed the lesser vibrations associated with my spell-transformed form. Beyond the storm, doing spellwork of any kind, from conjuring new storms to transforming into and maintaining alternate forms, could target my position.

So, once beyond the storm I descended to the ground and returned to my human form, in which, while evading detection, I determined I would have to, for a while at least, remain.

I landed deep in the forest near a small hut. I had taken nourishment earlier at the castle, but after my strenuous journey through the storm I intended to acquire new blood in order to maintain my strength at its peak. This time, however, my prey would have to be taken without my using any occult powers, including the use of my mental powers.

Thoughts of the hut Tzigane and I had visited on our first hunt came into my mind. I banished them. The remorse I had felt, now understandable, following my later attack on those in that same hut, I also banished.

Gathering my cloak about me, I quietly approached the small building, using the physical skills of a mortal hunter to move without sound.

I crept closer until I could use my Undead hearing to listen to those who were inside. Making use of my Undead *physical* senses and strengths would attract no occult notice.

From within I heard the voice of a man, and then the voice of a woman. I heard no children, but the sweet scent of a single child's blood told me one was also there.

I moved forward, intensely aware of my surroundings, alert for any indication that Satan, or those whom He had surely by now sent hunting for me, might be drawing near.

It suddenly occurred to me that even Satan's Enemy might be searching for me! But was the so-called false God of Light truly Satan's Enemy? I could no longer afford not to question everything I had learned from Tzigane, for surely she who had been so betrayed had also been tricked by lies. And I recalled that when Tzigane was taken, Satan's remarks had named her as some form of concession to the false God. But why—

I cut the thoughts short, upset with myself for having allowed my mental discipline to momentarily lapse. I must not think of those things! Not now. I must think only of surviving each passing moment, a predator ever conscious of also being prey to others.

With my Undead strength I could have easily broken through the barriers of wood provided by the hut's door and shuttered windows, but I was stopped, held back as I was by the maddening Rule of Invitation. And this time I dared not use my mental powers to provoke illusions that would trick an invitation out of my prey. There were, however, other, simpler ways.

I knocked on the door. After a moment of silence from within, I knocked again and the man called out, asking who was there.

I presented myself as an exhausted and distraught traveler from Bistrizia, the nearest village of any size. I said I had been stopped and robbed by forest thieves. I was injured. I begged them for help.

After they discussed what they should do for a moment, I heard the bar that held the door closed being slowly drawn back.

While waiting, I had made certain my hair and clothing were suitably unkempt, and just before the door opened I leaned against the frame as if weak and about to fall.

When the door had fully opened, I pretended to lose the ability to stand and slid slowly downward.

The man caught me and supported me and helped me move inside.

Once across the threshold, with bestial quickness I sprang to my feet and grasped him by the throat.

But then he vanished!

The woman, the sleeping child, the hut itself also vanished, and in its place appeared the cloud of Satan, surrounding me, engulfing me.

Darkness pushed into my mind.

Enraged, I fought unconsciousness but almost at once became too weak to stand, slipped to my knees, slumped onto the floor.

"Tzigane," I whispered weakly, "I have . . . failed . . ."

Satan's laughter rumbled thunderously within my mind as His crimson lightning lanced downward and struck me, searing, burning, destroying my Undead flesh . . .

56
Doomed

My consciousness was swept into darkness. I floated in nothingness.

The disorientation I had experienced in the disembodied state immediately after the death of my mortal flesh had been similar to what I was now experiencing, save that there had then at least been a sense of movement.

Was my soul imprisoned within the black sphere I had seen on my other journey into Satan's realm?

I had known defeat before. But there had always been some hope of later battle, or at least of revenge. And after meeting Tzigane, I had possessed a great secret that made mortal defeats seem insignificant, for always awaiting me had been the future glory in which Tzigane had so fervently believed.

But if Satan had destroyed my Undead flesh, as he seemed to have done, and imprisoned me in darkness, there was no such glory to which I could now aspire, no later victories, no revenge.

My defeat, it seemed, was total.

My vow to rescue Tzigane had been thwarted almost before it began. And so easily! Bait had been placed in my path, an illusion of easy nourishment, and like an animal unfamiliar with being hunted, I had fallen into the trap.

The horror I felt, to have failed Tzigane so! She would now continue to scream without end, without hope of release.

And what would Satan do to me?

But suddenly, in spite of horror and defeat made all but infinite, or perhaps because of it, I found the situation bordering on the *glorious*.

Doomed and short-lived my quest to save Tzigane might have been, but what a fine thing it was to have tried!

I had acted from the heart, not the mind, and vowed victory over impossible odds, even believed it possible to win.

I had rebelled against the will of Satan! *And God!* To save a woman that I loved.

Yes, it was a fine thing indeed, to have risked all on a hopeless quest without having once hesitated, without having once thought it foolish. A very fine thing. Or perhaps merely insane. My driving force mattered little now. And yet it was *all* that mattered, and it would have to sustain me through whatever lay in store. That, and my memories of Tzigane, the love we had known . . . but also memories of what she was suffering now . . . because she had been betrayed, wronged too greatly to ignore. And for me to have reacted by doing anything other than what I had done would have been equally as wrong. Indeed, I knew with a deep certainly that I would do the same again and yet again, had I the chance.

Total my defeat may have seemed, but at the thought of Satan's betrayal of Tzigane, and me, my hatred flared anew, blazed unseen in nothingness, warmed my imprisoned spirit.

Tzigane! Henceforth my battle cry. My prayer. My

reason for enduring and continuing, though doomed, to fight!

Satan! Hear me! Had I the power, I would destroy both You and the God of Light! But know this! I will love Tzigane and hate You, defy You, throughout all Time!

There was no response, just a continuation of nothingness.

Then I suddenly wondered, fighting down a surge of panic, if what I was experiencing might never end. Might this darkness, this nothingness, be my punishment? This complete isolation? Left totally alone with only my thoughts and memories separating me from nonexistence?

And might I in time then come to abhor the very thoughts and memories I now found so precious, craving their absence so that I might cease to exist? To think and feel no more?

Forever?

Anger blazed up within me. *I will never prefer forgetfulness over memory! I will never crave nonbeing over thought!*

Again there was no reaction, or so it seemed at first, but after what may have been moments or many lifetimes, it was impossible to tell the difference in that timeless realm, suddenly around me all was light.

I still floated in nothingness, but my fleshless consciousness was now adrift in an ocean of painful brightness.

Then there came a sound that grew rapidly louder, steady, high-pitched, and I began to sense movement.

The light no longer surrounded me but began to fall away beneath me, became a sphere of fire burning in the midst of nothingness, became a radiant glow in which there then appeared two eyes, staring at me, terrifying in their vastness, the eyes of a woman . . . beautiful . . . but not Tzigane's. I fought to remember whose eyes they were. But I failed. And the eyes closed, taking with them the light.

I floated in darkness once more, but I still heard the high-pitched sound. It grew louder and began to rhythmically change, became a haunting melody accompanied by a rhythmic pounding, a heartbeat . . . a song sung by a woman . . . her voice . . . so beautiful . . . so familiar . . .

Then suddenly I felt myself become other, elsewhere, enfleshed but weak and helpless, looking out at a hazy scene of light and shadows through eyes only barely able to see as, held by strong, protective arms, I hungrily sucked warm life into my body, strengthening myself while the beautiful song and comforting heartbeat went on and on. . . . Until above me, looking down from out of a realm of light, *I saw again the eyes* and knew whose eyes they were, and whose song, whose heartbeat, and with that knowledge came a change. Came helpless horror. As again I was four years old watching my mother die, seeing Katiasa's eyes fill with pain, consumed by flames, *my mother's eyes.*

And the song she had sung while suckling me suddenly became a scream, and within the scream a single word, *Lies!* that erupted from her mouth in the shape of a sphere of fire that engulfed me and left me floating in a universe of burning light once more.

Lies! I echoed with my thoughts. *Lies!* And I burned with hatred, became fire. *Lies! Tzigane!* And I merged with the light around me, became it, felt stronger than ever I could remember, and with that strength came the unshakeable knowledge that darkness and defeat could never destroy me, never extinguish my desire to remember my life and Tzigane's love! For I was now the sphere of fire itself . . . ignited by hatred . . . burning with anger, but also with love and a need for revenge against Satan and His Enemy. . . . And revenge for my mother's death, too, and so many others who had been and were being, and would be wronged by all of my Enemies' lies! *Lies!*

And I expanded, felt myself pushing outward through the darkness as if exploding, but growing stronger, burning even brighter, devouring the darkness that had tried to keep me prisoner . . . until suddenly agony lanced through me, the light vanished, and I opened my eyes and saw overhead a dark sky inhabited by stars . . . points of fire in the darkness above . . . as below was my soul a point of fire in the darkness of the night . . .

Pain coursed through me. I struggled to make my stiffened, death-chilled muscles obey. I fought my way to a sitting position. I battled agony to stand upright. A corpse that yet lived! That yet hated! That yet loved.

"Tzigane!" I cried, my voice a rasp of pain, and from far in the distance came a faint and plaintive scream.

Chapter Fifteen

57
Third

From the distance the scream came again. *Nearer.* But not a human scream as first I had thought. I recognized it now as the screech of a night-hunting owl.

Moments later, a white owl landed with ghostly silence in a nearby tree.

I tried to see it more clearly, but I could not, and with a shock I realized I no longer possessed the power of night vision.

If not for the faint light from a waning Moon I would have been all but blind in the dark. And I would never have thought the owl's cry to be human had my hearing been sharper.

Indeed, all of my senses had been reduced to what I remembered as mortal.

I strained to discern my surroundings, a forest clearing and the ruins of a hut. Then with a start I recognized those ruins as the ones near Targoviste where Tzigane and I had first shared passion.

How had I traveled there from the Carpathians of northern Transylvania?

And the night . . . the phase of the Moon was wrong I now realized, and the air was *warm*. There was no snow upon the ground. Wild flowers faintly scented the air. And looking above I saw patterns of stars only visible during the summer.

Not only many miles stood between me and where I had been before being taken by Satan, but months, while Tzigane . . . I felt horror and rage . . . months while her torture had continued . . . or even longer . . . I had no way of knowing, perhaps years . . .

Movement drew my attention back to the trees surrounding the clearing. Another white owl landed in a different tree. Then another silently glided to a perch, and others, until ten were stationed around the clearing.

The first owl then screeched and launched itself into the air, circled me once, and vanished into the dark forest while the other nine sat silent and motionless, watching . . .

Watching. Spying for my Enemies? Were Witches using spellcraft to see through the eyes of the owls? Was my location even now being made known to Satan?

I concentrated my will and spoke the proper words of power. The owls ignored my command to leave.

My night vision and heightened physical senses were evidently not the only things I no longer possessed. How many other powers had my defiance of Satan cost?

"All of them, and none of them," said a woman's voice nearby, a woman who had obviously just read my thoughts. A Witch . . . an enemy—

The voice came again, saying, "I am not your enemy, if you do not wish it."

From out of the trees she walked slowly through the weak moonlight, into the clearing and toward me, a tall figure in a dark cloak, the hood drawn up over her head.

Without my night vision, I could see nothing of the woman's face within the drooping hood. I tried to probe her thoughts but was not surprised when I failed, another power lost.

314

She said, "You think me an enemy because you think me a Witch, but you have been told many lies. Most Witches serve not Satan."

I could not imagine any Witch I had ever known serving Satan's Enemy.

"Nor do Witches follow the ways of the false God," she answered my thoughts. "Most Witches follow the way of the Mother."

"The Mother?"

"You have been told lies so vast that you do not even suspect their existence. Agree to share with me your knowledge of Satan's secrets so that I and my kind can strive to use them against him and his ally, and I will help you discover what is true and what is not."

I replied, "A woman who spent many years telling me what she believed true now screams without end, betrayed. Her pain is the only truth now that matters."

"Yes. Tzigane. Your love for her, your link to her, is stronger than one such as Satan could imagine. Not by hatred alone did you defy his power and escape to create new flesh for yourself upon the Earth, here in this place most sacred to your love. Even the ring she once gave you have you recreated upon your hand."

I paused, glanced down at the silver ring, then said, "You know of Tzigane, and it seems you know more of what happened to me in Satan's realm, and after, than do I. More reasons to mistrust you."

"Even so, I assure you that the true things I can tell you, and your knowledge of Satan's secrets, are your only hope of finding a way to stop Tzigane's pain."

"A line of reasoning no doubt intended to trick me into trusting you."

"One of the lies in which you still believe, Vlad Dracula, is that there are only two sources of true power, Satan and God. How then, if both are your enemy, could you hope to save Tzigane? But know you this, *there is a third source of power,* the force from which Satan and God have stolen much of the power they pretend is their own, the power of the Earth and Moon and Sun. Of Life. Of Nature. *Of the Mother."*

I said nothing, but my mind was racing forward with what her statement could mean if true.

She said, "I have risked much by appearing to you in this fashion. Your rebellion against Satan may only have been a trick by which he hoped to draw me out of hiding."

Her accusation angered me. "I will *never* do Satan's bidding again."

"Now knowingly. I studied well your thoughts before making my presence known. But he might have *allowed* your escape without your being aware. Nevertheless, I have risked this meeting."

She walked closer. "Tzigane told you of a War Beyond Earth in which Satan and God struggled for dominance, did she not? That so-called war is little more than an entertaining diversion to them. The *real* war is here, upon the Earth, a war in which they are allies in the struggle to destroy my kind and enslave yours, whether living or dead or undead, a war that has raged since Satan and God came from beyond Earth to replace the evolving partnerships of the Mother of Life with their ways of male dominance and Fear."

She took another step toward me.

"From beyond Earth?" I remembered the Vale of Fog and Flowers and the story Tzigane had told about Satan coming to Earth there upon a falling star. "From . . . above?"

"Yes. Satan did first curse Life on Earth in the valley of the Scholomance, as did the false God in the land he renamed Eden.

"For centuries upon centuries they have tried to usurp

our powers and destroy us, whom humans once honored as their native goddesses and gods, partners with the Mother in the cycles of Life and Death and Rebirth. And long have they sought to destroy the humans who strive to keep the ways of the Mother alive, hating most of all the power and knowledge of women, torturing and burning them alive by the hundreds of thousands in the name of the false God of love.

"But many of us yet survive and continue to fight as best we can, still defiant, though often weakened and in hiding on this part of the Earth where our enemies' efforts have, thus far, been most concentrated."

She approached to within arm's reach and slowly extended her left arm, thin and pale, from beneath the folds of her black cloak. "For the sake of your love for Tzigane, join us in our struggle. Of your own free will, begin now by touching my hand."

I hesitated. "Touching your hand would be rather foolish. Perhaps another trick."

"You well know that nothing is gained without risk. I have risked my freedom, possibly my existence, by emerging from hiding to meet you here. Will you not risk even a touch of my hand?"

I hesitated a moment more, thought again of Tzigane, then cautiously reached out and touched the woman's hand.

And suddenly I could see. My night vision had been returned to me.

"Look now upon my face," she said and pulled back the hood of her cloak.

Fear and wonder rose within me.

Her face was the face of my mother, but her hair was a writhing mass of slender white snakes.

"Be not afraid." Her voice I also now recognized as my mother's. "Whosoever gazes upon me sees first their mother's face and hears their mother's voice."

317

She removed her cloak. She was breathtakingly naked beneath. Desire rose within me, and as it did her face changed, became Tzigane's. I grew angry.

She held the cloak out to me. "Become my ally." Her voice was now Tzigane's.

"You dare ask that? You, who think to tempt me with Tzigane's face?"

"I control not whose face those who look upon me see."

"I do not know that to be true."

She still held her cloak, offering it to me. "Place my cloak about your shoulders. Join me and my kind in our fight against our enemies and yours. Be my ally, Vlad Dracula. Take my cloak and with it take back the powers you thought lost. Would an enemy offer you that?"

"Your cloak can return my powers to me?"

"Yes."

I gazed into the eyes I saw as Tzigane's eyes, and at last I quietly said, "For Tzigane."

I removed my cloak. I took hers and placed it around my shoulders. It had first appeared too small for my size, but now it fit as if made for me and me alone.

But even my Undead flesh was chilled as the cold within the cloak pierced my clothing and settled into my bones, until suddenly the cloak began to feel warm, and I felt occult power building within me. But not like before. The power I now felt was somehow different, somehow more . . . *mine*.

She said, "My cloak shields you from external forces so that your thoughts can be clear, and it has awakened your inner strength. A part of your mind, still partially controlled by Satan's lies, was blocking your powers, because part of you yet believed your defiance of him had cost you the skills you had struggled to master. But the powers were always your own, and never the Devil's to take or to give."

I looked at the ruins of the hut. I remembered what Tzigane and I had begun there, and the years after, so many years, and how Satan's betrayal had ended all our plans, our dreams. But not our love.

Fresh anger boiled within me, feeding my sense of power.

She said, "Although I have cast shields of protection around us, and my winged guardians watch well for our enemies, it would be wise for us to remain in the open not too long. One of my hidden dwellings within the Earth is near."

Another cloak appeared upon her shoulders, but this one was bone white, and her face, framed by writhing snakes, had again become the face of my mother.

I said, "You have not told me your name."

She smiled my mother's smile. "Living flesh cannot bear my true name. Your flesh, however, is neither living nor dead, and so . . ."

Her smile became a rictus grin, her face a skull. Her chilled thoughts mingled with mine.

After a moment, I said, "Your powers and mine will be most . . . harmonious, I should think."

Indeed, came her reply within my mind. And she laughed, a cold, brittle sound. *And now?*

Yes, I agreed, then transformed myself into the form of a bat, while the death goddess, for such I now knew her to be, returned to the form in which I had first seen her, a skull-white owl, and together with her nine guardians we left the ruins behind, traveling together upon silent wings toward her dwelling.

58
Goddess

The dwelling of the death goddess was within a wooded hill.

Just as it seemed we would strike the ground, an oval of darkness appeared and we passed through into her world below.

Down a spiraling, earth-walled passageway we flew, deeper and deeper into Earth's cool darkness, until finally we emerged into a large cavern. No candles or torches burned there, but neither I, the goddess, nor her guardians had need of light.

The cavern's stone walls were decorated with primitive paintings of animals and humans wearing animal masks, dancing among the beasts.

In the cavern's center a small pool glistened, its surface a dark mirror. It reminded me of the pool beneath the palace of Targoviste.

All such pools within the Earth were once sacred to me or one of my sisters, her thoughts told me, *but many are now claimed by our enemies, and upon them rest their sacred sites.*

I thought of the castle, but before I could ask the question, she answered. *Yes. Far below the crypt in which you slept was one such pool. But Satan made of it a pit in which He imprisoned the Old One whose power He most feared, she from whom he and the false God have stolen so much.*

I remembered Tzigane's mention of the castle's portal in connection with Old Ones who had once ruled the Earth in Satan's name.

Another lie, came the reply. *She who coils not dead but dreaming beneath the castle was never Earth's ruler. Ruling is something she would understand not at all. Evolving together was her way, and the way of all her children. She is the Mother. And she is the source of the third power.*

I saw the nine winged guardians one by one plunge into the dark water, where for a moment I glimpsed them as white serpents that slipped quickly out of sight in the water's black depths.

The goddess returned to her human form near a three-sided opening in the cavern wall. I returned to my human form beside her.

"Vlad Dracula, called Son of the Dragon and Son of the Devil, you were told Satan fathered your soul, and that Undeath was the Devil's gift of physical immortality. But your soul was not born out of Satan, and Undeath is not of the Devil."

"Neither of which is important to me just now. Stopping Tzigane's suffering is all that matters."

"I must tell you what I must tell you."

"And if it will help me save Tzigane, I will listen."

"Then know this. To free Tzigane, you must first free she who is the source of the third power, imprisoned beneath your castle. Only she can penetrate the barriers behind which Satan and the false God hide. That is why she is the one they most fear. That is why, using surprise, in the ages ago they attacked her and imprisoned her below."

I replied, "I assume you have already tried to free her and failed?"

"Long ago. Many were lost in the attempt, and with them much knowledge. We knew not, however, the secrets of Satan. Long have we waited for one such as you, that we might try again to set her free."

"*Waited?* You could have warned me of Satan's treachery before Tzigane was stolen from the Earth!"

"There were those who tried, but failed, with horrible consequences. Satan was most vigilante with regard to his chosen King. And it is doubtful you would have believed any warnings, had you received them, so accepting of Tzigane's beliefs did you swiftly become."

She motioned to the triangular opening in the cavern wall. "You must now risk trusting me again. You must enter the darkness and remember all you have ever been.

"You have lived other lives, Vlad Dracula, before this one. But you are not unique in this. It is the way of the Mother. Even Satan and the false God cannot imprison souls forever. All those they capture in time escape to be reborn in new flesh."

"Then, Tzigane will in time escape?"

"No. Not only her soul has been imprisoned, but also her Undead flesh. Rebirth into new flesh is lost to the Undead. Vampires exist immortal in the flesh, but their souls are trapped in that flesh and thus denied the healing rest within the darkness of my womb of death."

I responded, "There can be no rest while Tzigane is in pain. Each moment I waste brings new screams. A year passed before I broke Satan's mental chains and remembered what had happened, and several months more have passed since He captured me, if not longer." A sadness came into her eyes. I tried to read her thoughts, but even my restored powers could not penetrate them. I asked, "How long?"

"More than a year."

Despair. Rage. Fists clenched at my sides I said,

"Then we must waste no more time. If I must trust you again, I will."

"Then enter my darkness. But before you do, I would also have you know this, that you have loved Tzigane in other lives, and she you. Yours is an old love."

"And Satan knew, of course."

"So it would seem."

"And He used what He knew we would feel for each other to further His Evil, and then sought to destroy the bond between us. But . . . why? If what you say about other lives is true, have I served Him well in another life to be thus chosen in this one?"

"Not Satan, but his enemy did you once greatly serve. Enter the inner darkness and remember your other lives. You must have complete knowledge of yourself, whom you have been, what you have done, your other memories, other knowledge, from your first life as a self-aware intelligence until this current life. The remembering in itself will reveal much of what is true. Truth does not change from one life to the next, merely the perception of it."

She walked to stand beside the three-sided opening. "If you are ready?"

Thinking of Tzigane, I walked into the darkness.

And into life. *Lives.*

Memories.

Emotions.

Dreams.

All mine and yet not mine. The realities of the other people I had once been flashed through my mind, my soul, stretching back and back to the dawn of human-kind.

And Tzigane . . .

Again and again, though our names and appearances were different our souls always recognized each other, recognized our love as we sometimes spent many happy years together, raising children, growing old, knowing the pain of loss when one or the other of us died first. But other times, though in love, we were kept apart by circumstances beyond our control. And sometimes our togetherness was cut short by early death.

Until this life, in which we conspired to become immortal, so that Death would separate us no more.

And I saw, and then knew, that *this* had always been the real motivation behind Tzigane's allegiance to Satan and my willingness to become Satan's king. Not my desire for power. Not Tzigane's belief in Satan's lies. Our desire to be together always in the only way we thought possible.

Satan was more Evil than even I had guessed. And He hated us, our love for each other, more than I could imagine. As did His Enemy. *His Ally in Tzigane's punishment, and mine.*

How many times before had They secretly conspired to separate us? And why? Did our love in some way threaten Them?

I searched through my memories, all of my memories, of the people I had been, looking for other clues, other possibilities, on and on, until finally, exhausted, I felt sleep enclosing me and had not the strength to resist.

I awoke in the cavern. Nine women in bone-white robes knelt around me, watching over me. Nearby stood the death goddess.

I sat up. My head throbbed with pain. "So many," I whispered. "So many lives."

She responded, "And yet only one."

I nodded. "Yes. Only one. What must I do next?"

"I would now have you share your knowledge of Satan with me. Open to me your thoughts."

And gladly then I did.

Chapter Sixteen

59
Journey

Time soon lost meaning in the dwelling within the Earth.

I did not grow hungry for nourishment. I did not feel a need to sleep when the Sun was above the horizon. But I knew time was passing, knew Tzigane's suffering was continuing, and that knowledge pushed me to master all the death goddess taught as quickly as I could, until at last we had decided what I must do.

On the night I left the dwelling, the air was cold and the trees were losing their leaves, but I had been assured only a few months more had passed, not years.

As I walked away, alone in the night, I kept tightly woven around me a spell of protection I had but recently learned. It did not partake of the occult vibrations associated with the spellwork Tzigane had taught me, and I therefore hoped by using it to avoid detection.

Behind me I left the goddess in her dwelling, forgotten by the humans who had once honored her with their prayers. Humans stripped by her Enemies of their rightful knowledge of her truth of rebirth. And mine.

When I was a good distance from the mound that marked her dwelling, I strengthened my spell of protection and took the form of a bat.

I flew northward and traveled undetected through the Pass of the Red Tower that led from Wallachia into Transylvania, arriving at Hermanstadt before dawn.

I again took human form, but not the form by which I had been known as Vlad Dracula. Instead, using skills taught to me within the dwelling of the death goddess, I assumed the appearance of a man I had been in a former life not too far removed from my present one. Further, rather than arousing suspicion by using spellwork to prevent my thoughts from being read by some agent of my Enemies, I kept the memories of my former life in the foreground of my consciousness to conceal my identity.

Before dawn, I took nourishment and appropriated some coins from a wealthy Saxon merchant sleeping within a large house near the center of town.

When the Sun rose, I risked using another spell recently learned from the death goddess, rather than the one Satan had taught to me, in order to walk forth in the sunlight unharmed. The death goddess had not thought it nearly as great a secret as Satan had pretended.

With the stolen coins I purchased a horse, the provisions a mortal man would need, and a sword, then set out on the next stage of my journey, endeavoring to appear as normal as possible and determined to use spellwork and my alternate forms as little as possible while within Transylvania, where I deemed any search for me would be most intense.

Not long after noon, I felt myself far enough from Hermanstadt to dismount in a shadowy forest well off the main road. Maintaining the spell of protection from the Sun was tiring me quickly, but I was determined to last the entire day in the open, though out of direct sunlight.

I rested in the shadows until sunset, then found nourishment from a woodsman's family in an isolated hut, and afterward, strengthened, rested until dawn.

After sunrise, again using the spell of protection, I set out upon my horse once more, and thus did I pass several days until finally I reached the Danube River.

I sold the horse in a village and in bat form crossed the wide river after dark. Tales you may have heard about the Undead being unable to cross running water are but other lies you have been told.

Once safely out of my homeland, though still cautious not to arouse attention or suspicion, I nonetheless felt less apprehensive.

I was surprised to have come so far without encountering trouble. Had the nearly two years since my disappearance dulled Satan's desire to recapture me? Or *was* he even searching for me? Could it be possible that He was unaware of my escape? Such a thing might well have been unthinkable to Him, and He might have consigned my memory to oblivion once He had imprisoned me, never to relieve my isolation by so much as checking to see if I were still there.

It was an attractive idea. But I could not afford to assume it was true. There was no evidence to support the notion, other than my lack of trouble thus far. And if I relaxed my guard and was discovered, all would be lost. Tzigane would be lost.

So I continued to make my way cautiously across Hungary and then beyond.

As I traveled onward, in secret, I sought out various sites the death goddess had suggested might harbor portions of knowledge lost to her kind since the coming of their enemies, knowledge that might prove useful both to me and to them.

Occult barriers placed upon such sites by Satan and

the false God kept her kind away. But they did not keep me away, and piece by piece, the knowledge I possessed slowly grew.

Often I used the disguises of former lives to acquire information by normal means. But sometimes it was necessary to use, under strong shields of protection, my occult powers, occasionally even to the awakening and questioning of a corpse, whether that of a respected scholar or the remains of one who had studied obscure elements of the occult.

In great libraries and centers of learning did I search, and in places of occult darkness no mere human could have survived.

In the courts and great halls of the aristocracy of many countries I plundered knowledge from noble, educated minds, and in the maddened minds of obsessed seekers of forbidden lore did I also find information I hoped would prove useful.

As I continued on my search, always traveling in a generally northward direction toward a far distant goal, I happened now and then upon Satan's Own whom I had seen at my castle. But they recognized me not in my disguises, and when I probed their thoughts, though not too deeply lest I arouse suspicion, I found no knowledge of a search for me. Indeed, their surface thoughts indicated they thought I still sat the Throne of the World, Satan's King.

Had Satan placed an impostor on the throne? Perhaps my father or brother? Or was it all part of the continuing deceptions and lies by which He manipulated His followers?

I also visited sites of ancient power the death goddess had suggested might be useful, vast caves with primitive paintings on the walls like those in her own cavern, haunted mountaintops where sacred rites had once been performed, pools of deep water in sacred groves within dark forests where occult echoes of lost truths lingered still.

Others of the death goddess's kind did I also seek out when I could, that they might know of my quest for surviving fragments of ancient knowledge that, when combined, would hopefully aid us in the struggle to free the imprisoned one beneath my castle. And with those others I shared what knowledge I had acquired, in return for other knowledge they possessed.

Northward, gathering more and more knowledge as I went, I traveled on, and the farther north I went, the longer the nights of the oncoming winter became.

Then finally I arrived at my destination, and there, with the winter solstice near, I was troubled not at all by the Sun, for while above, shimmering in the sky, glowed the glorious Northern Lights, the Sun did not rise above the horizon all day long.

60
Wisdom

My destination in the north was a site long sacred to the natives of that land before the coming of Satan and the false God to the Earth, and so remote was it from the lands to the south they had all but conquered, it survived as yet relatively unscathed.

An old man clothed in the skins of animals, in his hand a great spear, awaited me there. Two wolves stood guard at his feet. Two ravens circled watchfully overhead.

He had only one eye. Legends said he had plucked his left eye from his head in exchange for knowledge. Other legends said he had hung upon a tree for nine days and nights in self-sacrifice to acquire the knowledge of the Northern Mysteries known as Runes. And other tales of his exploits told of many other quests for knowledge.

I was hoping that, if he were indeed the relentless seeker of knowledge the old tales claimed, he might know much that others of his kind had lost.

Though his left eye was gone, his right eye blazed brightly, a hot coal in the darkness of that far northern night, as also my own eyes glowed.

"Welcome, warrior," he said, his voice like the whisper of winter wind scattering pellets of snow. "I have seen your deathless soul in dreams. You return with much knowledge."

"Return. Yes." I remembered the life I had lived in that land, the life when, as one of my own ancestors, I had honored the one-eyed god before me with prayers and become a Berserker in battle while shouting his name.

And I remembered how that ancestor had in time traveled eastward and then to the south down great rivers and over the land with others of his tribe to trade at Constantinople, passing near Transylvania and later dying there, leaving behind a grieving wife and strong children in whose veins flowed the essence of his wild northern blood.

I said to the ancient one before me, "You honor me with your presence, Wisdom Seeker. Will you exchange knowledge for knowledge?"

He smiled, showing wolf-sharp teeth. His one eye blazed brighter. "I will. Welcome home."

"Only one of many homes I have known."

"And you *remember all*, I can tell. Much do I value thought and wisdom, but memory I value even more. I would know who taught you to remember."

"Her name cannot be spoken aloud."

He laughed, a deep and booming sound. "Ah. One of *those*. I have known a few myself. And bedded them. Save for one."

Thinking of all I had seen and learned in the dwelling of the death goddess I responded, "Or perhaps they bedded you?"

He laughed even louder. "Aye. Perhaps they did at that, Deathless One. Perhaps indeed they did."

61
Mountain

Much knowledge did I acquire from the one-eyed god, and many connections between pieces of knowledge I had gained did he help me to see.

While in his dwelling, hidden atop a high mountain much like the castle I had fled, I also spoke with others of his band. There was his quick-tempered, red-bearded son to whom the old tales attributed the power to make lightning flash and thunder roll when he wielded his massive warhammer. But little in the way of the knowledge I needed could the hammer-wielder offer.

Much of value, however, I learned from a goddess of great power and knowledge, more ancient than the one-eyed god himself, a goddess still honored by the prayers of a few stubborn northlanders determined not to allow all of their ancestors' beliefs to be swept away.

From others, too, did I learn, and with others shared what I knew. But until my last night spent atop the mountain, of the one-eyed god's mate there had been no sign.

I had asked if I might talk with her, but to no avail. If the legends about her being the wisest of them all were true, so also it seemed were the stories that said she always kept her vast knowledge secret.

But then she appeared and looked at me, stared into my eyes, and without saying a word touched my forehead. My flesh warmed beneath her touch. I stood still as stone. After a moment she withdrew her hand and said within my thoughts, *I have listened from afar to all you have said. I have felt with my heart all you have felt. And I deem you worthy of my aid. I too shall ride forth with the host and use my knowledge to help you save the woman you love.* Then she turned and walked away.

My thanks! I said with my thoughts, but she moved from my view without once looking back.

My host laughed. "Often have I struggled to obtain new knowledge, only to discover that she possessed it all along."

Chapter Seventeen

62
Fury

I returned to my homeland that very night, but I did not return alone. Nor did I return in stealth. I returned upon a spectral steed, riding the howling winds of a crashing storm.

The Wild Hunt of the one-eyed god raged above the Earth as of old.

Many gods and goddesses of the northlands, warriors all, rode at my side, among them the ancient goddess of power with her nine warrior women, their piercing battle cries rising shrilly above the din of the thunderous storm, while the red-bearded son of the one-eyed god followed closely behind, lightning streaking earthward from his warhammer. And of course with us too rode the one-eyed god's mate, her face of fury breathtaking to behold.

And as we moved ever southward above the Earth, the call went out to the places I had found where hid others of their kind, until from within the Earth and atop mountains and out of dark forests did arise more and more of those too long robbed of their rightful power by fear and isolation, hungry to be free once more.

Among those who joined us as we neared our goal was the death goddess and her nine guardians, all now having taken the form of white-scaled serpents with leathery wings, pale dragons with burning venom dripping from their fangs.

Moving faster than the winds in our wake, and with surprise on our side, as hoped we met no resistance until within sight of our goal. Then, with Castle Dracula but a short distance ahead, there appeared before us in the sky the two boiling clouds I had last seen the night Tzigane was taken, the black cloud of Satan shot through with crimson lightning, the white cloud of the false God writhing with serpentine streamers of dark energy.

With Satan and His supposed Enemy also appeared many of Their servants. White-winged creatures brandishing glowing rods emerged from behind the manifestation of the false God, even as bat-winged creatures, like the one who had bestowed upon Tzigane the crimson kiss of Undeath, flew from behind Satan's cloud.

As the battle began, as we had planned I slipped away under a shield of protection and took the form of a bat.

The roar and crash of the battle in the sky continued behind me as I flew to the castle. But I did not attempt to enter the fortress. Instead, I landed near the base of the mountain upon which the castle was built and resumed my human form. Then, concentrating my will, I spoke words of power gleaned from fragments of knowledge Satan and His Enemy had hoped lost for all time.

The Earth trembled. A vertical fissure appeared in the mountain. Taking the form of glowing mist, I slipped through the narrow opening and into the darkness within the pinnacle of rock. Once inside, I took human form once more.

I was heartened to confirm that, as portions of the knowledge I had gained had suggested, the base of the mountain was hollow, forming a vast cavern in whose center, revealed by my night vision, gaped a circular opening, once filled with icy water and, if what I believed proved to be true, soon to be filled with cleansing water once more.

Standing beside the opening in the cavern floor, I concentrated my will and focused my occult powers as never I had before until my body trembled with the effort. I shouted words of power, again and again, endeavoring to unravel the spell of imprisonment cast there by Satan and the false God long ages in the past when They usurped the ancient power of the Mother for Their own.

And from deep within the Earth, the imprisoned one below stirred, uncoiled from her centuries-long slumber, took advantage of the fraying fabric of the spell of enclosure, and broke free.

Up she rose, the Earth trembling as she neared. And preceeding her came the cleansing water that was her element.

I retreated to the side of the cavern. I feared for a moment the quaking Earth would collapse the ceiling, but it did not. Instead, suddenly into view came the imprisoned one, eyes of fire, scaled body glistening with energizing water, glowing with power, driven by fury.

Her eyes found mine. Her thoughts touched mine. And she vanished from the cavern.

Taking on the form of glowing mist, I slipped back through the fissure to the outside.

The battle in the clouds was still raging, but now joining the fray was the imprisoned one, and against her unrestrained power her enemies could not stand.

They and Their forces retreated until directly above the castle, then began to disappear. But the imprisoned one shot forward and into the cloud of the false God before it had entirely vanished, *disappearing with it*.

In bat form I flew to the castle where my victorious allies were coming to ground.

The battlements of Castle Dracula, broken by the quaking of the Earth below, showed a jagged outline against the sky. In some places roofs had collapsed. But to my occult senses and those of my allies, no trace of Satan's power remained.

Inside I found only the three women I had taken as my wives. They had been mistreated badly by my father and brother, whom Satan had, indeed, placed on the throne in my stead. The three further told me that my father and brother had fled, along with several Witches from the Scholomance, on Strigois during the confusion of the aerial battle.

I asked the three why *they* had stayed. They replied that they had stayed to await my return. They had never given up hope I would come back. They assured me that their allegiance had always been to me, not to Satan, and looking into their thoughts I found they were telling the truth.

Leaving them in the care of others, I ascended Tzigane's Tower. It had escaped the shaking of the Earth relatively unscathed. And there I waited alone, hoping for Tzigane's return.

63
Tiamat

The imprisoned one had been the most ancient of all her kind, a power of creation from the ancient oceans where first appeared life on Earth.

Many had been her names throughout history, but the earliest name my research had discovered was Tiamat.

Again and again in the fragments of knowledge I had collected, references had been made to an All Powerful One, the Creatrix of the Waters of Life, the Most Ancient Mother of All.

But would Tiamat succeed? Or would I wait and wait atop the tower, never to see her return? I tried to stop such thoughts, but as I paced to and fro over the stones, I could not banish the possibility from my mind.

Even if she did succeed and return with Tzigane, how long would I have to wait? I remembered that a few moments in Satan's realm had meant months upon the Earth.

As dawn neared, the death goddess and the one-eyed god of my ancestors joined me atop the tower. And they were still with me there when, shortly before the rising of the Sun, the skies over Castle Dracula exploded with light and from within the burst of white radiance appeared Tiamat, a woman's body clutched tightly in her coils.

"Tzigane." Cold tears stung my eyes. "Tzigane!" I shouted. *Tzigane!* I called with my thoughts. But within my mind came no reply.

Tiamat changed to a human form, and placed Tzigane, unconscious, in my arms. Her flesh appeared unharmed.

I healed her body, Tiamat said in my mind, *but the pain, the horror, the endless cruelty, it was more than her sanity could stand. When I found her, I called to her by her name, but she knew it not. Only time can now heal her mind.*

I held Tzigane tightly against me. *My thanks, Most Ancient One,* I said with my thoughts. *If time she needs to heal, time she shall have, here with me, immortal.*

But Tiamat replied, *Her mind will never heal frozen in flesh. Her body itself will remind her of the horror. She will never be at peace Undead. Only the healing rest of death's dark womb can place her soul at peace and make whole her mind once more.*

In stubborn denial I refused to admit it might be true. I remembered all the lives we had shared together. I remembered the love that had again and again been ours. And I said, "You say we cannot heal Tzigane's mind. But I believe I know one who can. Tzigane herself."

64
True

We took Tzigane to the dwelling of the death goddess and I carried her within the darkness where she could remember her other lives.

She stirred in my arms and moaned softly as the process began. But I did not leave her alone to face all that she had ever been. I kept my mind linked with hers, and together we shared the lives we had once lived.

When came a life in which we had not met, I pulled back from the stream of memories and waited and watched over her as she remembered those years, that lifetime. Then I would enter the river of time with her once more, sharing again a life we had lived in different lands, in different flesh.

Then finally came the most dangerous memories of all, those of the life just passed.

Carefully did I watch over her as she slipped closer and closer to the night when she was by Satan betrayed. Stubbornly then did I stay with her and share her horror and pain as her endless torment began, and continued, on and on.

But this time she did not suffer alone. This time always was I there in her mind, with her in her agony, speaking of my love, of our life together, our *lives* together, again and again, gently reminding her of the pain from all of the lives we had known, and all of the joy. So that the torture to which she was being subjected became less and less a thing unendurable, became more and more a torment among many others she had known over the cycling span of her lives.

And then came the moment when Tiamat broke the barriers behind which Satan and the false God hid, when Tiamat in rage did attack and destroy those who served our enemies there, when Tiamat did free my beloved Tzigane and returned her to my arms.

And Tzigane's mind returned . . . to the present. But with an awareness of all she had ever been. Though still wounded, she had indeed begun to heal.

In the darkness her eyes were ruby stars, two points of light that then misted with tears. "Vlad? Is it true? Is it over?"

"Tzigane," I whispered, holding her closely. "It is true. You are safe. And now we can begin to share the centuries to come."

We kissed. "My love," she said.

And I laughed. "So it would seem, Tzigane. So it always would seem."

WARNING

My revenge is not yet complete. I shall yet find a way either to destroy my alien enemies or banish them from the realm of Earth for all time. Their evil shall not go unpunished. Their lies shall not go unchallenged.

When Tiamat broke the other-worldly barrier and rescued Tzigane, she was unable to destroy either Satan or his ally directly. And afterward, our enemies strengthened the barriers with energy so alien that even Tiamat and the combined power of all the reunited goddesses and gods of Earth and Moon and Sun could not break through. But with each passing year our combined power grows as we find and awaken or free ever more of the Mother's vanquished children, so that in time we *will* have the strength to break our enemies' barriers and take the battle to them once more.

Until that day, however, on the Earth itself and in the eight realms upon which it borders, in one form or another the battle rages on.

Many battles have been lost, and many lives lost too, both living and Undead, with too many of them innocents caught between opposing forces, as is always the case in war.

At times, battles in our secret war have escalated into

the wars of history. Most often, though, history has been influenced in secret, and in ways that may not outwardly seem battles at all.

Indeed, many of our most effective and enduring successes have involved quiet struggles to inspire the minds and souls of humankind, and in those struggles some of our greatest warriors have been and continue to be the creators of human art in all its forms, warriors of artistic truth that, like the Undead, lives on through the centuries, awakening generation after generation of humankind to the limitless potential of the human spirit, free and indomitable, the birthright of all those born of Earth and Moon and Sun.

Few listening to the climactic ninth symphony of Beethoven, who like myself was born under the Archer's sign, fail to be uplifted and inspired in often nameless ways, and to hear the opening movement in his so-called "Moonlight Sonata" is to experience the music of a death goddess native to his homeland whom he once met, thinking it but a dream, in a moonlit cemetary as she sung her ancient song, calling to and comforting the souls of the newly dead.

And as you undoubtedly know, approximately one hundred years ago a work of art, a book of fiction by an Irishman named Stoker, made of me a monster.

Stoker's *Dracula* was Tzigane's idea. She is even mentioned within its pages, more than once, if you but know how to look, even to the title, which she arranged to have misspelled, giving my name, in my native tongue, a feminine rendering, one of her mischievous jokes she still finds humorous. A more masculine rendering of my name is shown in the painting created for the cover of the first edition of the book you have just read.

Drakulya.

Although the truth Stoker's book contains was disguised as required by the expectations and conventions of his time, he responded admirably well to the influences Tzigane arranged. His tale is, I find, overall a worthy and amusing one. And, as Tzigane says, it is not as if I cannot at times *be* a monster! In particular to my enemies, and to them a monster shall I ever be! And to those who serve them as well, I am merciless and cunning in my revenge, and more monstrous, if need be, than the monsters I yet endeavor to destroy.

Are you among *their* number, I wonder? Or mine?

Tzigane was, as she is overly fond of pointing out, of course right about influencing the creation of Stoker's fiction. It proved so popular that it has never been out of print, and now, a century later, instead of my name being known only to scholars of fifteenth-century history, there exits a multitude of stories and motion pictures inspired by my legend, as well as several serious books by historians detailing what is to them my *real* life.

So, then, my name is now known around the world, and that notoriety has led, as Tzigane and I intended from the first, to the book you have just read, the *truth* finally made manifest in its most direct form. But first its audience had to be properly . . . prepared.

Of course I have not told you *everything* that has transpired in the five centuries since I became Undead. Perhaps I shall tell you more, in time. Or perhaps not. All that matters now is the truth in this book, *and you who have just read it.*

Verify the historical accuracy of what I have said with books by historians, if verification you require. And verify the reality of the Ancient Mother Goddess with recent books by noted archaeologists and scholars.

But once you have verified what you must, what then will you do?

As Tzigane told me five centuries ago, so now I tell you. Release your inner truth and allow it to be your guide.

Choose wisely. Choose well. Be not my enemy. Join me in my fight. And in time our Earth shall again truly be ours, and, children of the Mother all, together shall we thrive!

About the Author

C. DEAN ANDERSSON is a critically-acclaimed author whose Zebra novel, *Buried Screams*, was recommended for the Horror Writers of America Bram Stoker Award, as were his *Torture Tomb* and *Raw Pain Max*. Other works include five novels written under the pen name of Asa Drake, and short stories, one of which, "Horror Heaven," co-authored with Nina Romberg, appears in Zebra's *Dark Seductions* anthology. Dean holds degrees in physics, astronomy, and art. He has worked as a professional artist, musician, robotics programmer, and technical writer. He lives in the Dallas/Fort Worth Metroplex where he recently completed *Fiend*, his new Zebra novel, and is now writing his next. But once upon a time he was a child encountering the horror of Dracula for the very first time and wondering (when the initial terror had passed) how Dracula *became* a Vampire, a Great Secret he eventually (obviously) learned. And revealed. For you. In this book.

About the Other Author

VLAD DRACULA was born in the third decade of the fifteenth century in Sighisoara, Transylvania. His current address is unknown, but rumors recently placed him near your home.